Sound Proof

Barbara Gregorich

This is a work of fiction. Any resemblance to actual people, places or events is purely coincidental.

Printed in the United States of America

Cover design by Robin Koontz

Gregorich, Barbara
Sound Proof
Philbar Books
Chicago, IL

For Phil,
the music in my life

1 Monday

Shelby Stubbs stepped onto a bale of straw and looked down on the group of musicians. I leaned against a porch rail and watched everything in sight. Even Stubbs, though he wasn't the thief.

Stubbs hooked a thumb through his belt, puffed out his chest, and repeated his announcement. "No sir. Absolutely not." This was directed at Vance Jurasek, who was balancing a string bass on its endpin. "Only fiddles, guitars, and banjos," Stubbs lectured. "No other instruments allowed. That's 'cause no other instruments belong."

"You're kidding." Jurasek settled his bass against the rail and scowled.

"No sir. You don't see a bass in old-time music. It's not traditional. You never saw an old-time player carrying a bass around. No bass in my class."

Jurasek, his thin ponytail hanging limp in the prairie heat, waved a small emerald-green instrument bag at Stubbs. "You'll accept a mandolin, though, right? Bill Monroe played the mandolin."

Stubbs glared. "Don't tell me what Bill Monroe played. I don't dispute that mandolins have a *fine* sound. Fine for bluegrass. But they don't belong in old-time music. 'Sides, I heard you playing that mandolin as we drove in, and either you or the instrument is off key."

Face flushed, Jurasek shot Stubbs a murderous look.

My eyes scanned the two dozen people agape at Stubbs'

announcement. Ranging in age from late teens to early seventies, they had one thing in common: folk music. Make that two things: folk music and T-shirts that advertised the festivals they'd already attended: Augusta Heritage, John C. Campbell Folk School, Summer Solstice, Swannanoa Gathering.

This week they were attending Midwest Music Madness where, based on what happened the two previous years during Old-Time Music Week, at least one of them would have an instrument stolen.

"Waydell Ames would have taught us," someone said.

"Waydell's dead," Stubbs retorted.

The bluntness of the remark stopped conversation cold. Stubbs and his band had been signed as a replacement after Ames had died of a heart attack three weeks earlier.

Seconds ticked by, then argument started in again. "The hammered dulcimer—"

"*No!* No big old hammered dulcimers. The sound is much too rinky-tink, it just piddles around in the high end. A hammered dulcimer can't *drive* the music." Stubbs pointed a finger at the dulcimer player. "Only a fiddle can *drive* the music."

I glanced at the name tag of the musician who had just spoken. *Guy Dufour, Maine.* Sensing my scrutiny, he turned and stared at my tag in return, seeing *Frank Dragovic, Chicago*. Dufour's name tag didn't identify which instrument he played. Mine didn't identify me as a private eye.

"Hammered dulcimers play in old-time music band all over New England." Dufour shouldered two large gig bags easily. Maybe back in Maine he was a lumberjack. Didn't matter, because I wasn't here to watch him.

"That's contra dance, not old-time," Stubbs barked, wiping the sweat off his forehead with a yellow bandana.

Not even 9 A.M. in downstate Illinois and the temperature had allemanded past 90° and was eager to do-si-do with 95°. Sweat percolated down my neck and into my White Sox T-shirt.

"Hammered dulcimer in a contra band is fine *if* you can get a good player. But it ain't an old-time instrument."

On the opposite side of the porch, Kofi Quay and Booker Hayes leaned against a rail. Quay held an African drum and observed; Hayes softly plucked a banjo and grimaced. If they were pondering the antics of white folks, I couldn't blame them.

"Nothing in the literature excluded other instruments," Dufour insisted. "I paid my money, I am going to take your class."

Sneering at the word *literature,* Stubbs patted back his salt-and-pepper hair and hitched up his pants. He breathed deeply, his belly stretching out his dark blue T-shirt. *Any Old-Time You Wanna,* it offered. Unlike most of us, who wore shorts to fight off the heat, Stubbs — who had not arrived Sunday night with everybody else, but during breakfast this morning — wore chinos. "Old-time music is fiddle, guitar, and banjo," he reiterated from his wobbly pulpit. "The fiddle plays the melody, the guitar holds down the rhythm, and the banjo fills in. That's the way it is." He looked down at the group. "I'll be touring France later this year, and that's what I'll be taking with me — my fiddle, a guitar player, and a banjo player."

"What about autoharps?" asked Jurasek angrily. Standing with his left side facing Stubbs, the better to see him, he removed a minidisc player from his pocket and flipped it open. Jurasek's right eye was glass. Last night he'd worn a black patch, this morning he didn't. He was one of those I was here to watch. I looked around to see if he carried an autoharp in addition to his bass and mandolin. Apparently not.

"Autoharps are for ladies who like to strum and pluck. So are mountain dulcimers."

The sound of a vehicle driving over gravel made me glance left. An old blue Ford pickup bounced across the parking lot. A nylon tarp covered what I surmised was camping equipment and an instrument or two. From the dining hall behind us plates and silverware clattered. People ambled by on their way to class, staring at Stubbs on his bale of straw. Under a massive sycamore tree a boy of about ten practiced "The Battle of New Orleans" on his guitar. To my untrained ear, he sounded good.

The group around Stubbs milled restlessly, its din reaching crescendo.

"I will come to your class," repeated Dufour, who was dressed in a long-sleeved shirt, jeans, and heavy boots. July in Maine must be a nippy month. I wondered if he'd make it through a hot and humid week in the Midwest.

Craning his neck, Stubbs studied Dufour's second bag. "What've you got in there — a pregnant mandolin?"

"I build and play the hurdy-gurdy."

"Ohhhh!" wailed Stubbs, throwing back his arms in mock despair. "The hurdy-gurdy is nothing but a substitute for *bagpipes*. Now if you like *bagpipes*, you have another problem."

I felt a finger tap my arm. "What's happening?" whispered Suzanne, the main reason I was here.

"Madness," I whispered back.

Mary Ployd, the organizer of Midwest Music Madness, and my employer for the week, emerged from the breakfast area, winding a thick guitar strap around one hand. "What's going on here?" she demanded.

"He's telling us we can't take his class. We signed up and paid our money and he's telling us we can't take his class." Lafayette Wafer bounced up and down in indignation. He was another one to watch. "I paid to play the bowed psaltry in Waydell's class, and now Shelby—"

"The *bowed psaltry!"* roared Stubbs. "I liked it better when you scratched away on that miserable little fiddle of yours, Lafayette. The bowed psaltry ain't even a real instrument! It's a Christmas tree gone bad! *No* instrument — I repeat, *no* instrument — deserves to be in a class with a bowed psaltry." He shuddered dramatically. "Compared to that thing, the hurdy-gurdy sounds good."

Mary pushed her way through the group. "Shelby," she questioned, "are you trying to exclude these students from your class?"

Stubbs barely looked at her. "They don't belong in an old-time class, Mary. You should know that."

"What are you talking about?" she demanded, swinging a long braid of brown hair over her back. Her voice lowered. "You signed a contract to teach old-time ensemble. I sent you a list of twenty-five students, with the instruments they played. Our agreement was that you teach them."

"That's right!" shouted Lafayette Wafer in a reedy voice. Mary scowled at him over her shoulder.

Stubbs shook his head. "Didn't get no such list. Wouldn't have agreed to it if I had."

Mary unwrapped the web strap from one hand and wrapped it around the palm of the other, like surgical tape. Or brass knuckles. "Be that as it may, you signed the contract, the students paid their money, and the best thing for everybody is that you accept them into your class. *Next* time, I'll make it clear that only fiddle, guitar, and banjo are permitted in your class." From the way she looked at Stubbs, I doubted there would be a next time.

He shook his head. Avoiding eye contact with Mary, he gazed out over the heads of those gathered on the porch.

"Let's go to my office and discuss this." She turned to go.

"No."

She turned back to Stubbs. Unwrapped the strap from her hand. Clipped it around her waist. "It would be better if we discussed this in private. We're upsetting everybody out here."

"I am not upset," shouted Dufour. "Nobody can keep me out of the class I signed up for."

Mary turned in a circle. Caught my eye. I half-expected a sign that she wanted my help. Dealing with big-headed musicians wasn't what she hired me for, and I didn't think she wanted me to blow my cover, but I was willing to drive a charge against Shelby Stubbs if that's what she wanted.

No sign came.

"Shelby," said Mary softly. "Please step down from that bale."

He considered it. After a moment, he acquiesced.

"I want you to think about this." She touched his arm. He flinched. "This is the kind of thing you could end up regretting. Imagine driving along on a dark, rainy night. Twisty roads, nobody in sight. Fog everywhere. The kind of night that makes you look back on your life, you know?"

Stubbs stared at her.

"There you'd be, all lonesome and sad, just you and the dark and the rain. What would you be thinking? I know you'd be wishing you could do things over. This would be something you'd wish you had done different." She paused. "But then it would be too late."

I stared at Mary, whose words carried an overtone of threat.

Stubbs cleared his throat.

"So do the right thing now, Shelby. Teach these students what you know about old-time music."

Nobody spoke. Sensing her advantage, Mary pushed on. "Half of them — *more* than half — didn't sign up until they heard you were going to be here. They came because of you, Shelby. They aren't beginners, they're all advanced students, and they want to take a master's class from *you*." Again she paused. "Please don't disappoint them."

Stubbs worked his jaw. "It ain't right," he croaked. "It's against my principles."

I heard Mary grit her teeth. Sounded like four-four time to me. "I understand that," she soothed. "But what if you didn't do it for yourself? What if you dedicated this class to Waydell's memory? An honorable gesture from one musician to another."

Stubbs shifted from one foot to the other.

"You knew Waydell long ago. Played with him way back then."

A truck door slammed. Stubbs jumped as if he'd been stabbed with a psaltry bow.

"All right," he grumbled. "All right. I'll do it. Just this once."

"Good," said Mary.

Good?

I had my doubts. *Ako laze koza, ne laze rog*. A Croatian saying my mother is fond of repeating. *If the goat lies, its horns don't.*

Wafer and a few others picked up their instruments and headed toward the barn. Jurasek balked. "I'm not taking his class! The son of a pup is closed-minded and musically unimaginative."

Not saying *son of a bitch* struck me as prudish, if not closed-minded and verbally unimaginative, but I wasn't here to spice up anyone's expletives.

Mary pushed Jurasek in front of her, back toward the farmhouse. "You can take my class, Vance. You'll be a welcome addition, with your knowledge of music."

I turned to Suzanne, who I had met when she came to me with a case last October. I wanted us to live together, but she wasn't saying yes. "You were right," I said to her. "It won't be dull."

Behind us, somebody tolled the bell. Suzanne hurried off to her morning class, as did the other 200 or so students. I strapped on my tool belt and headed toward the barn. For this particular gig, I was undercover as a carpenter.

2

I was a city kid, but I had spent my summers on a farm. Rudy, one of my mother's nine brothers, left Chicago in his youth and bought a farm near Galesburg, home of Carl Sandburg. My parents believed that children should know what it's like to help the land produce, so every summer for ten years they sent my sister and me downstate to live with Uncle Rudy and Aunt Angie.

Out there on the prairie I learned how to raise soybeans and corn, milk cows and slop hogs, muck manure and bale hay. My sister and I and our cousins built tunnels in the stacked hay and swung from hay trolley ropes. When nobody was looking we hurled pitchforks at targets and dueled with scythes. Each morning when I woke and looked out my bedroom window, the first thing I saw was the barn. Massive. Permanent. A shelter for animals, harvest, and humans. A place warm with the smell of living creatures and the gentle tang of cured hay.

Mary's barn brought back these memories. Entering her barn through the south side, I noticed that all six double doors — south, east, and north — were rolled back, the few windows propped open with sticks. The entire bottom floor hosted the old-time ensemble class. Clustered around a pine stage built against the north wall, most of the students perched on rusty folding chairs. Others took a big chance with chairs cobbled together out of branches and twigs. I suspected Mary might host a rustic furniture festival during the winter.

Over in a corner, Raven Hook stood with a cup of coffee in her hand, talking to Guy Dufour, who hefted a large trapezoidal instrument onto a stand. I wondered what she was doing in the barn — didn't she have a class to teach?

"Be very careful around here," Raven warned Guy. "Don't leave your instruments out at Mary's festival. My autoharp was stolen last year."

Guy looked at her as she touched a hand to her breast. "Part of my heart is missing," she said, "gone with my autoharp."

At the Sunday night orientation Mary had introduced me as a carpenter she hired to improve the buildings. I'd be walking around, she announced, sitting in on classes and observing what space people needed. I'd also be taking Kofi Quay's drumming class, she added, because I liked pounding on things. That drew a chuckle from everyone. The carpenter cover was my idea, the drumming Mary's. "You can't pass as legitimate without taking a class!" she had insisted.

"That is too bad!" Dufour commiserated, removing his long-sleeved shirt. His T-shirt shouted *Blowzabella*. Whoever or whatever that was. From his accent, syntax, and name, I thought Guy must have grown up speaking French. When he introduced himself to Raven and pronounced his name the French way, hard *g* and long *e*, I gave myself points for observation.

"Be careful," she warned again, trailing her fingertips down his arm. "That looks like a very expensive hammered dulcimer."

Raven was in her forties, dark-haired and lean. I guessed that Guy was a couple of years younger than my thirty.

"It is," he agreed with a smile, oblivious to her good looks or touch. "But I think my dulcimer is safe because it is large. You cannot tuck it under your arm and walk away with it. You would be seen — especially this case would be seen!" The arresting purple nylon case, nearly four feet wide at the top, looked like Barney skinned and stitched.

"As for my hurdy-gurdy," he continued, caressing the smaller instrument, "it would be impossible to sell. Who would buy it but another hurdy-gurdy player? Believe me," he said with a laugh, "that is a small community of people. Everybody would recognize my instrument and report it to me."

I stepped closer. The hurdy-gurdy resembled a large, fat mandolin with a pot belly. The body appeared to be maple, the top spruce. Beautiful inlay work testified to Dufour's woodworking skills. A wheel sat perpendicular to the flat top, with four strings stretched across it and through a trough. A dozen or so wooden keys, something like piano keys, projected from the trough. A stainless steel crank protruded from the bottom end. The crank no doubt turned the wheel, which vibrated the strings. All in all, it looked like an instrument of torture from the Inquisition.

Raven tossed back her head, her long hair cascading over her shoulders. She blew across the top of her coffee and stepped to the side, surveying the room.

I hung near Guy, studying the hammered dulcimer. Mary had hired me with twofold instructions. One: catch the thief who had stolen instruments at each of her two previous old-time weeks and who, she was certain, would try again at this one. Two: make certain that whatever else happened, Shelby Stubbs' performing fiddle and bow weren't stolen. "Shelby wouldn't agree to teach at Madness unless I underwrote his precious fiddle," she had complained. "If it's stolen, he'll end up owning part of my farm."

Catching a thief involves thinking like one, so I observed the instruments, calculating their value. "How much does it weigh?" I asked Guy, examining the trapezoidal instrument better. I wanted everybody to take my asking questions for granted.

"Oh, thirty pounds, give or take a few."

"Well, I'd best be getting off to my class," Raven announced. "I just wanted to warn you all about the thefts that occurred here last year. A guitar and my autoharp were stolen."

She sipped her coffee. "And the year before that, a mountain dulcimer was stolen."

Raven Hook was one of my suspects for instrument thief, along with Vance Jurasek and a small number of others who had been at each of the previous Midwest Madness festivals during Old-Time Week.

Lafayette Wafer, another suspect, shuffled across the floor with bowed psaltry in hand. "You should know better than to leave your autoharp alone overnight," he told her as he examined a Leatherman tool that hung from his belt. Guy wore a similar small tool on his belt. I guess stringed instruments needed frequent repair.

"How are you, Lafayette?" Raven offered, ignoring his remark. "I'll see y'all later." She moved toward the door.

"Oh." She stopped in front of me. "Frank — just the man I wanted to see." She touched my hand. "The corn crib, where I'm teaching, has a stuck door that we can hardly open or close. I wonder if you could fix it."

"No problem. I'll stop by later this morning."

"Much obliged."

Stubbs and his band walked in just as Raven was on her way out.

"What are you doing here?" demanded Stubbs. "Shouldn't you be teaching the ladies to press buttons for chords?"

"You are so ignorant, Shelby. Besides which you are rigid, pompous, and downright *wrong*. Anybody listening to you would think Maybelle Carter and Kilby Snow weren't *real* old-time musicians because they played the *autoharp*." Raven shook with fury. Storming out the door, she spilled coffee over her white cotton shorts.

The rancor was thick, but I didn't know why. I'd have to ask Mary more about Raven who, according to Mary, was "at the very top of your suspect list, Frank."

Up until last week I'd had no suspect list at all because the only thing I knew about Mary Ployd was that she was a folk singer from the Sixties. Old ballads came to mind, stories of lust, betrayal, murder. She had faded from sight until a couple of years ago, when she reemerged with a new song, "Jealous Man." Although Mary was a good singer with a deep, husky voice, it was the song more than the singer that grabbed public attention. At least one performer in every genre you can think of covered the song — country-western, bluegrass, rock, rhythm and blues, maybe even jazz and pop. Probably not hip-hop, but I couldn't swear to it.

Until Suzanne brought it to my attention, I hadn't known Mary Ployd lived in Illinois, owned a farm in Auralee in Iroquois County, ran a music festival, or needed the help of a private eye.

Back when Suzanne had been a frizzy-haired four-year-old growing up on Madeline Island, Wisconsin, Mary Ployd had been her preschool teacher and later her babysitter. Mary left Wisconsin, but she and Suzanne met up again at the Old Town School of Folk Music in Chicago. Mary told Suzanne her problems, and Suzanne called me.

Anything I could do that would help Suzanne, I would. My good deed might even persuade her to move in with me, which I'd been urging for weeks. Or me with her. I wasn't particular about where. It was Suzanne I wanted.

"Not until I have a job," she kept saying. "I can't move in with you without a job."

I didn't ask her to explain that. I assumed her refusal was based on pride. If it was something else, maybe I didn't want to know.

Suzanne had been laid off from her Internet graphics design job weeks ago and was looking for one related to her true calling. Wood carving. This made me think we'd never move in together: how many wood carver jobs were there, even in a city as big as Chicago?

Shelby Stubbs snapped me out of thoughts of Suzanne. He

chuckled as he watched Raven walk away. "I know how to press her buttons," he announced. "Just love it when she uses those ten-dollar words! Brains and beauty together."

Stubbs picked up a fiddle case that he had laid nearby. Snapped it open and removed a fiddle and bow. I studied the fiddle as carefully as I could. The top was spruce, the sides maple, part of the neck looked like ebony. The luster came from age and use. It was a beautiful instrument. The bow was made out of a wood I didn't recognize, its grain running lengthwise.

Stubbs turned toward a long-legged twenty-something with blonde hair cut close to her scalp, cropped almost as short as mine. "Pay attention, Bliss. Beauty *and* brains."

Bliss wore decidedly new-time clothes: a leather halter top, shorts with a two-inch inseam, and wedge heels. Her left arm sported an armlet tattoo and she carried what looked like a cosmetic case in one hand. She ignored Stubbs. A tall thin musician standing on stage strumming a guitar watched Bliss and Stubbs like a hawk watches its hunting territory. Who was Bliss, I wondered: the banjo player? Mary hadn't briefed me on the Shelby Stubbs Band, only on Stubbs' $20,000 fiddle and his $10,000 bow. I watched as he held the fiddle and bow in one hand and looked around the barn.

"Where's our banjo player?" he demanded of everybody in general. "My band's between banjo players right now, and Mary promised me a professional. Where is he? You," he barked, studying me and my tool belt. "What're you doing here?"

Several quick retorts came to mind, but I saw no need to antagonize him. "I'm just observing." He frowned at that, but festival policy was that anybody could observe any class, as long as they didn't interrupt.

Stubbs was about to reply when Booker Hayes walked in the south door, strumming his banjo and singing "The Bluetail Fly." His version was about as far from the rollicking one I'd learned in grade school as Midwest Music Madness was from the

Chicago Symphony. Booker's rendition was blues-y, and when he sang *"De pony run, he jump, he pitch / He threw my Massa in de ditch / He died an' de jury wondered why / De verdict was de blue-tail fly,"* I had no doubt Booker considered justice done. All eyes were on him as he approached the stage, climbed the five stairs, walked the planks, and finished the tune as he took his place alongside the guitarist.

Several students clapped. "Yea, Booker!" Lafayette's reedy voice cheered.

I took time to study Fonnie Sheffler, Mary's fourth suspect — after Vance Jurasek, Raven Hook, and Lafayette Wafer. Fonnie sat in the last row of students, tapping her fingers against her guitar. Her light brown hair was cut in a single-layer, as if somebody had inverted a bowl on her head and trimmed away. She wore a tan short-sleeved Henley, navy blue shorts, and dirty white walking shoes. Alongside her chair sat a beat-up old guitar case: black cardboard held together with duct tape. Fonnie stared at the musicians as if memorizing them. Or maybe their instruments.

"What are you doing here?" Stubbs demanded of Hayes.

Booker replied that he was the band's stand-in banjo player.

"No sir! You're no banjo player of mine! Get off this stage!"

Booker moved toward Stubbs. "Mary asked me to help out. I'm doing this for her, and for the students. Now why don't you just act like a man — I mean a *real* man — and let's get on with our business."

"No sir, I'd rather have no banjo player than have you. Minstrel music ain't got no place in old-time."

Booker got in Stubbs' face so fast Stubbs nearly tripped backwards. "I don't play no *minstrel* music. And I'm sick and tired of you goin' up and down the country saying you represent old-time music, cause you *don't!* Old-time is black music and white music all mixed together."

The guitar player stepped in and bumped Stubbs toward a corner of the stage where I couldn't hear what they were saying. Booker paced the stage, fuming. Bliss walked down the stairs and into the group of students, smiling at Guy Dufour, whose eyes lit up.

After a few minutes, Stubbs returned to center stage. "Let's get this lesson started," he said, glaring at both the guitar player and Booker. "I haven't introduced the members of the Shelby Stubbs Band. This here tall gentleman on my right is Edric English. You can see by what he's carrying that Edric plays the guitar." His voice dropped a notch. "Know what you call a guitar player with half a brain?" He paused.

"Gifted."

That drew a few chuckles from the group. None from English.

"Course, I'm kidding, folks, just kidding. Now we're going to have a good old-time class and a good old time here today, but all breaks will be limited to fifteen minutes." Stubbs paused again. "That's so we don't have to retrain the guitar player."

Edric turned his back on the group and bent over his guitar, maybe tuning up, maybe tuning out.

"Now, you all know the banjo player Mary has loaned me, so I won't bother introducing him, no sir." Stubbs paused and looked around.

"Now my new wife Bliss Beckins — Bliss, come back here on the stage so these good folks can see you." He waited until she complied. "That's good. Bliss has a banjo joke she wants to tell you. Being a blonde, Bliss is good at the basics." He wiggled his eyebrows. Behind his back, English shot him a dirty look.

Diamond ear studs sparkled as Bliss toyed with her ear lobe. She glanced back at English. "What do you say to the banjo player in a three-piece suit?" she asked the students.

"Encore, encore!" suggested Dufour.

Bliss smiled in delight. Booker grinned to himself.

"No sir." Stubbs glared at Guy. "What you say to a banjo player in a three piece suit is, 'Will the defendant please rise.'"

Shelby Stubbs' played an acoustic instrument, but his personality was electronic squawk. I could understand that Waydelll Ames, Mary's first choice to teach the old-time class, had to die before she would stoop to hiring Stubbs, who was still telling bad jokes as I wandered out the north door.

After Suzanne and I had arrived at Mary's farm Sunday afternoon, I drove off to case the town of Auralee, looking for a place to stow stolen instruments. The town consisted of two bars, post office, church, bank, pizza parlor, and police station. And a woeful bus depot which housed eight lockers. Almost every building, including the red brick police station, sported a cupola. Late last night I had walked the farm, and now I studied the barn.

Like the outbuildings, the barn was aligned with its long sides facing east and west. Along its old stone perimeter I looked for possible hiding places, checking for chinks below, loose boards above. If I were the thief, I'd swipe an instrument and hide it immediately, so I couldn't be caught with it.

Mary's barn was in serious need of painting. Its weathered gray wood was probably last painted when Bob Dylan was a teen. Back in Chicago the aged siding would fetch a fortune as ambience in a restaurant or private home. The barn's east wall faced a small creek, Raccoon Run. No hiding places I could see. And the south wall was unlikely because it could be seen from the dining hall. High above me, below the peak of the gambrel roof, the hayloft door stood open. Music from a guitar class drifted down.

Bisecting the barn's west wall, a long earth ramp led to the second floor. My Uncle Rudy's barn was similar, a Pennsylvania-style barn, with one side protected from storms by a hill of mounded earth. As pioneers moved west from the Atlantic seaboard they eventually abandoned the Pennsylvania style somewhere in Indiana. Most of the barns in Iroquois County were smaller structures than Mary's, with no earthen wall and no ramp.

Lots of cupolas, though. Every barn we'd passed except Mary's sprouted a cupola. She should have hired me to figure out who had done the desecrating.

A quick walk up the gravel-filled ramp and I stood in a doorway large enough to admit tractors, combines, and threshers. Bales of hay, hundreds of them, were stacked along one wall. Gathered close to the open loft door to catch any breeze, the guitar class practiced. The teacher hadn't been there before, so Mary didn't consider him a possible suspect. "Mark my words, the thief is somebody who keeps returning," she had said.

I listened a while as the class played "Careless Love." The ten-year-old kid held his own.

Two tunes later I walked back down the ramp and toward the sales area. Several vendors had set up their tables between the dining room and the barn, where all human traffic would pass sooner or later. The guy who had arrived just after breakfast was unloading his truck.

I asked if he needed a hand.

He looked at me from under the brim of his low-slung cowboy hat. The outfit was completed by a western shirt, jeans, and cowboy boots. Bucking bronco Wyoming plates were fixed to his ancient truck with rusty wire. What was with all these people in the heavy clothing: didn't they know how hot and humid a Midwestern summer could be?

"Wouldn't refuse if you offered," he admitted, lifting a box from the truck bed. "Jeff Glover's the name."

"Frank Dragovic," I returned. The box I lifted must have weighed seventy pounds.

"Just stack them here," he indicated. Glover looked to be in his fifties. He walked slightly off kilter, favoring his left leg.

While helping Glover I studied the other vendors: seven of them. The one I was interested in was Kim Oberfeld, who had attended the two previous Madness festivals at which the thefts occurred. Being an instrument dealer, she had a good opportunity to sell stolen instruments. Steal one here, sell it four or five states away at another festival.

"What're you selling?" I asked Glover, just to make conversation.

"Fiddles and mandolins. Sheet music. Cowboy albums. Spoons. Hand-forged knives. Best bones in the West." He pulled a chamois bag out of a box and tumbled the contents onto the table, "Eight pairs," he said, "each different. Each beautifully laminated. This one's my favorite." He thrust two thick sticks at me, maybe eight inches long, an inch wide, half an inch thick. "See that sky-blue streak on the end? Beautiful."

I admired Glover's knives, which were beautiful. So were his bones, which I knew were percussion instruments.

"You're the first here," he said, "you should take advantage of that and buy them. They won't last long, not with that sky-blue color."

It wasn't the sky blue that attracted me, it was the gray triangle in the corner of each bone. The same shade of gray as Suzanne's eyes. I shelled over $40 for a pair. A present for Suzanne, who seemed to like only instruments she could stuff into her pockets: a penny whistle, a jaw harp . . . and maybe bones.

"What about the tool box?" I asked.

"I'll get it later." He thanked me and I moved toward my destination.

Kim Oberfeld sat behind her table, picking a tune on a mandolin. The vendor sign indicated she was from Milwaukee. I approved of her apparel: sandals, shorts, a sleeveless shirt, and a sun visor. "Chicago," she said, studying my tag. "Like Milwaukee, just a bit further south. You're the carpenter."

"On my way to a job." I placed a hand on one of the two-by-fours that held up a roof. "When was this breezeway built?"

"I'd call it a walkway," she said. "Breezeways connect things."

Right.

Covered by a roof, the long wooden walkway provided the vendors with good ventilation while protecting them from the sun.

"It wasn't here the first two years," she replied. "Nice, isn't it?"

I nodded. According to Mary, all the royalties she earned from "Jealous Man" went into improving the farm as a festival site.

"Can I interest you in an autoharp?" Kim offered. "It's a good instrument for beginners."

"How do you know I'm a beginner?"

She smiled. "Oh, just a good guess. The way you look at the instruments, as if you wish you could figure them out."

"Maybe later," I replied. "I promised Raven I'd fix a door for her."

My arrival at the corn crib coincided with what Raven called a break. She and the students lounged outside the crib, fanning themselves with sheet music or wiping down their instruments with cloths. A hammer lay on the dirt floor near the door. I didn't like tools lying on the floor. "Yours?" I asked as I handed it to Raven.

"No, it's from Mary's wood shed. Now don't you go telling her I borrowed it, Mary gets all excited over little things."

I examined the door, surmised that the recent pounding it had taken came from Raven, who probably belonged to the if-it-doesn't-work-whack-it school. I shimmed the bottom hinge and tightened the top one, all in quick time, which earned me another touch on the arm by Raven.

I was conscious of the students watching us. So was she. "What did I tell you?" she asked them. "I knew it could be fixed." She paused. "Of course, at my festival we take care of such things in advance, so we don't disturb the students."

Her festival?

"You run a festival?" I asked.

"Well, of course! The Hoosier Folk Music Festival. The entire month of August, every year."

"Uh, where?"

"Oh, about forty miles southeast of Indianapolis. You're coming, I hope?"

"I didn't know anything about it," I said truthfully. "How long have you had it?"

As Raven explained that her festival began only last year, I was silent, pondering the fact that Raven and Mary must be rivals for the same students. Which explained Raven letting everybody know her autoharp had been stolen. Which also explained why Mary had relegated Raven to the corn crib: a tall, narrow, airless boarded building with no windows except the cutouts near the top, designed for dumping corn into the crib. If I were corn, I'd be popped and buttered by now.

Why did Mary keep inviting Raven back?

Raven interrupted my thoughts. "I hope you didn't buy that pitiful autoharp I saw Kim trying to sell you."

So Raven had her eye on what was happening at the vendor tables. "Not my style," I said.

"I think what you need is a good used autoharp."

"Ummmm," I mumbled. "Not sure I can afford one."

"Let's talk about it later," she said. "This evening."

3

Turquoise, purple, burgundy, yellow, blue — a hundred or more tents bloomed on the camping field like giant wildflowers. Many were inexpensive nylon dome tents with fiberglass poles, the kind anybody could pop up in a couple of minutes. Not the kind you'd want to take on a serious expedition. I peeked into open tents, looking for tarps, boxes, or storage containers of any kind. Lafayette's tent was a scout master's nightmare: three jagged tears on one end, sloppily-tied guy wires, and a mud-spattered front flap. Cindy Ruffo, whose mountain dulcimer had been stolen two years ago at Mary's first Midwest Music Madness, was a seasoned camper. She had even tied pieces of cloth on the guy wires, making them more visible so people wouldn't trip over them.

I checked out the RVs and campers next, but they were harder to look into. Fonnie Sheffler's grizzled Chesapeake camper was anchored next to Stubbs' Roadtrek, and next to him stood Kim Oberfeld's Chevy truck with a Coleman folding trailer attached to its bed. I lingered a moment at the truck and trailer, then glanced down toward the covered walkway, where Kim still stood behind her vendors table. What Kim lacked that the other suspects had was mobility. So far, she was spending every minute at her table.

From the camper area I reached the recently built cement-block showers, and from there I walked toward the dining hall.

When the thief stole his next instrument, he'd have my well-worn path for his getaway.

"Cody Thompson, you watch how you climb." Tansy Thompson, one of the festival's two cooks, stood outside the kitchen squinting up the trunk of a shagbark hickory. As if in reply, a chunk of bark fell from on high.

"He's always climbing," she said, turning to me. "And stay away from the black walnut tree, you hear me, Cody?"

A mumbling from above.

"What's wrong with the black walnut?" I asked.

"Oh," she whispered, "he fell from it the first day of the first Madness. Broke a leg."

Cody scrambled down, swung from the lowest branch, dropped to the ground, came up grinning. He was the guitar-playing ten-year-old. "Can I see Jeff now?" he asked his mother. "He promised to show me his knives. Can I?"

"Yes," she sighed, " but be careful."

Cody was gone before she finished speaking.

"I don't know what these vendors are coming to. That Jeff Glover has knives out on his table. Knives aren't musical instruments."

"Hand-forged," I replied. "I saw quilted purses and vests for sale at one of the tables."

Tansy frowned. We returned to our respective jobs.

My meeting with Mary was scheduled for noon in the farmhouse. An old tractor tire filled with day lilies stood near the back door. The first floor of the farmhouse had been converted to offices. Bedrooms on the second floor housed four instructors: the morning guitar teacher and the afternoon harmonica teacher as well as Raven Hook and Booker Hayes. The third floor constituted Mary's living quarters.

The thermometer on the back stoop read 92°.

Directly under the thermometer, leaning up against the house siding, a nylon instrument case stood unprotected.

I couldn't tell by looking what instrument it housed because the case was long, wedge-shaped and blue — like a Cheesehead after a Green Bay winter.

Lifting the wedge I unzipped it. Inside was a guitar, Tippin by name. A brand I'd never heard of, but I wasn't a musician. Rosewood sides and back, spruce top. Tortoise-shell inlay under the sound hole. Beautiful construction. Worth a few thousand for sure. What was it doing out on the porch in the sizzling heat, at a festival where a thief supposedly picked instruments with the same ease he picked notes? Zipping the case closed, I leaned it against the siding.

A loud grunt made me jump.

I turned and found myself facing a pig.

A five- or six-hundred pound one. Yorkshire, by the looks of it: a white pig with a pinkish hue. Its little eyes looked at me. Its wet snout quivered. Its bristles looked hoary in the sunlight.

Pigs, my Uncle Rudy always lectured, are not dirty animals. Provided with adequate space, clean bedding, and good eating conditions, pigs remain clean. Except in hot weather. Cursed with inefficient sweat glands, pigs cool themselves in water or mud. The pig confronting me looked as if it had been cooling itself a long time, probably down by the creek. Snorting, it jumped sideways and thundered off in the direction of the old tractor shed, its corkscrew tail bouncing.

Wouldn't happen in Chicago, I thought, entering the air conditioned farmhouse.

Sitting at the front desk, Nola Grayson had a phone pressed to her ear. She was local, an attorney by trade, Mary's friend. Music lover and volunteer festival worker. That much I'd learned from Sunday night's socializing. Without missing a beat, she pointed at Mary's office and motioned that I should go in. As Mary's good friend and attorney, Nola wasn't on Mary's list of suspects. But she was on mine, for the simple reason that she had attended each of the two previous Midwest Music Madness festivals, and instruments had been stolen while she was there.

I entered Mary's office, closing the door behind myself.

Mary was also on the phone. "That's right, Mary," she said. "You take care, now. Call me if you need me. Bye."

"That was Mary Ames," Mary explained. "Waydell's sister. She's feeling bad."

I nodded, unstrapped my tool belt, laid it on the floor, pulled a chair closer to Mary's desk, and sat.

"Well?" Mary demanded. "Have you been watching Raven?"

"I have."

"And the others? Vance, Fonnie, Lafayette, and Kim?"

"I have. But I don't agree with you that the thief is necessarily one of those five."

Mary stood and stretched, her purple tunic top pulling upward. Exhaling, she lowered her arms and readjusted the top over her floor-length lavender skirt. I couldn't see her red clogs, but assumed she was still wearing them. Mary Ployd was short and sturdy. She wore her long hair, once dark, now graying, in a single braid down her back. I remembered she was Welsh, second-generation American. In another era I could see her leading demonstrations, protesting the conditions of Welsh miners.

"Yes," she conceded, "you said that last week. But they're the ones I want you to watch. That's what I'm paying you for."

Paying me she wasn't. Because she was Suzanne's friend I had cut my fee in half, asking $200 a day for the five-day gig, throwing in Sunday for free. Mary had poor-mouthed and folk-traditioned me into doing the job for free room (the tents) and board and tuition for both Suzanne and myself. Plus a token $100 fee. I guess the $100 still bothered her.

I tried another tactic. "What you say makes sense — that the person who stole Cindy Ruffo's mountain dulcimer the first year also stole Raven's autoharp the second year."

"And the Martin guitar the second year, don't forget that.

The student whose guitar was stolen hasn't returned. I even offered him one free week, but he refused." She frowned. "That is *very bad* for business, Frank." She plopped into her chair angrily. "I think she'll try for *three* instruments this year. But you'll stop her." Mary was convinced that Raven Hook was the thief.

"I have to tell you, Mary, it could be anybody. Could be that the dulcimer, autoharp, and guitar were stolen by three different people. And it could be no theft at all occurs this year."

She frowned.

"I met Tansy Thompson this morning."

She sighed. "I told you before, Tansy is a local, she's not going to steal instruments. She's the *cook,* for pete's sake! She won last year's cooking contest, which got her free tuition for Cody this year." Her dark eyes narrowed. "And even though she won only one week free tuition, I'll have you know I threw in two. Cody practically lives at Midwest Music Madness."

"What about Cindy Ruffo?"

Pulling open a desk drawer, Mary took out a webbed strap and wrapped it around her hand. My questions were annoying her.

"Cindy is a full-time mother. Seven kids. Drives a beat-up old van. Makes her own clothes. It took her five years to save for that dulcimer." Mary grimaced. "I placed ads in the papers, paid for any leaflets Cindy wanted to put out. I looked for it on eBay, warned local music stores. Nola even thought to list the instrument on stolen instrument web sites."

"It's strange she keeps coming back."

"It's *not* strange!" protested Mary. "This is the best damned music festival in the Midwest! I'm up to eight weeks of music this year, and I think I can afford ten next year. *If* you solve my theft problem."

Nobody had swiped instruments during Mary's other weeks — Cajun, Blues, Celtic, and more. Only Old-Time Music Week had a thief at work.

"I'm on the job," I assured her. "Which brings up the drumming class — I really think I should be working instead."

Another vigorous shake of her head, "No, no, no! You take the drumming class, I insist. It's part of your pay. It'll look more natural, you'll fit in. And the thefts occurred on Thursday and Friday the last two times. You don't have a thing to worry about this early in the week."

I disagreed, arguing that the thefts were most likely crimes of opportunity — that the thief was on the lookout for what came to hand easily. Sure, guitars would be the *easiest* instruments to resell, there were as many guitars as there were weeds in the roadside ditches. But if a dulcimer or autoharp was handy, why not take it? That's why I should be patrolling the grounds, studying everything. We sparred a few rounds, but Mary still insisted I take the drumming class.

As I got up to leave I remembered the guitar on the front porch. Mary informed me it was hers.

I stared at her.

"What's wrong?" she asked too innocently.

"Won't the heat buckle it?

She waved a hand, dismissing my concern. "It's just been there for half an hour. I'll bring it right in."

"Aren't you tempting fate?"

"Meaning?"

"Meaning, do you *want* the thief to come by and lift your guitar, case and all?"

"Certainly not," she replied, looking down. She studied the web strap, uncurling it and examining the swivel end. Liars always give themselves away.

"Don't you think you should keep the guitar with you?" I asked. "Isn't that what you've warned everybody else to do: keep an eye on their instruments?"

"Frank, listen to me. I want to prove that Midwest Music Madness is a perfectly safe festival. Folk musicians in general are kind, considerate, friendly people."

That, I suppose, justified my token fee. "You're kidding yourself. My advice is, keep your guitar with you. If you don't, the students won't, either."

She waved a hand, dismissing my suggestion.

I left her office, closed the door behind me, and strapped on my tool belt.

"Goodness, there must be more carpentry work on this farm than I thought," chided Nola.

"More than I can finish in a week," I agreed, stepping out of the indoor madness.

Suzanne waited for me on the stoop. She had pinned her hair up, but a few red tendrils escaped, giving her the look of a carefree devil.

I draped an arm around her shoulder. "How was your class?" She had signed up for Mary's "History of Old-Time Music" in the morning and Booker Hayes' "Old-Time Songs in Black-and-White" in the afternoon.

"Outstanding." She grinned.

"Anybody interesting in your class?" — *interesting* being our code for one of the suspects.

"Whose guitar is this?" Suzanne asked, staring at the blue wedge.

"Mary's. She says she wants it there."

Suzanne frowned. "It's going to warp. I'll take it inside." She picked up the case and deposited it inside the farmhouse. "Vance Jurasek and Cindy Ruffo are interesting," she whispered as she returned. "Cindy stole my chair when I wasn't looking."

I grinned back at her, shifted my tool belt, slipped the bones out of my pocket. "I have a present for you."

She admired the bones, stroked the wood lovingly. "Thank you," she said. "Where'd you get these? They're *beautiful.*"

As I led Suzanne toward Jeff Glover's vendor table, I talked and Suzanne examined her new bones. "This is a whole area of wood working I haven't considered," she mused. "Musical instruments. Bones. Shakers of all kinds, guiros, spoons, wooden blocks, just think—"

"Highway robbery!" Shelby Stubbs blocked the path between us and Glover. Fiddle case in one hand, he was planted in front of Kim Oberfeld's booth. "Highway robbery!" Clutching a shiny new fiddle by its neck, he pointed the body end at Kim.

"Get real, Shelby," Kim retaliated. "It's worth every penny. And be careful — you damage it, you pay for it."

"Where'd you get it?" Stubbs snorted, examining the fiddle. "Steal it?"

Kim deliberately and carefully removed the instrument from Stubbs' grip. "Only a cheapskate accuses an honest instrument dealer of theft," she replied.

Bliss, who had been hidden by Stubbs' bulk, stepped forward to examine one of Kim's autoharps. "Leave that goddamn autoharp be!" Stubbs spun on his heel and marched to Glover's stand.

Raven Hook and Vance Jurasek stood at Glover's table, Raven sipping coffee and Vance examining one of Glover's fiddles. Instead of taking a fiddle off the table, Stubbs reached for the one Jurasek was holding. Jurasek backed off and Stubbs advanced, grabbing for the fiddle. "Gimme that fiddle," he growled.

"Wait your turn, you son of a pup." Jurasek, who was considerably taller than Stubbs, managed to keep the fiddle out of his reach. "*If* I don't buy it right out from under you."

Stubbs' face darkened. "Aren't you the bass player? Mandolin, too? Didn't you ask about autoharps? Give that fiddle to a man who knows what to do with it."

"No sir," mocked Jurasek, keeping the fiddle elevated.

Stubbs made a desperate leap for the fiddle just as Glover, who had been talking to another customer, turned with a scowl.

Stubbs gasped like a fish out of water and staggered

backward, clutching his chest. He fell off the walkway, creating a cloud of dust as he landed on his ass. For a moment everybody stared. I moved toward him, thinking CPR all the way. But Raven stepped in, kneeling alongside him.

A dozen people moved forward. "Stand back," I said. "Let him get air."

"I'm all right, damn it, stop making a fuss!" Stubbs propped himself up on his elbow, but in another second he was flat on his back again. "Just woozy, that's all. It's the heat," he muttered.

"C'mon," said Raven, helping him up. "Why don't you lie down in my room? It's air conditioned."

Stubbs swayed back and forth. "Might just do that."

I watched them walk toward the farmhouse, then turned to see Jurasek put the fiddle down and step away from it as if it were red hot. Glover looked white. Over at Kim's booth, Bliss was staring at Raven and Stubbs as they walked slowly toward the farmhouse, Raven holding Stubbs' fiddle case in her left hand. Mary stepped out onto the stoop just as they entered. She pointed at the fiddle case, said something to Stubbs, who said something back. Raven and Stubbs went into the farmhouse and Mary marched toward the vendor area.

Toward me, to be exact.

"Frank! Richard has escaped again. You've got to do something."

Richard?

"Who's Richard?"

"My pig. Come with me," she commanded, marching off toward the pigpen.

A porch bell clanged loudly to announce lunch. "I'll save you a seat." Suzanne laughed, joining the crowd heading toward the dining hall.

I caught up to Mary.

"You've got to help me, Frank. I can't have Richard

running around the festival. He could hurt somebody, destroy an instrument."

"I've seen Richard. He could destroy an entire building."

"He must have broken through his pen. Or somebody let him out."

We cut a short corner around the showers and turned left at the old tractor shed. Ten yards beyond the tractor shed stood the pigpen. The only way you could miss it was if you'd lost all sense of smell. In the Midwest smart farmers located pigpens east of the house. Downwind. Mary's farm had once belonged to a smart farmer.

A cupola topped the roof of the low shelter inside the pigpen. The way I figured it, some nineteenth-century farmer had come west to Iroquois County, erected the most serious building first — the barn — then abandoned the county to head west again. Somebody else had come by and started erecting outbuildings, each with a cupola.

The pigpen door was still fastened. I had seen no pig inside the pen on my earlier trips: it must have been in its shed when I walked by. Probably admiring the cupola from the inside.

"Here's the problem," I called. A bottom board had rotted away. A closer look told me it was chewed through, not rotted. Richard was one hungry porker.

Mary hurried around to examine the board. "You've got to fix it."

I looked at her to see if she was serious.

She was.

"You're the carpenter!" she said, reading my expression.

"Think again."

"Well, but, Frank — you've *got* to fix it. Who else can I count on? What if Richard harms someone? I mean, he *is* big."

"I'll fix it right after lunch," I grumbled.

"Maybe you should fix it now," she suggested. "I don't know where Richard is or what he's doing."

"Creek," I replied, walking away from the pigpen. "Wallowing."

A dark thought ran around my brain: what if she hired me mainly to get a carpenter, cheap? I turned to look at her. "You don't know much about pigs, do you?"

"Richard's an indoor pig. I wasn't sure about putting him outside, but I couldn't very well keep him in the house during the festival, could I?"

"An indoor pig," I repeated.

"Yes, a pet. Pigs are very intelligent animals. They—"

"I know all that," I interrupted. "I'm surprised he hasn't crashed through the floor boards."

"I keep him in the back room, a new addition. It's concrete. Are you going to fix the pen after lunch?" She huffed to keep up with me.

I gritted my teeth. "Yes."

"Good. Wait 'til you see what's for lunch," she said, putting on a burst of speed.

Instrument cases — presumably with their instruments intact — lined the walls of the dining room. As did backpacks and purses. Unbuckling my tool belt, I deposited it carefully in a corner and looked around for Suzanne.

She had chosen a table wisely: two suspects, Vance Jurasek and Lafayette Wafer, sat there, along with Edric English and Bliss Beckins. The table was filled with Amish salads. Cold beef in sour cream; broccoli, cauliflower, onion, and raisin salad; cold pasta, chicken and peas in cream sauce; an extra-large bowl of lettuce, spinach, and carrot salad. The food did a lot to improve my mood. Maybe I should move to Iroquois County, run my business from there and commute to Chicago for Sox games now and then.

"Mary's festival has the best food *anywhere,*" Vance said as he reached for more cold beef. Piling his plate high, he put his eye patch on and settled in to eat. I wondered how he'd lost an eye.

Edric shoveled down his food and pulled out a pack of

cigarettes. Looking around, he observed the No Smoking signs and extracted himself from the bench, which was attached to the table. "Anybody here finds a pair of running shoes, they're mine," he said in parting. "Left 'em outside my tent this morning, they weren't there after the class." He eyeballed me as if taking my measure. "Hope nobody boosted 'em. I don't take kindly to theft."

"Nobody does," Lafayette muttered into his iced tea. His skin was pale, his sharply pointed nose covered with burst capillaries. I caught the whiff of alcohol when I leaned his way. Also the odor of stale sweat. His clothes, old khakis cut off below the knee, a graying T-shirt, and old leather sandals, spoke of neglect. Pushing his tea away, Lafayette fidgeted with the multiple parts of his Leatherman — screwdriver, awl, wire cutter, pliers, saw, scissors.

"Problems?" I prodded.

He thrust an awl point into the side of the table. "Shelby Stubbs doesn't deserve to teach the old-time class." He pocketed his tool, grabbed his bowed psaltry and marched out of the dining room.

"Shelby picked on him all morning," Bliss said softly.

Nobody said anything. Bliss reached under the table, picked up an instrument case, and said goodbye.

"Notice he lets his wife play the mountain dulcimer," sneered Vance as he watched Bliss depart.

I assume he knew from the size and shape of the case which instrument it contained.

Suzanne frowned. "She probably lets *herself* play the mountain dulcimer."

Vance rubbed his bad eye. He removed the eye patch and put it in a pocket. "I really wanted the old-time ensemble class. But Shelby insulted me."

I eyed the instrument cases lining the wall, figuring the dining room was not a theft area: too many people watching. That didn't keep me from hoping somebody would swipe my tool belt so I wouldn't have to repair the pigpen.

Over in a far corner Jeff Glover, still wearing his cowboy hat, left the table and headed toward the vendor booths. Maybe to sharpen his knives. Kim Oberfeld followed suit from another table. Almost as if by signal, other vendors headed toward the door. Competition.

Suzanne pulled out the bones I had given her and held them loosely in one hand. She and Vance began discussing what Mary had covered in their morning class. I went to the food window and brought back cookies and iced coffee.

"Peanut butter cookies! I love this place!" Suzanne clicked the bones, blew me a kiss, and passed the plate to Vance.

Chowing down two cookies and gulping down some coffee, I excused myself.

"Don't go!" Suzanne protested. "Classes don't start for another half hour."

"Carpentry work," I grunted.

4

The pigpen needed more work than I could accomplish in thirty minutes, but I tore out the chewed-through board, replaced it with a new one, and nailed on a cross-brace to strengthen that side of the pen. I double-checked to make sure I had clinched each nail — if Mary's pig intended to chew up the new board, he wouldn't bite into any protruding nails. Whether the pig would deign to return to an improved enclosure was another matter.

No time for a shower. I wondered which was more socially unacceptable: showing up late the first day of class, or smelling like a pig sty. Wafting eau de swine in all directions, I hurried toward the pole barn.

Farmers like my Uncle Rudy and whoever had owned Mary's land before her constructed pole barns quickly and cheaply: one story high, gable roof, round poles as the main structural support, siding hung from two-by-fours. The life expectancy of such barns was thirty or forty years: a one-generation solution to hay and machine storage problems. Mary's pole barn, its two short sides sagging toward each other, stood at the brink of its life cycle. One long side slumped on its own door, and a lone, dust-covered window blended in with the weathered wood.

Between the pigpen and the pole barn, clumps of butterfly milkweed still bloomed in the blazing sun. I wondered if Mary had considered restoring these few acres to prairie: it could be an additional attraction of her festival.

The beat of a drum, deep and powerful, rolled over the distance as if its destination were the Mississippi River. Even if I hadn't wanted to reach the pole barn, the drum beats would have pulled me there.

Skittering above the drumming came a high, thin screech. Mosquitoes? My eyes turned toward the creek. Under the shade of the massive black walnut tree sat Lafayette Wafer, bowing his psaltry.

Lafayette was on Mary's list of five prime suspects. I walked over to him.

He lifted his head at my approach. Wrinkled his pointed nose, tensed his bony shoulders. His pale skin was lightly freckled, his goatee brown and wispy.

The bowed psaltry was shaped like a long isosceles triangle. I didn't know if psaltries came in sizes or not. Lafayette's was about two feet high, maybe eight inches wide, two inches deep. A string ran from the apex of the triangle to the base, with other strings following to the left and right. Each string was attached to a silver peg at its top end and an identical silver peg at its bottom, resulting in rows of silver pegs down the two long sides of the triangle. Shelby Stubbs had called the instrument a Christmas tree gone bad.

"Beautiful instrument," I said. Which wasn't a lie. The sides looked like birdseye maple, the top cherry. Some sort of iridescent material shimmered around the sound hole.

"You stink," Lafayette replied.

I looked up at alternating branches of the black walnut and counted to ten. The heat was getting to me. "Mary asked me to repair the pigpen."

"Stay out of my tent."

"Huh?"

"You're always walking back and forth by the tents and campers. Stay out of my tent."

The lowermost branch of the tree was about six feet off the ground. "I have no intention of going into your tent," I lied.

"If my psaltry is stolen, I'll know it was you."

I looked at the tree, looked at my watch, looked toward the pole barn. "That doesn't make sense, Lafayette. I wasn't here when the instruments were stolen." I paused. "You were, though."

"So was Vance. I don't trust him."

"Don't trust him?"

"He has too many instruments. Raven was here, too. She'd like it if Mary's festival went under. Where are you going?"

"African drumming." I left him behind, resolving to pursue the conversation another time. Footsteps indicated he was following me. We walked into class exactly on time.

"I see you have arrived." Kofi Quay looked us over. "Please choose a drum and pull a chair up into the circle." He was dressed in an open-necked short-sleeved shirt patterned with orange, green, and buff-colored triangles, khaki shorts, and sandals. He sniffed at me.

"Sorry," I explained. "I had to repair the pigpen."

Kofi nodded, waiting in silence while Lafayette and I selected drums from what remained. The barrel drums were all of a type, staves bulging out about two-thirds of the way down. Skin stretched taut across each drum, with rope strands connecting the skin to seven or eight evenly-spaced pegs projecting at an angle several inches below each drum head. I grasped that the drum was tuned by pounding the pegs to tighten the skin.

The instruments ranged in height from fifteen inches to three feet, with head diameters from six to twelve inches. I chose a substantial one with a ten-inch head. Lafayette followed suit. I pulled a chair into the circle between Cody Thompson and Jeff Glover, who was apparently taking time off from selling bones, fiddles, mandolins, and knives. "Kim's watching my booth," he explained as if reading my mind. "Don't get much African drumming out in Wyoming."

I dropped my tool belt alongside the chair. As usual, sawdust and more important contents spilled out — an occupational hazard of carpenters. My father, who taught me carpentry, also taught me to look around for any dropped items before picking up my tool belt.

Glover edged away from me and Cody giggled.

Next to Cody sat Bliss. I wondered why she wasn't with her husband. Not that I would be if I were her.

My hands were sweating. I rubbed them against my shorts. Having to perform music made me nervous. I felt comfortable with beat and could recognize many tunes and instruments, but I never could play music.

Obviously the head of the circle, Kofi stood. "We are ready now, except for the drum sizes." He approached each of us, examining our drums. Removing Cody's large drum, he replaced it with a smaller one. He did the same with Lafayette, who protested that he wanted a big drum.

"It is not right for you." Kofi returned to the head of the circle. "We will begin. First, if you are wearing rings or watches or bracelets, remove them. They will scratch the skin of the drum, injuring it." He waited until we all complied. "Now, tilt the drum away from you, in this manner." He illustrated and we copied. "Good." He looked around at each of us.

Kofi held up his hand, showing us how his fingers were together, thumb cupped. His right hand slapped the center of his drum, creating a deep boom. We tried the same. Something jumped inside my chest when I hit the drum. Again he made the booming sound, again we copied. The same with the left hand, and we imitated him. Soon he had us playing in a drum circle: he created a pattern of booms and each of us repeated the pattern, first singly, then as a group.

In between the drumming Kofi talked about Africa, Ghana, the Ewe people. He told us a bit about himself, that he grew up playing African drums and was a master drummer. "In my language," he said, "there is no word for *music*. Music just is, like the air we breathe. It is always there, for everyone."

After a particular pattern, Bliss asked him to count out the rhythm.

Kofi shook his head. "We do not count. People trained in western music come to Africa and the first thing they want to do is write down the 'count' of the drum songs. That is not how we learn in Africa, that is not how we play. We listen." He played a pattern. "Listen to the sound. Say the sound in your head. Play it."

"But I've got to be able to count it." Bliss pouted.

"It is not about counting, it is about the sounds and the space between them. They create a pattern. It is not a one-two-three-four pattern."

We continued, and when Kofi announced that the two hours were up, we all moaned in disappointment. I didn't know if it was customary for students to thank their teachers, but we all thanked Kofi Quay enthusiastically. I lingered over my drum, touching the wood and the skin, not wanting to leave. I held my drum, wanting to know it. This would be the drum I used in tomorrow's class.

I wondered how Suzanne would feel about an African drum or two in the house . . . if we ever ended up living together.

We were all still communing with our drums when the sound of a man howling in despair rolled across the fields and into the pole barn. Before the others could even leave their seats, I was out of mine, racing out the door and up the hill.

5

Guy Dufour raged in the tent area, screaming hoarsely. Cindy Ruffo cowered before him. In contrast Vance stood shirtless and sullen outside his large burgundy tent. Several others gathered round.

"What's wrong?" I asked.

"Ma vielle!" moaned Guy. *"Ma vielle!* My hurdy-gurdy is gone!"

"What do you mean, *gone*?"

"Stolen! That is what I mean!" He glared at Cindy.

"I'm sorry," she whispered. "I'm so sorry, I didn't . . . ."

"You promised you would watch it!" he shouted.

"I know," she replied. "I know, but . . . ."

"Exactly what happened?" I asked. I sensed Kofi and several students from the drumming class behind me, Lafayette among them. Suzanne and Booker arrived at a run from the farmhouse.

"We are wasting time! Come," Guy implored, "help me search — we must find my hurdy-gurdy!"

I grabbed his shoulder. "Wait a minute. We can search, but first let's hear exactly what happened, so we don't go off half cocked."

Cindy, maybe sensing that Guy was too agitated to speak, stepped in. "Guy had to drive to town," she started, "and he didn't want to leave his instruments in his car, not in this heat.

"So he asked me to watch his hammered dulcimer and hurdy-gurdy," she continued, wringing her hands. "I said I would, he put them in my tent, and I stayed just outside my tent, learning a tune. Then I felt sick, nauseous, I don't know what, maybe it was something in the chicken salad, I had to, uh . . . leave, so I asked Vance if he could watch the instruments."

I turned to Vance, who thrust both hands into the pockets of his shorts. "I did," he said, curling his nose at my pigpen scent. "I brought them into my tent and put them in front, right there." He pointed to the mesh vestibule projecting from his tent. "I sat inside, but I could see the instruments."

Vance's tent was more than twice the size of my sleeps-two expedition tent. Not only did it have a vestibule, it had a central room and a bedroom. Maybe he had a family that didn't attend festivals with him.

"And then you fell asleep!" Guy bellowed. He and Vance squared off like bulls preparing to charge. I stepped between them.

"Come!" Guy's eyes flicked left and right. "We are wasting time! I will *kill* the person who stole my hurdy-gurdy!"

"Guy," I cautioned, putting a hand on his shoulder, "calm down."

Without a word he swung at me. I dodged the punch, grabbed his hand, twisted it downward, and with my other hand pushed down on his elbow, locking it.

"Let me go!" he gasped.

"Calm *down*," I said quietly. "Somebody should tell Mary, and she should call the cops."

"I'll tell her," said Suzanne.

I nodded and Suzanne ran back toward the farm house.

"The rest of us can start looking for the hurdy-gurdy," I said evenly. I looked around to see if anybody would protest or ask what the hell business it was of mine. Nobody did. "If we're going to find your instrument," I told Guy, "we have to be methodical." I waited. He nodded curtly and I released him. "Did anybody see anything?" I asked the group around us. "See somebody in Vance's tent, maybe? Did you see anybody carrying the hurdy-gurdy?"

Nobody spoke up.

I turned to Vance. "What time was it when you put the instruments in your tent?"

He thought about it. Looked at his watch. Took his time. "Around 2:30."

"That sounds right," Cindy agreed.

It was about 3:45 now. "Did anybody see anything suspicious in the last hour or so?" I asked. "Let's all help each other out here."

When nobody replied, I asked Kofi and Booker to help me search the grounds. With Guy, and Suzanne when she returned, that made five of us. "Let's be diplomatic," I instructed. "Remember that only one of these people is a thief: the others are all innocent. We want to cover the entire festival area, look into every possible hiding place — in buildings, in cars if the owners let us, in tents and trailers if they let us, outbuildings, trees, shrubs."

Kofi nodded, but Booker counted himself out. "Nothing doing, man. I don't want to be part of asking people to prove they're innocent." He studied me a moment, started to say something, but didn't.

Suzanne returned. "I've told Mary," she said.

"Good." I explained what we were doing and Suzanne agreed to help. I deployed her, Kofi, and Guy — again warning Guy to assume innocence, not guilt. He rubbed his elbow and looked depressed as the reality of his loss sank in.

Me, I was thrown off balance. Why was the hurdy-gurdy stolen anyway? Hadn't Guy announced that it was a speciality instrument, highly traceable? And why a theft so early in the week? The thief must feel very confident about not being caught.

I watched Kofi head toward the pole barn and creek; Suzanne to the farmhouse; Guy toward the vehicles, where I thought he would do the least harm. I stayed in the camping area and turned to Cindy. "Do you mind if I search your tent?"

Startled, she stepped back. "My tent? You want— oh, I see, sure, go ahead."

I stepped in, checked out the tent, poked into a few piles of clothing. No hurdy-gurdy or anything like it.

Vance was next.

"No."

Can't say I was surprised. "No?" I repeated. "Why not?"

"For one thing, you stink, and you'll stink up the tent. For another, general principals." He had been belligerent from the moment I arrived. Before that, probably.

"Look, if I just pop inside and check things out, you'll be clear and I can go on to the next tent."

"No. And who the hell are you, anyway? Nobody put you in charge. This is your first time here and you don't know anything." Vance turned on his heel, dropped to the ground, and crawled into his tent porch. Then he turned around and stuck his head out. "Guy's hammered dulcimer is here. Tell him I'll keep an eye on it until he's ready for it."

Right.

The hurdy-gurdy might be inside Vance's vast tent, case and instrument tucked inside a pillowcase or camping box.

Then again, people have plenty to hide that has nothing to do with the matter at hand.

I expected the small crowd to stand around discussing the event, the way crowds do. Instead there was a general exodus of people away from the tent area and toward the sycamore tree near the back porch. Some sort of class, I remembered, but couldn't recall what. Their departure made my job easier. When nobody was home in a tent, I looked around quickly, then bopped in uninvited.

Lafayette had moved on with the crowd. The interior of his tent smothered me in the smell of dirty linen and something cloyingly sweet. Candy wrappers lay scattered along one side, along with empty bags of shelled peanuts. A cracked red plastic cooler held four bottles of Gallo Fairbanks, a cheap sherry. The hurdy-gurdy was nowhere in sight.

I was just finishing the tents when Mary found me. "Frank! Say it's not true."

"It is," I said. "Somebody stole Guy's hurdy-gurdy."

"But that makes no sense!" she cried. "No sense at all! That's a five-thousand dollar instrument, unique! Do you realize how hard it will be to sell such an instrument? No pawn shop would take such an odd thing. Any honest instrument dealer would suspect it!" She stamped her foot, sending up a small cloud of dust. "Where was Raven?" she demanded.

"It's probably a crime of opportunity," I muttered. "There's a hammered dulcimer and a hurdy-gurdy out in plain sight, nobody around, the thief can't resist taking one of them, he takes the smaller one — which makes sense of course — he'll deal with how to get rid of it later. As for Raven, last I saw her she went off to the farmhouse with Stubbs."

Mary plopped to the ground and sat there, pounding her fist on the grass. "It's not fair, it's just not fair!"

After a moment, she looked up at me. "Where were you when this happened?"

I started to speak. Tried again. "In the drumming class."

"Oh." Mary hung her head, looking like a kid in a sandbox. "What am I going to do?"

"Get up." I gave her a hand and pulled. "I'll search the campers and RVs. Did you call the sheriff?"

Mary nodded. I saw Guy leave the parking lot and head toward the barn. He looked my way and I signaled he should enter the barn. Kofi, coming from the pole barn, looked my way also. I signaled he should take the ramp to the barn's upper level.

Mary walked off and I stood there a minute, wondering whether the thefts were more than thefts. Whether they were designed to disrupt or even destroy Midwest Music Madness. That was when I noticed Fonnie Sheffler sitting cross-legged on the roof of her camper. Had she been there the entire time? I walked toward her.

If the theft was a crime of opportunity, then the thief must have seen not only that the hurdy-gurdy was ripe for plucking — he, or she, must have seen that the coast was clear for a quick getaway. I remembered that Guy's hurdy-gurdy case was charcoal gray: a color that wouldn't stand out, so the thief didn't have to worry about carrying a brightly colored case around.

"Hey, Fonnie," I greeted, craning my neck to look at her.

"I've been watching you," she said in a warning tone. "I know what you're doing."

"What's that?"

"You're going into people's tents without their permission. I've seen. I'm going to tell."

"How long have you been sitting up there?" I asked.

Her lower lip came out in a pout. "About an hour. I was taking the harmonica class but didn't like it, so I left."

Fonnie was prickly. I wondered how best to reach her. "Guy's hurdy-gurdy was stolen from Vance's tent," I said. "In the last hour, probably. If you saw anything, you could be the hero of the day."

She shook her head vigorously. "No. I've been meditating."

"Did you see Guy leave the instruments with Cindy?"

"No. But before I went to my harmonica class, I heard Guy talking to Tansy about driving to town. He wanted to know where there was a butcher."

"A butcher?" I repeated.

Fonnie nodded. "Yeah, a butcher. Then I went to my class. You smell like a pigpen."

I lowered my head to relieve the pressure on my neck, swung my head in a circle a couple of times and looked back up at Fonnie. "Did you notice anything when you came out of the harmonica class?"

"Nobody was around. It's hot as blazes."

So what was she doing on the top of an aluminum camper, getting toasted like a crostini, top and bottom? "You didn't see anybody go into Vance's tent?"

"I already told you, no. I've been meditating. I don't remember anything until I heard Guy shouting."

I didn't believe her.

"Here comes Guy," she said.

Guy lumbered up, head down. His Blowzabella T-shirt was drenched in sweat. So was my White Sox shirt. Dejected, Guy asked if I'd found anything.

I shook my head. "I'm just about to ask to see the trailers. Starting with Fonnie." I looked up at her. "Do you mind if we search in and under your camper?"

Fonnie jumped out of her meditation as if Buddha had zapped her. "Stay out of my camper!" Assuming a straddle-legged pose, she extended her arms. I half-expected thunderbolts to shoot from her fingertips. The camper swayed a bit, then settled down.

The words inflamed Guy. *"You!"* he shouted. "You stole my hurdy-gurdy! You waited until the coast was clear, then you took it! It is in your trailer." He struck the side of her camper with his fist, nearly sending Fonnie overboard. Guy was a big guy.

"Hold on," I warned. "You don't want to overturn the camper."

Ignoring me, Guy tried opening the cab door. Locked. He peered into one of the jalousie windows.

"Stop that!" Fonnie shouted, swinging herself off the roof onto the ladder. She scrambled down and hurried to the camper door, spread-eagling herself in front of it. "You have no right to search me!"

She was raising such a ruckus that a few others peered out of their campers. I was wondering how to handle Guy when I saw the sheriff's car pull into the parking lot. I pointed it out to Guy, who hesitated, then took off to meet the law.

Turning my back on Fonnie, I turned to Stubbs' RV, which stood between her camper and Kim's truck-bed attachment. I gave the door of Stubbs' Roadtrek four hard, rapid knocks.

Edric English opened it, a cigarette dangling from his lips, a beer bottle in his hand. "Yeah?" he demanded. "*Jesus,* what happened to you, Carpenter? You smell like pig shit."

Bliss Beckins stood behind him, sipping something from a frosted glass.

I summarized, then asked for permission to search the inside and outside of the RV. Edric shook his head. "Can't give you that permission," he said, "it's not my RV, belongs to Shelby."

I leaned around him the better to see Bliss. "Will you give us permission to search?" I asked her.

Edric turned his head and Bliss locked eyes with him. He gave her an almost imperceptible signal. "No," she answered. "Shelby wouldn't want me to."

I turned away, but English called me back to remind me somebody had, as he put it, *boosted* his running shoes. A lot of things about him, not the least of which was his vocabulary, pegged him as an ex-con. If so, he wouldn't be the first or the last musician to have spent time in prison. Glancing down at his feet, I noted the scuffed-up chukkas. Size eleven, maybe larger.

He looked down at my feet, judging my shoe size. Ten-and-a-half. "I find who took them, they'll be one sorry sonuvabitch." He closed the door firmly.

Kim's truck-bed camper was locked, as was her truck. A locked truck-bed struck me as a very good place to stash a stolen instrument. I'd have to ask around, see if Kim was at her vendor table the entire afternoon. Nothing inside the cab that I could see, so I walked to the back of the truck and crawled under it.

Nothing. I crawled back out to find Kofi and Suzanne waiting for me.

They had found nothing.

"The appetizer class starts soon," Suzanne said. "Do you want us to keep searching?"

I shook my head. "The sheriff wouldn't like it. He'll want to run the investigation. We should go about our normal business."

Kofi nodded his approval and strolled off.

"Really?" Suzanne asked when he was out of earshot. "Are you going to stop searching?"

"What do you think, Suzie Q?"

She punched me on the arm: either because she didn't like being called Suzie Q or because she wanted to move in with me. With the name Suzanne Quering, what did she expect? "I think you're going to keep looking." She smiled. "What should I do to help?"

"Go to your class. Console Mary. Whatever seems right."

She scratched one leg with the foot of the other. "Are you going to shower?"

"Right away. As soon as I get my watch and tool belt from the pole barn."

Nodding, she departed for the sycamore tree.

When I arrived at the pole barn, Kofi had my watch and tool belt ready.

"Where's the hammer?" I asked, looking around on the floor.

"No hammer," he replied. "This is all there was."

I walked around the perimeter of the chairs anyway, looking for my straight-claw hammer. When it didn't appear, I broadened my search to the area outside the chairs. "Somebody took my hammer," I said.

"Mary has hammers," Kofi replied. "She will loan you one."

I frowned at him. I didn't want Mary's hammers, I wanted *my* hammer, the one my father had given me, a Klein smooth face heavy-duty straight-claw.

En route to the showers I stopped by the vendor area to ask Jeff Glover if he'd seen my hammer. He said he hadn't. "I'd offer to loan you mine," he said, "but Guy Dufour borrowed it this morning."

I moved down the line of vendor tables to Kim Oberfeld's booth. A straight-claw Klein was lying on top of a stack of song books. I picked it up. Not mine. I returned it to its paperweight function. "Somebody took my hammer," I explained, "right after the drumming class. Have you seen anybody walking around with it?"

She shrugged. "Not that I recall."

"You were here all afternoon?"

Kim nodded. "Haven't left my booth since lunch. Jeff asked me to watch his, then when he came back business increased because classes had ended, so here I am. I'd ask you to spell me," she sniffed, "but I think you'd drive away the customers."

In the showers I threw my swine-scented clothes under one stream of water and washed and rinsed off under another. I dressed in a clean pair of shorts and plain T-shirt. Back at the tent I cleaned off my black running shoes, spread my wet clothes on the grass to dry, and laid out the clothes I'd be working in tonight: an old "Good Guys Wear Black" Sox T-shirt and a pair of black jeans. Too hot for them now.

I looked toward the barn, which sported three lightning rods and one weather vane — which stood absolutely still.

Guy and the sheriff continued to talk in the parking lot. My watch read 5:00. Time for the thirty-minute "appetizer" class, which I had no appetite to attend. Maybe it shouldn't bother me that I didn't know who the thief was. Maybe it shouldn't bother me that an expensive instrument had been stolen the first day of old-time week while I was drumming away. But it did.

Still, I went to the appetizer class because it gave me another opportunity to observe.

Under the sycamore tree thirty people sat or stood listening to Nola Grayson, who was teaching them how to play the jaw harp. I was surprised to see her outside the office: since Suzanne and I had arrived on Sunday, Nola had been rooted to the check-in desk. Unlike most of the people present, she wasn't dressed casually. In addition to a gray linen suit she wore T-strap shoes, gold earrings, bracelets, and rings. Her toenails and fingernails were blood red. Seriously overweight, she moved slowly. I figured she'd be pretty conspicuous walking around with somebody else's instrument: people would have remembered seeing her. Still, Nola was intelligent and efficient, and I didn't rule her out altogether.

Booker stood off to the side with a guitar, playing whatever tune Nola wanted as she demonstrated some principal of jaw harp playing. I wondered where Booker's banjo was. Locked in his room if he was smart.

Suzanne saw me and grinned, twanging the tongue of her jaw harp. Then, sensing my miserable mood, she furrowed her brow.

I watched as Nola opened and closed her mouth to change the pitch of the jaw harp on "Turkey in the Straw." If I tried playing the jaw harp, I'd slice my tongue into deli portions with the sharp metal prong.

I was just turning to go when Nola stopped. "Carpenter, don't go," she called. "We could always use a rhythm section."

"Well," I hesitated, "I don't know. I—"

"No, no," she said, pointing to one of the small African drums. "Everybody learns, everybody plays, everybody enjoys. Let's go. 'Cotton-Eyed Joe.'"

I knew the Michelle Shocked version and hoped it fit in here.

"Four-four time," Booker whispered to me, pounding out the beat on his guitar.

What the hell. I pulled up a chair, placed the drum between my knees, and followed along with the song. Tried to, anyway. If I missed a beat here or there, it's because I was thinking about the hurdy-gurdy.

And my hammer.

6

Dinner was hot: hot outdoor temperatures, 200 hot bodies crowded together in the dining hall, vats of hot burgoo. Tansy Thompson announced her creation and explained that burgoo was a Kentucky and southern Illinois special, a kind of a stew made with chicken, pork, corn, okra — whatever meats and whatever vegetables were handy.

Not an ideal dish to serve on a 92° day.

Suzanne and I sat with Booker, Fonnie, and a couple from Kansas City who were attending Madness for the first time. I had hoped to snag a table with more than one prime suspect sitting at it, but no such luck. Fonnie glared at me, maybe still remembering Guy's assault on her camper.

My tool belt, with the curved-claw hammer I had borrowed from Mary's shed, lay beneath the bench. Fonnie stubbed her toe on it and deepened her glare. At a table near the serving counter Mary sat with the sheriff and Guy. I expected Yale Davis, the sheriff, to question me about the hurdy-gurdy, but he hadn't yet. When she hired me, Mary told me that Davis had failed to catch the thief the two previous years. Scanning the long dining hall, I spotted Cindy Ruffo with Kim Oberfeld. Another scan of the room told me that Raven Hook wasn't there. Neither was Stubbs. Lafayette Wafer was missing, too. Maybe they knew something about burgoo I didn't. Bliss and Edric were sitting together at a table near Mary's.

I noticed that Suzanne was following my gaze. "Mary looks upset," she said softly.

More than upset, I thought. The corners of Mary's mouth turned down, the lines in her face were crevices. In the short time I watched her, she dropped her silverware twice. Between bites of food, she held her head in her hands. I wondered if there was something else bothering her — something besides the theft of the hurdy-gurdy.

The musician from Kansas City was saying something about a second helping of burgoo.

"Probably got possum in it," chirped Booker.

Kansas City hesitated. Booker chuckled and helped himself to more.

Despite the heat, maybe even despite the ingredients, the burgoo was tasty in a peppery way, and Tansy's cornbread and salad were good accompaniments. So was the home-made strawberry ice cream. "She's got my vote for best meal of the week," I announced.

"You can't vote until Friday morning," Booker snorted. He finished his second helping leisurely, then excused himself. "Promised Vance he could see my guitar."

Fonnie blew her lips in derision. "Vance wants every good instrument he sees. Fiddles, basses, autoharps, mandolins, he's got a new one at every festival. What's he want them for?"

"I promised Vance he could *see* my guitar, not *buy* it. My guitar ain't for sale." Booker nodded at Fonnie and left.

Part of my brain registered what Fonnie had said, the other part was stuck in the gear called Failure. Not only hadn't I prevented the theft of an instrument at Mary's festival, but the theft had occurred the very first day.

Another part of my brain wondered about Mary's distress. I had a feeling there was more bothering Mary than the theft of the hurdy-gurdy. The sheriff kept looking at her as if waiting for an answer. In fact Guy Dufour, despite the fact his instrument had been stolen, seemed the happiest of the three.

Fonnie departed, leaving the table clearing to Suzanne and me and the couple from Kansas City. After we finished I glanced at my watch. "I think I'll take a walk before the dance," I told Suzanne, hoping she understood I meant *search*, not *walk*.

Outside, I walked the perimeter of the farmhouse, peeked into the new back room to see if the pig was lurking there. Richard wasn't to be seen. I kicked baseboards, prodded loose stone blocks, examined eaves and rafters everywhere. Unlikely that the thief had gotten this far, or even stashed the hurdy-gurdy anywhere other than his — or her — personal quarters. I was overcompensating: trying to make amends for drumming away during the theft.

Toward the west the sun glowed orange behind a row of poplars. Wispy columns of dust shimmered along the county road.

When the sound of music drifted out of the barn, I ceased roaming and joined the crowd heading toward the music. I listened to snatches of conversation, all of them praising Mary, the four nights of free dancing, the festival.

Inside, I found Suzanne. Sitting next to her was Jeff Glover. Wearing his cowboy hat, of course. Did women find cowboy hats sexy? He was too old for Suzanne anyway. The barn was full of people I knew weren't part of the festival. County residents, I surmised, here to dance.

Booker Hayes was the staff performer. He gave us nearly an hour of nonstop music, including a lot of numbers I recognized, like "John Henry" and "Follow the Drinking Gourd." Afterwards we applauded loudly, stacked the folding chairs, pushed aside the twig furniture, and lined up to dance.

Edric English took the stage. That surprised me: the festival schedule listed him as playing Friday night, not Monday. Guy Dufour lugged his hammered dulcimer onto the stage. Vance Jurasek on mandolin rounded out the group, which called itself the Monday Night Special. Mary, looking a lot less stressed, called the dances.

I was no stranger to contra dances, having attended them since my summers at Uncle Rudy's. Even in a cosmopolitan center like Chicago, barn dances were held weekly. We lined up, took hands four, and head couples changed places. "Form long lines," Mary called in time to the music, "together and back." Despite the heat, the barn was full of twirling couples, some of whom had showered, some of whom hadn't. As Suzanne and I twirled, I looked around. Where was Lafayette Wafer? And Raven Hook.

Suzanne poked me in ribs. "You're supposed to make eye contact with your partner!"

I did, but soon returned to observing everything around me.

Guy played the hammered dulcimer with power, driving the music in a way that Stubbs might have envied — had he been here to witness it. The trio played so infectiously that Bliss, who had changed into a short dress and cowboy boots, stood in front of the stage in rapture until somebody — Guy, or perhaps Edric — invited her to join them. When I next looked their way, she was scraping a stick across a gourd. "Guiro," explained Suzanne when she caught me looking. "I can make one out of wood."

We do-si-doed and swung our partners and swung our corners and opposites and had a grand time. At ten o'clock the county residents left. The band wound down half an hour later and the dancing came to an end. Some people scattered quickly, others lingered. I was in the mood for another kind of do-si-do with Suzanne. "Let's go back to the tent," I said.

Suzanne shook her head. "I'm going to meet Jeff and learn more about the best bones west of the Mississippi."

"Like I said, let's go back to the tent."

Suzanne smiled.

"Anything he can do, I can do better," I said.

"We'll see," she said, leaning into me. "Later tonight."

She kissed me and left.

I walked to the farmhouse in search of Raven.

"She's not here," Nola informed me. "You can try her room if you want, but I saw her leave just before dinner. Her car's not back."

"You keep long hours," I commented.

"I'm a night owl. How was the dance?"

"Great."

"I *love* dancing. I always miss the first night, though, there's so much work to do on registration. It's a shame about Guy's hurdy-gurdy, isn't it?"

"Mary seems really upset," I offered, wondering how Nola, who I assumed was her confidante, would respond.

Nola nodded but said nothing.

Trying another avenue, I told her I admired Vance's huge tent and asked if he ever brought his family to Madness. She informed me he was single.

"What do you want to see Raven about, if I may ask. Perhaps I can help you." She looked straight at me. Mary, at my insistence, had not told Nola, or anybody else, that I was a private eye.

"She wants to convince me to buy an autoharp."

Nola studied me in silence. "No," she said at last, "I would say the autoharp — it's more proper to call it a chorded zither, you know, but nobody does — is not your style. I hope you're enjoying the drumming class."

I admitted I was, then left to walk the parking area, checking out cars. Raven's red Miata convertible was gone. Vance's Volvo was still there, as was Lafayette's battered Chevrolet. Mary's Toyota pickup was present, and so was Cindy's van. Over in the RV area, the campers were all in place, most with lanterns hanging from the extended porch awnings, almost all with small groups of jamming musicians. Stubbs' trailer was dark. Lafayette's tent was unoccupied. In Vance's two-room, one-vestibule tent a silhouette hunched over an instrument. I stood still, listened. Guitar. Maybe Vance needed the extra tent space just to store all his possessions.

Around midnight I checked my tent. Suzanne sat on top of a sleeping bag, examining three pairs of bones. The ones with the sky-blue streaks and two others. "I see you found Glover."

"Nope. Kim was working his booth and I bought these." She rattled a pair in each hand.

I changed into my black clothes. "I'll be back in about an hour," I said.

"I'll be here." She yawned.

Back in the parking lot I removed a belt pack from the trunk of my car. Infrared binoculars, bug spray, a few other items. Two days ago I expected the kit might come in handy to help *prevent* a theft. Now the best I could do was find the hurdy-gurdy and prevent a second theft. If I got lucky.

I walked around the farm slowly. Listening. Looking.

A car drove down the frontage road and turned left on the country road: sheriff's vehicle.

Back at the farmhouse Mary's guitar case was once again on the porch stoop. What was she up to? I put the case inside the main room. Nola had gone home at last. No lights were on downstairs. Outdoors I circled past the showers, keeping to the shadows. All was quiet. Skirting the edge of the small woods, I observed the RVs and tents. A figure wearing a long dress strode through the tent grounds.

Cindy Ruffo, carrying her mountain dulcimer.

Keeping back, I followed her as she walked toward the creek. Removing her shoes she crossed the water, slipped her shoes back on, and walked north, toward the county road.

I took up my station under the black walnut tree, fairly certain that if I stood still I could see without being seen. Half an hour later, a figure came walking along the creek. She passed within fifteen feet. Cindy. I watched her as she returned to the tent area and, presumably, to bed.

A car drove into the parking area: the slamming of its door echoed across the silent land, mixing with the sound of bullfrogs and locusts. The final camper lantern was turned off and the sound of music stopped. At 1:30 A.M. I left the tree and walked alongside the creek out to the county road.

Raccoon Run fed a larger creek, which fed the Iroquois River, which flowed into the Illinois, which flowed into the Mississippi north of St. Louis. My eighth grade Illinois history teacher, Mrs. Varsogio, would be proud of my knowledge, though probably not of my prowling around at night.

By the time I reached the parking area again, all the farmhouse lights were off.

Back at our tent I noticed my T-shirt and shorts were gone from the grass. Suzanne must have taken them in earlier to protect them from the morning dew. She was asleep atop one of the sleeping bags. I stripped and lay down next to her. She remained asleep. Eventually I rolled over to my own sleeping bag.

"Ouch!" I yelped as something sharp dug into my ribs.

I reached around and pulled out one . . . two . . . four . . . six curved pieces of wood. Bones.

Maybe I pushed them aside, maybe I didn't: I fell into sleep fast and deep. I had a disturbing dream in which Guy Dufour stuffed Stubbs' head into the hurdy-gurdy and turned the crank while Bliss laughed.

In the pitch black night I opened my eyes to the realization that somebody was moaning.

7 Tuesday

The moaning came from Bliss.

Shelby Stubbs lay on the couch of his RV, his head smashed in, blood splattered on both couch and wall. I checked his pulse just to make sure. Dead. The body was still warm, but on a night like this that meant little.

Only two places to sit: up front in the driver and passenger compartments, or in the dinette directly across from Stubbs' body. I moved Bliss toward the front of the vehicle, pulled aside the pleated curtains separating the front from the back, and sat her in the passenger seat. "Stay here," I said, hooking back the curtains so I could keep an eye on her.

A cell phone rested on the sink counter. I took a kerchief out of my shorts, held the phone with it and dialed 911. Behind me, the microwave clock read 3:30 A.M. Turning away from Bliss I reported the murder, then replaced the phone on the counter. I thought of calling Mary but decided against it for the time being.

"Somebody will be here soon," I told Bliss. She was shaking. "Can you hold on?"

She stared out the window into the dark. When I arrived, she had been moaning in the doorway.

I returned to the living quarters, if they could still be called that, and looked around. One of the dinette benches held Bliss's mountain dulcimer case, a couple of small cosmetic bags, and an African drum. One of Kofi's drums, I was sure. On the other bench lay a bright red fiddle.

The fiddle was in fine fettle — except for its four strings, which somebody had snipped off and twisted round and round the fiddle's neck, as if strangling it. I looked but didn't touch. A bow lay on the floor. I squatted to examine it, expecting to find its horsehairs cut through, but the bow looked fine.

The red fiddle wasn't the one Stubbs' had played in class. That had been the $20,000 fiddle and $10,000 bow Mary wanted safe at all costs. I looked around for his black fiddle case. Using the kerchief, I lifted the handles of storage areas, peeking inside. No fiddle case. No $20,000 fiddle. No $10,000 bow. In fact, there was no fiddle case anywhere, not even for the strangled red fiddle.

I rubbed my forehead with both hands. Stolen hurdy-gurdy, stolen fiddle and bow, and a murdered man. I was standing at the plate looking as the strikes blew by me.

And something else was missing.

The murder weapon.

Stubbs' head was smashed in, his skull cracked wide open. Flecks of brain dotted the couch and the window above it. As far as I could see, no weapon in sight.

I went to sit in the driver seat. "Tell me what happened," I said.

"Is he dead?" Bliss breathed.

"Yes. Where were you?"

She stared at me without answering.

"Bliss," I prodded. "The sheriff will want to know."

"Just out. Hanging — " She shrugged.

The cigarette smoke clinging to her clothes suggested she'd been with Edric English. "Who were you with?"

"Nobody. By myself."

"Where were you all this time?"

She told me she had been out walking the ground, but I told her that wasn't true, I had been walking the grounds and hadn't seen her anywhere.

"Leave me alone!" she implored.

"Bliss?" The door rattled, then opened. Edric English stepped in. He too was fully dressed, wearing the same clothes he'd worn at the dance.

"Holy Christ!" Edric stared at Stubbs' body. His shock seemed genuine.

"He's gone to the barn," he said, so low I barely heard him.

I'd heard the expression before. Understood its weight. Death and barns are serious business. For all the shelter they provide, barns can be deadly places. Within their walls farmers have been gored by bulls, crippled by machinery, or killed by falls out of hay lofts.

"I've called the sheriff," I told English. "Don't move, you'll contaminate the crime scene."

"Sheriff?" He looked at me, looked at Bliss. "Are you gonna be okay?" he asked her.

She nodded.

"Don't say anything," he warned her. "I told you what the law is like." He glanced at me, started to say something, thought better of it, and left.

"Did he do it?" I asked her.

"What?! No, don't be crazy! Edric would never do anything like that! Why should he?"

I thought maybe English was packing up his tent this very minute. Ex-cons don't feel too cooperative with the law.

Blue flashers in the parking lot indicated two police vehicles had arrived. In the stillness of the night I heard the car doors close, heard the crunch of footsteps on gravel, could tell at which spot the two pair of footsteps reached the grass. Silence. Then the rustle of pant legs, the slight jingle of metal: keys and handcuffs. No squeak of leather indicating heavy holstered pistols. The cops had their guns in hand.

"Sheriff," announced the law. "Step outside, please."

He used the dark for protection, standing off to one side. We were exposed, lights on in the RV.

"We're coming out," I said. "Unarmed."

"Keep your hands up where I can see them."

I went first, motioning to Bliss that she should follow. We stepped into the dark. One lawman stood on either side of the door, gun drawn.

"Identify yourself," the one in charge demanded. Sheriff Yale Davis was dressed in full uniform.

Just beyond him, in the dark, I sensed other people. Not many. Other festival goers, I surmised, awakened by the sounds.

I kept it short for the sheriff, gave him my name, told him who Bliss was, explained about the moaning that had wakened me, told him I had called 911.

Davis gave the two of us a once-over, taking in Bliss's short dress and tear-stained face, the fact that I was shirtless and shoeless. Hitching up his belt, he stepped inside the RV. He was there maybe five minutes.

"Touch anything in there?" he asked.

I told him about the kerchief and the cell phone, left out the part about opening the storage areas.

"Stay here," he commanded.

"She needs a jacket," I said. "She's shaking."

Davis looked at Bliss, then stepped inside the RV, came back with a sweatshirt that he handed to her.

He left us standing there while he placed a few phone calls. He and his deputy conferred. Finally the deputy was assigned guard duty in front of the trailer door, and Bliss and I were marched to the back porch of the farmhouse and from there into the dining room, where the sheriff flipped on the light switch as if he were very familiar with the place.

Ordering me to a table near the coffee machines, Davis ushered Bliss to a spot at the other end of the dining room. He sat down across from her, pulled out a pen and notebook, and began the questioning. He kept his voice low, so I couldn't hear what he was asking her. After half an hour he took her into the main part of the farmhouse, using the back hallway — the one that led to Mary's private staircase.

Just how friendly was Mary Ployd with the law? And if she was *that* friendly with Davis, why hadn't she told him she hired a private eye?

The darkness outside the window turned to pale light. Slowly a porcine shape revealed itself. Richard stood staring into the dining room, moving his mouth back and forth. Beyond the pig, a few human shapes stared into the dining room. I wondered who they were, and if the killer was one of them.

The sheriff returned and stood across from me just as a car pulled into the driveway. His summer uniform consisted of a white short-sleeved shirt, black tie, olive trousers with a black stripe down the side, and black polished brogans.

He positioned himself with the rising sun at his back, so that any rays shining through the windows would hit me in the eyes. He watched as an African-American woman walked from the car to the kitchen. I surmised she was Aja Freeman, the cook in competition with Tansy Thompson. She entered the kitchen by the back door. When pots and pans began to rattle, he turned to me.

"I'm Sheriff Yale Davis," he informed me. "Please state your name and address."

I'd already given him my name, but I gave it again, with my address.

He studied me in silence.

Davis had two problems, I could see that. The first was a matter of numbers: somebody had murdered Shelby Stubbs, but — unless Davis solved the case quickly — the 200 festival goers were free to leave at week's end, no matter how much he might want to question them.

His second problem was me, and I understood that. A murder, two people present, no murder weapon found. Did the person who reported the murder perpetrate it? If not perpetrate it, then at least remove the murder weapon? And if neither of those, who was this take-charge person who preserved the crime scene? Cop? Military? Freelance? Nosy busybody, uptight citizen? Somebody who's read too many detective novels? Davis wanted to know where I fit.

"What are you doing here, Mr. Dragovic?"

I chose to assume he meant Midwest Music Madness and told him I'd come down with a friend who was taking classes.

"Mary tells me you're a carpenter."

"I've made some repairs."

"Name some."

I gave him the corn crib door and the pigpen.

"Tell me again what happened this evening, Mr. Dragovic. Start with what you did after the dance." His eyes were dark brown, almost black. Difficult to read any expression in them.

I noticed he wasn't taking notes, which meant he'd ask me to repeat my words many times during the week. I reported my movements.

He studied me. "Seems to me you spent a lot of time walking the grounds at night."

I shrugged.

"You're the person who organized the search for the hurdy-gurdy. I didn't get around to interviewing you yesterday." He waited. "Now we meet." Another pause. "How did you know what time it was when Miss Beckins screamed?"

"She didn't scream," I corrected. "I heard moaning. That's what woke me up. As to the time, I looked at the clock on the microwave."

Davis studied me. "Tell me again how she looked when you entered the trailer."

"Her back was to me," I replied. "She had a hand on the door, holding it open. She was stiff — shoulders back, body rigid."

The sheriff, standing straight and stiff himself, studied me.

"And you did what?"

"I moved her aside, stepped into the trailer."

"You didn't ask her what was wrong?" Davis hitched his left hand over his belt and rested his right on his holster. "How did you know she needed help?"

"Body language." Too late I realized *body* might not have been the best word choice, but if Davis picked up on it, he filed it away for future use.

"So you went to Ms. Beckins' assistance."

I nodded wearily and waited for more. Cops are all alike: they go over and over the questions, trying to trip you up. Outside the window, Midwest Music Madness slowly came to life. A few instrument-toting early risers headed for the showers. Each of them looked at the two cop cars parked in the lot. The pipes of the old farmhouse creaked. Aja Freeman stepped into the dining area to put on the first of many vats of coffee. She and the sheriff exchanged greetings.

"Did you recognize the dead man?" he asked me when she left.

"Yeah, I did."

"How?"

"He was wearing the same Saucony running shoes he'd had on Monday, and chinos, and from what I could see of his T-shirt, it was the same one, and from what I could see of the body, it was the same body, beer belly sticking out over his belt."

The sheriff sucked in his stomach, though he didn't need to. He stood about 5'10" and had no gut. Late fifties, square jaw, hook nose, black hair streaked with white. A thin, faint scar ran from his left eye toward his jaw. The jaw was noticeable, the scar barely.

"Also," I added, "there was enough of the face left that I recognized him."

For the third time this evening — morning — he asked me what I did next. I told him I moved Bliss to the front of the RV, where she couldn't see her husband's body.

Davis mellowed a bit, like an iceberg shedding a drop of water.

"How much experience have you had with dead bodies, Mr. Dragovic?"

"Enough to recognize one when I see it."

He jutted his jaw out, squaring it even more. If I'd dropped plumb bobs from both corners, they'd have registered true vertical. "How did you figure Stubbs was killed?" he demanded, stepping closer.

My eyelids were closing, my stomach grumbling. I'd had enough.

I stood. "Two things you need to know in addition to the fact that Edric English showed up fully dressed." I waited, but Davis said nothing. "One: somebody took the hammer from my tool belt yesterday afternoon, when I went to help Guy Dufour find his hurdy-gurdy."

He studied me a long time. "Are you saying Stubbs was killed with a hammer?"

"I don't know what he was killed with. I'm just reporting that somebody took my hammer."

"So you're missing a hammer, and you didn't find the hurdy-gurdy."

An admirable summary of the situation.

I continued. "Two: when I entered the RV, I looked around. As far as I could tell, Stubbs' fiddle and case weren't there. Based on how he behaved earlier Monday, I'd say he wasn't one to let the fiddle out of his sight."

Davis turned red. "Let's cut the crap, Dragovic. Who are you?"

Despite the fact that Mary apparently hadn't told him, there was no way I couldn't.

"I'm a private eye, working undercover. Mary hired me to find the instrument thief."

Whatever reaction I'd been expecting, it wasn't the one I got. Davis's body language softened instantly: hand off holster, shoulders loose. He seemed at a loss for words. He pointed at the table I'd just vacated. "Let's sit down," he suggested, straddling the bench. "Are you getting anywhere?" he asked.

"Not yet," I answered, hesitating. What accounted for his change in manner?

Finally I lowered myself back onto the other bench.

"Tell me what you think," he demanded, placing his hands on the table, leaning forward.

I thought briefly of noncompliance — my gut reaction to cops ordering me around. But I realized that Mary Ployd was in deep trouble, the theft of instruments being little compared to the murder of a musician teaching at her festival. Murder, most likely, by one of the other festival participants.

In working for Mary, I was working specifically to identify the instrument thief. But a substructure lurks beneath every specificity, and what I wasn't getting paid for — saving Mary's festival from ruin — was far more important than what I was getting paid for.

If you could call it pay.

Glancing out the window I noticed Suzanne walking toward the showers, a puzzled look on her face. She wore cargo shorts, a white tank top, and sandals. Her red hair hung loose. Coming here was probably a bad idea. No way were my actions convincing her she should move in with me. I wasn't there when she went to sleep, wasn't there when she woke up.

Suddenly I realized that Mary hadn't shown up. Where was she? Didn't she see the cop cars?

Coffee perked behind me. I stood and helped myself to a mug. The brew enabled me to give Davis a quick summary of what I had observed Monday, both before and after the theft. He asked what I thought of Mary's belief that Raven was stealing the instruments. "No telling yet," I hedged. He asked specifically about Lafayette, Vance, Fonnie, and Kim — a sign that either Mary had shared her theories with him, or that he had shared his with her. I went over everything, ending with the bright red fiddle with cut strings twisted around its neck.

Davis pounced on the fiddle, asking me what I made of it.

"Whoever did it hated Stubbs. Or fiddles. Or both."

Vance Jurasek walked into the dining room, empty mug in hand. He nodded to the sheriff and maybe even to me, I couldn't tell. After filling his mug, he left. A guitar case was strapped bandoleer-style over his back. How many instruments did he own? Were the others unguarded in his tent?

The sheriff looked at his watch. "I'm glad Mary hired somebody on the thefts, Dragovic. You keep me informed on what you find." He waited for a reply. I gave him a nod. "And," he warned, "keep your nose out of the murder investigation. Ongoing case, no interference — you know the rules."

I nodded again.

He stood. I stood.

"It's sad," he informed me, "Two deaths in two years — I don't know if Mary's festival can survive."

8

Outside my tent, Mary sat keening to Suzanne. The morning had been hard on Mary. Dark circles lined her eyes. Her hair hung uncombed and unbraided.

"Frank, this is terrible," she moaned softly. "Terrible. Shelby is dead. Terrible things are happening. "

I squatted down beside the two of them. "Terrible things happened before you hired me, Mary. And you didn't tell me about them."

Mary coughed. "How do you . . . what do you mean?"

I kept my voice down. "Who died here two years ago?"

Suzanne inhaled sharply.

Mary turned pale. "Who told you that?" she demanded. "Edric?"

"No," I answered, "the sheriff."

Mary pressed her lips together.

She remained silent. I waited.

"Now is not the time or place," she responded at last. "I'll tell you about it in my office." She stood, brushed off her shirt and skirt.

Suzanne and I got to our feet.

Mary looked at the ground, then back at me. "Shelby's fiddle and bow . . . ."

"What about them?" I asked.

"They — they're safe, aren't they?"

"I don't know, Mary. As far as I can tell they weren't in the trailer with Stubbs."

Grabbing her hair, Mary pulled it over one shoulder and twisted it around and around. The motion conjured up images of the red fiddle with the strings wrapped around its neck. "You've got to find that fiddle and bow, Frank."

That I knew. "Let's go to your office," I said to Mary.

Suzanne and I walked with her. Mary made a point of greeting every one of the masses heading toward the dining hall. She wiped her hands on her skirt and turned back to me "Lafayette is missing," she informed me.

"He wasn't in his tent," I agreed. "And I don't recall seeing him at dinner last night. Or at the dance."

Her head wagged back and forth. "You've got to find him."

"Why?"

Her mouth gaped.

"He's an adult," I explained. "He's probably ripped, sleeping it off."

"I want you to find him, Frank." She frowned at me. "He needs his breakfast, he needs to go to Shelby's class. Oh god, what am I saying? Who's going to lead Shelby's class?" She looked at us in horror. "No, never mind, I know just who." She cleared her throat. "Lafayette needs to have a good time at this festival, so he'll come to next year's — and he can't do that if he's soaked."

"Mary, I can't stop him from drinking."

"No, no, I mean soaked *wet,* from spending the night outdoors!"

I snorted. "From the dew?"

"I'll double your pay," she said, forcing the words through her teeth.

Suzanne raised her eyebrows.

"I don't like being a nursemaid," I said.

"Please?" Mary forced the word out. "He's an old friend, a

loyal supporter of folk music, and he harms no one."

In for a note, in for a song. "All right, all right," I grumbled. "I'll look for him."

Mary smiled weakly. "His car is still here, so he must be on the grounds. Suzanne will save breakfast for you. Come on, Suzie, we'll go in together."

Suzanne placed a restraining hand on my arm. "In a minute, Mary," she replied. "You go ahead, I'll catch up." When Mary was out of earshot, she turned to me. "You saw Raven carrying Shelby's fiddle case after he fell. Remember?"

I nodded.

"Well, maybe Raven still has it. Maybe he never took it back with him."

I nodded. "Did Raven let you into her room when you were searching the farmhouse?"

"No. She said Shelby was asleep in her room and she didn't want to wake him up."

"What was she doing — sitting there while he slept?"

Suzanne shrugged, gripped my arm a little tighter. "How did Shelby die?" she asked..

"He was murdered," I answered, "but I'm not sure the sheriff wants that known yet."

"Is this dangerous? I don't want you helping Mary just because I asked you to — I never thought there was any *danger* in this," she offered.

"I can't quit," I replied.

Suzanne gave a small smile. "Yeah," she said, "I understand. But I'm worried about you — you're going to investigate the murder, aren't you?"

I nodded.

"But you aren't supposed to, are you?"

I nodded again.

She sighed. "I don't want your life in danger."

"It's not."

We looked at each other steadily. "I'm going to solve this," I told her.

She believed me.

"I'd better go," she said. "Do you want me to skip Mary's class this morning? Can I help in any way?"

I shook my head. "Take the class. Keep an eye on Vance and Cindy." I didn't add, *and Mary.*

Suzanne left reluctantly. I entered our tent and pulled on a T-shirt and shoes, wondering where Lafayette might be. What was so important about him that Mary was doubling my pay? I doubted he was in the barn or chicken coop or corn crib. I doubted he ever took a shower. That left the pole barn, the small stand of woods, and the cornfields.

The woods lay to the south of the farmhouse and fields. I hadn't seen any festival members frequent them yet, so I skipped them for the time being. The pole barn, which housed Kofi's drums, seemed a good bet, but no Lafayette. From there I followed the path alongside Raccoon Run.

A raspy sound like an insect with an attitude floated through the thick summer air.

The bowed psaltry.

The music was distinctly non-modern. Medieval. Images of knights and wenches filled my head. Facing the cornfields, with all the farm buildings behind me, I could have been standing in a field from five hundred years ago in England. Or Croatia.

Except that Croatia, one of the few Slavic nations to experience a Renaissance, wasn't home to the bowed psaltry.

Natural superiority, I supposed, setting off in the direction of the vibrations.

A few stepping stones later I had crossed the creek. The path curved north, then crossed the east-west frontage road. The corn was as high as a six-hundred pound pig's eye. Somewhere in the hundred acres of maize was Lafayette Wafer.

Farmers plant their crops in neat rows so that it's easier for the tractor to drag the cultivator over the young plants, ripping out the weeds. After the corn is thriving, farmers carefully squeeze between corn plants and follow the rows if they need to check something other than the outer stalks. Recently broken stalks of corn told me Lafayette wasn't a farmer.

He must have been tanked before he reached the cornfield: his path staggered from one row to another, then back again. Mary wouldn't be pleased with the loss of her crop. Then again, maybe she wrote off a certain number of rows each year as normal destruction by folk musicians.

Psaltry balanced across his bony knees, Lafayette sat cross-legged, dressed in the same clothes he'd worn yesterday. An empty bottle of sherry lay on the dirt beside him.

"Good morning," I said.

"Do you like my playing?"

"Uh, the sound attracted me."

He nodded. "It has that effect on people." He frowned. "*Discerning* people. Not like Shelby Stubbs." He drew the bow across the strings, producing an angry squawk.

"Were you out here all night?" I asked.

He plucked a loose hair off the bow. Across his lap lay a second bow. "The nights are mild."

"You spent the whole night here?" Could he have been there at midnight, when I was making my rounds?

Only if he wasn't playing the psaltry.

"A tune was calling me." He pronounced it with a long-u, *tyoon*. "When a tune calls, I follow."

"Uh-huh."

"Listen," he said. "I'll play it for you."

Before I could demur, he launched into a sprightly number, stroking two bows quickly across the strings. I watched as the bows moved rapidly between the silver pegs. It surprised me that he could sit in a cornfield all night slurping sherry and still compose a brisk tune. I'd been expecting something melancholy.

The tune was over in no time.

"Did you like it?"

"I enjoyed it," I answered truthfully. "What's it called?"

"I call it 'Mary's Cornfield.'"

"Mary will love it," I assured him. "In fact, she wants to see you."

He shook his head.

I looked at my watch. 7:45 on the dot. Breakfast was being served. My stomach growled. "Why?" I asked. "Don't you want breakfast, a change of clothes?"

"No."

"What about your class, the old-time ensemble? You wouldn't want to miss Stubbs' class." I watched him carefully.

Not carefully enough — he drew the bow across the strings violently. I refrained from plastering my hands to my ears just in time.

"I was looking forward to that class. Waydell was supposed to teach it." His lips quivered. "But Stubbs insulted me. I don't know why Mary hired him, she never had him before, she doesn't need him now."

"Waydell died," I reminded him.

"Oh." He seemed to be remembering something. "Waydell. Mary loved Waydell. They went back a long way."

"Listen, Lafayette: Stubbs is dead."

He looked up at me.

"He died last night. In his trailer." I paused to let that sink in. "When did you last see him?"

Stroking his psaltry, he stared into its sound hole. If a *tyoon* was calling, I didn't hear it.

"Was he at lunch?" Lafayette asked. "I didn't see him at lunch. I looked, because I didn't want to sit near him."

"He wasn't at lunch. Did you see him after drumming class?"

A shake of his head was all the answer I got. He didn't

appear interested in Stubbs' death. I remembered something: I hadn't seen Lafayette since the drumming class. "Do you know that somebody stole Guy Dufour's hurdy-gurdy?" I asked.

Another shake of his head.

"That's what the shouting was about — at the end of our drumming class. Remember?"

No response.

"Somebody borrowed my hammer," I tried. "Right after drumming class. Do you know who?"

"Shelby was a bully all his life. He picked on little kids, made fun of them. He took things away from people."

"You grew up with Stubbs?"

"I grew up. He was a bully, always a bully. He took the woman Edric loved." Lafayette pushed himself up, wavered. "I don't want to talk about it anymore. I want breakfast." He zipped his psaltry and bows into a case of tattered black nylon. Clutching it to his chest, he marched unsteadily toward the festival buildings, his chin bobbing.

I picked up the empty sherry bottle and shepherded him to breakfast, sort of like Uncle Rudy's Sheltie used to bring in the woolies.

From the subdued atmosphere in the dining room, I inferred that the sheriff or Mary had announced Stubbs' death. Maybe not his *murder*, though the local paper would eventually report it as such. People milled about, some lined up at the counter for seconds, some for coffee. Others picked up their instruments and headed for the door. His large purple hammered dulcimer case slung over his shoulder, Guy Dufour ambled back to his table with a cup of coffee.

Nola Grayson, sitting with Suzanne and me, added sugar and cream to her coffee, stirred it, and settled the spoon alongside the cup. "Mary and I have talked about Shelby's death," she said, "and while it is tragic that somebody has died at Midwest Music Madness, it's important for the festival to continue in the spirit intended. A spirit of fun, relaxation, friendship. And good music."

I nodded absentmindedly, wondering if I had missed any clue . . . Bliss smelling of cigarette smoke, Edric English fully dressed, the cut strings twisted around the red fiddle. . . .

". . . do you agree?" Nola asked.

Suzanne prodded my thigh.

"Huh? Agree with what?"

"That we want the festival to be a positive experience for everybody, so we should proceed like we usually do."

"Sure," I said.

Nola nodded. "Good. That's what I told Aja, and so she wants to talk to you."

I stared blankly at Nola. "Aja Freeman?" I asked. "One of the cooks?"

"*Yes,*" said Nola in exasperation.

"What about?" I asked.

Nola smiled and leaned forward as if we were conspiring. "Aja *really* wants to win the cooking contest this year, and she's got it into her head that more table space will help. Do you think you can build a table for the kitchen staff?"

Build a table. I thought about it for a long minute.

"Sure," I said at last. "That's what I'm here for," I lied, wondering if Mary had carpentry work planned for me every day. "I'll talk to Aja this morning."

"Mary told me you found the body," said Nola. A sideways look. "How did he die?"

That confirmed the sheriff hadn't announced that Stubbs was murdered. Waiting for somebody to slip up.

"I wouldn't know."

"I see." Nola's eyes were shrewd.

Suzanne stood. "There goes Mary," she said. She patted her pockets for whatever instruments were there.

"Have a good time," I said automatically.

Her smile had a touch of sadness in it. "I'll try." She pulled the bones out of her pocket and rattled them at me. The motion looked easy: maybe I could learn to do it.

After I determined who stole the hurdy-gurdy.

And the fiddle.

And my hammer.

I also wanted to know who killed Stubbs.

And who had died two years ago.

And why.

9

Stubbs was dead, but the old-time ensemble class continued. Booker walked the stage, strumming his banjo. Vance, apparently eager to return to the class now that Stubbs was gone, hurried in carrying a fiddle and mandolin. Over near the south door Raven leaned against the wall, autoharp strapped to her chest, ear bent to the strings. Did she need a barn to tune up in, or was she just avoiding the corn crib until the last possible minute?

Today felt even hotter than yesterday. Around me the musicians complained about the heat and wondered why the sheriff and his deputy were still present.

"They are looking for who stole my hurdy-gurdy," Guy informed them. "I think the best thing is if the thief just returns the instrument to the dining room late at night. It is unlocked all the time. I will be so happy to have *ma vielle* back, I will ask no questions."

It was a good tactic: make the suggestion loud and clear, announce it everywhere. If the thief got nervous with the law around, he just might return the instrument at night. I edged my way toward Raven with the intention of asking her if she had seen Stubbs' fiddle.

Edric interfered simply by entering the barn. Raven touched his arm and said something to him.

I had half-expected Edric to bolt. But that would have been the surest way to have the law after him.

Scratching out irritating sounds on his psaltry, Lafayette followed me.

"She's with Mary," I heard Edric say. Raven said something I couldn't catch and Edric walked away with a "No" over his shoulder.

"Little bitch!" Raven muttered

"What have you got against Bliss?" I asked.

"Everything." She turned and walked away.

Lafayette stood beside me, shaking his head. "Raven was married to Shelby Stubbs. Everybody knows that." He wandered off to find a chair.

Raven? Married to Stubbs? That explained the familiarity as well as the rancor. But why hadn't Mary told me?

Edric stood on stage and mumbled something about how sorry they all were to lose Shelby. Then he announced that Vance Jurasek was taking over as fiddler for the duration of the class. Edric explained that Bliss wouldn't be there, considering the circumstances. He laid on a few more words about how lucky they were to have a musician of Vance's caliber, somebody Edric had played with at other festivals, somebody who, he hoped, could help them honor Shelby's contract to tour Europe in September. Maybe, Edric continued, the group could include a fine banjo player, none other than Booker Hayes.

Nothing like dividing up the perks before the corpse is cold. As I headed toward the kitchen I passed Vance's tent. Thought of entering it. But somebody was sitting nearby practicing "Go Tell Aunt Rhody" on the guitar. Kindergarten was the last time I'd heard the tune.

The old outdoor kitchen, now attached to the dining hall, had little in the way of counters. Aja showed me where she worked, at a small chopping table. What they needed, she said, was two long tables to put platters, food, and supplies on.

While I measured I questioned her about a typical working day at Madness. By using "you and Tansy" as often as I could, I got her to tell me not only about their work habits, but about Tansy's role in the community.

"Her husband's the deputy, you know. Saw him standing out there by a trailer early this morning, when you and the sheriff were inside. Toby Thompson."

"Uh-huh," I answered, writing down some measurements.

"They own the land next to Mary's. Wanted to buy the old Mitchell farm — that's this one — when it went on the market, expand their holdings like, but Mary was willing to pay more money so she got the land."

I looked at Aja. "Do people think that's a good thing, that Mary got the farm?"

"Don't know about people, but I do. There's not much to do down here. You want some real excitement you gotta drive all the way to Chicago. Mary's festival gives us something to do. Blues week is my favorite. If I win the cooking contest, I'm gonna take me a blues class."

I wondered about Tansy Thompson — where she had been when the hurdy-gurdy was stolen. When Suzanne had checked the farmhouse for Guy's hurdy-gurdy, had she checked the kitchen? Lots of storage spaces in and around the kitchen.

With the wood Mary had in the shed I could have constructed two permanent trestle tables for the outdoor kitchen. But that would have taken time, and carpentry wasn't my job here. I knocked together four horses, set them up in the kitchen space, cut particle board to shape, dropped the particle board on top of the horses, and earned thanks, as well as chocolate chip cookies, from Aja and her helper.

By the time I finished, morning classes had let out. I looked for Suzanne but couldn't find her.

I leaned over the pigpen railing and watched Richard explore the empty trough with his snout, rooting for food that wasn't there. *"Po jutro se dan poznaje,"* I told him. *The morning shows what the day will be like.* Richard returned to the shed. I was so tired I considered joining him, catching a few winks.

Maybe I did, because next thing I knew somebody had come up behind me.

"Frank." Vance placed a foot on the bottom rail of the pen. Size ten shoes, I judged. Opening his minidisc recorder, he stared inside. I half expected him to record our conversation.

"Vance." I eyed him. "Good of you to fill in for Stubbs." I kept my voice neutral.

"Sutbbs was too high strung. Personality type A-plus, know what I mean?"

"He was harsh," I agreed.

"And what did it get him? A heart attack, that's what."

I replayed his words and tone in my head, trying to figure if he knew things he wasn't saying.

Scraping the sole of his shoe along the rail, Vance bent to examine both rail and sole. The pig trotted our way. Vance reached down to scratch behind its ear. "A few of us —Cindy, Booker, Kim and me — were going to put together an open stage performance for Mary. The new guy from Maine, too. We were going to play all pig tunes. 'Pig Town Fling,' 'Four Little Pigs,' things like that."

The tunes meant nothing to me.

"Now that Stubbs is dead, I don't know if it's right."

"Why?" I asked.

He looked sheepish. "Doesn't it strike you as frivolous?"

"No," I answered. "I think Mary wants the festival to proceed as usual. And if you're putting together the tunes to show how much you appreciate her and the festival, it's even more important that you play them."

"You think so?"

"I just wouldn't play them tonight," I advised.

He thought about it. "Well, I see what you mean." He started to say something, then stopped. "I feel guilty about Stubbs." He looked away.

"You feel guilty?"

"You were there, you saw. He practically keeled over when I wouldn't give him that fiddle. The argument precipitated his heart attack."

It was hard to tell if Vance genuinely believed Stubbs had died of a heart attack. "You aren't responsible for the kind of person Stubbs was," I said.

"Yeah." Vance looked back over his shoulder.

I followed his gaze. Over in the parking lot Mary and the sheriff were having what looked like an earnest discussion. She leaned forward, close to him. Davis pulled back, said something, got into his cruiser, slammed the door, and spun out of the parking lot. Mary stood there a long time, staring after him.

Vance interrupted my observation. "Look, there's something else." He cleared his throat. "I'm sorry about yesterday, when I wouldn't let you into my tent."

"Why wouldn't you?" I asked.

His shoe scraped the rail a few times. The pig lost interest and rooted in the corner, enlarging a depression. I was tempted to let Richard loose so he could trot down to the creek and cool off.

"Doesn't matter," Vance insisted. "I didn't steal the hurdy-gurdy, but I just didn't feel you had a right to barge into my tent."

He was right of course. I didn't. "Big tent," I commented.

He flushed. "Yeah. I like to host jams."

There hadn't been a jam in his tent last night. "I heard there were instruments stolen last year and that most people had their cars searched."

"Yeah, that's right," he agreed, brightening. "I let Nola search my car before I left."

Maybe Vance's tent was full of pot. "Who do you think took the hurdy-gurdy?" I asked.

"I don't know," he muttered, glancing over his shoulder. "Who in their right mind would steal a hurdy-gurdy?"

"I hear it's worth a lot of money," I said, watching him.

He pulled away from the fence. "Time for me to go."

I left, too, plodding toward the barn. My feet felt like lead. I doubt I'd had two hours' sleep.

In the winter barns provide warmth, in the summer coolness. On the hottest days of summer my sister and cousins and I would sit on the barn floor, our backs to the foundation stones. That was our favorite place to eat ice cream cones: to slow their melting in the heat of the day. Apparently musicians had an intrinsic understanding of the coolness of barns: a stack of instruments, each in its case, occupied the northwest corner.

Although the old-time class was over and the teachers gone, a few students grouped near the stage, practicing a tune. Guy stood near the stack of instruments, playing his dulcimer and singing a song about four little pigs. I applauded when he finished. Guy laughed. "Thank you," he said.

For somebody whose hand-built instrument had been scooped, he was unusually cheerful. "Any word on the hurdy-gurdy?" I asked.

"No," he answered, still playing the tune, "but you heard what I said this morning about returning it to the dining room? The sheriff suggested it because a stolen hurdy-gurdy is not easy to sell. I will give the thief every opportunity to return it."

I liked Guy and admired his positive outlook, though I doubted the thief would return the instrument.

Today Guy wore a bright red T-shirt with a silhouette of a man behind a team of two mules. *I Sing Behind the Plow,* it read in an arch across the top of the silhouette, and in a straight line across the bottom, *John C. Campbell Folk School Brasstown NC.*

"Do you go to a lot of folk music festivals?" I asked.

"Of course."

"Are instruments stolen at other folk festivals?"

A solemn shake of his head. "No. I wouldn't say they are *never* stolen, but a theft is a very rare occurrence." He clicked his dulcimer hammers together as he spoke and rocked back and forth on his feet.

I looked at the instruments stacked in the corner. "What I don't understand is, if instruments are being stolen at Mary's festival, why do people still leave them where they can be lifted?"

"No, no," Guy protested, "it makes sense." He sounded defensive. "Everybody needs a place they feel free, where they can lay down their briefcase or instrument and come back hours later and it is still there. Folk musicians feel they are safe and free at folk festivals, that's all." He looked at my tool belt. "I have seen you leave your tool belt on the ground and walk away."

"My hammer was stolen yesterday," I informed him. "Klein, smooth-faced, straight claw."

Guy shook his head. "I bet it was borrowed, not stolen. People are always borrowing my tools. Eventually they return them."

"I went to borrow Jeff Glover's hammer," I told Guy, "but he said you borrowed it first."

"Oui," said Guy. "I will return it by tomorrow morning."

"Did somebody borrow your hammer, that's why you had to borrow Glover's?" I asked.

"No. I forgot my hammer. You can borrow one from Mary, she has many," he informed me.

I gave a noncommittal grunt. Hanging with the pig was rubbing off on me. "Do you run into many of the same crowd at the other music festivals?" I asked.

"Some. Raven is usually at Augusta and Swannanoa, and Mary used to be before she started running Madness."

"I imagine the teachers circulate from festival to festival?"

Guy thrust the striking end of his dulcimer hammers between a set of strings so that the handles projected out at about a thirty-degree angle. "Good players who can teach are always in demand."

"I think Vance has been to other festivals," I tried. "Does he teach?"

"I have not seen him much," said Guy. "I see Lafayette a

lot, he probably goes to more festivals than I do. Fonnie has been to a few. I have seen Edric, too." He frowned. "Is Bliss going to be all right, do you think?"

I told him I thought she would recover, then I walked around the barn until I found a spigot.

Guy followed me. "What are you looking for?"

"A hose. The pig is hot and I want to fill its trough and pour water into its favorite corner. I thought Mary had a hose here, but I guess not. I'll have to carry the water in buckets."

Informing me that the temperature-humidity index was 100°, Guy volunteered to help. He zipped his dulcimer into its case, stashed it with the other instruments, asked the group of musicians to keep an eye on it, and helped me look for buckets. We found four in a corner, filled them, and hauled them toward the pigpen.

I walked evenly, balancing the buckets. Guy walked boisterously, sloshing water everywhere.

"Regardez! Regardez ce porc! Très grand!" Guy set his buckets down and jumped onto the pigpen rail. "I cannot believe Mary lets that thing in the house!"

I set one bucket down and dumped water from the other on Richard as he lay in the dry wallow. Richard squealed, jumped up, looked at me, then turned his attention to the hole, showing me how enthusiastically he could mix dirt and water. I let the water from the second bucket flow slowly into the beginnings of the mud hole. "You can pour one of those buckets into the trough over there," I told Guy.

"Excellent!"

Guy acted like taking care of the pig was a treat, not a chore.

The two of us hung over the rail and watched Richard root for a while, then we returned the buckets to the barn. Guy stayed to practice more pig tunes while I walked to the office, looking for Mary. Neither she nor Nola were there. I thought of climbing the stairs and entering Raven's room, but the sounds of a banjo told me somebody was upstairs.

Over by the trailers Fonnie was descending from the roof of her camper. I found it hard to believe she meditated in this heat.

"*Cody!*" she shouted angrily. "Stop that!"

Cody was retrieving a pitchfork from under Fonnie's camper.

"Hey, Cody. What's happening?" I greeted.

"Hi, Frank. Nothing. I was throwing a pitchfork."

"What were you aiming at?" I asked.

"My camper!" Fonnie glared at both of us.

"Was not!" he denied. Under his breath he muttered something about Fonnie being clueless.

I put out my hand and Cody reluctantly turned over the pitchfork.

"Let's go down by the woods," I said, leading us to a small stand of trees.

Nothing wrong with wanting to toss a pitchfork javelin-like. I'd done it, my sister had done it, my cousins too. I was just surprised that Cody, being a farm kid, didn't have better technique. I gave him a few pointers, tossed the pitchfork a few times myself.

"Fonnie's clueless, is she?" I asked.

"Yeah. Cindy's cool, though. She helped me when I fell from the tree and broke my leg. Jeff's cool, too. He's going to show me how to make bones.

"Hey, Frank."

"Yeah?"

"You're cool, too."

Cody treated the pitchfork toss as if it were an Olympic event. I left him to his practice and walked back to the farmhouse. I wanted to know who else had died here.

10

"There's an autoharp out on the stoop alongside your guitar," I announced, walking into Mary's office and closing the door.

"What? Whose? Never mind," she frowned. "Wait here."

She returned with the autoharp case. "Raven's. What does she mean by putting her instrument out there like that? Her Fladmark 'harp was stolen last year."

I studied her. She was serious. "Mary, your guitar has been out there at very opportune moments."

Her eyes narrowed. "Did you put my guitar away last night?"

"Yup."

"Don't *do* that!" She waved her hands back and forth across the desk, laying down orders. "I told you, nobody is going to steal my guitar."

Mary's behavior was odd. So odd that I was beginning to wonder if she was missing a few notes on the scale. "I guess Raven feels the same way about her autoharp," I replied.

"No! This is another one of her devious little tricks. She *wants* her autoharp to be stolen!"

Now we were getting somewhere. "Why?"

"Because! If Madness fails, she thinks she'll get more people to her festival. Even though, I might point out, she started hers *last* year, after Madness was already up and running."

"If she's such a rival of yours, why do you keep inviting her back?"

Mary clammed up.

I waited.

"I feel sorry for her," she replied at last.

"You feel sorry for her," I repeated.

Mary rolled her eyes. "The divorce was rough on her. She and Shelby had been married almost twelve years. Raven was the singer for the Shelby Stubbs Band, then Shelby divorced her, kicked her out of the band, and put Bliss in as the singer. Now Raven's got to make a living starting all over again. It's hard for her to get booked as a single act: autoharp players aren't that much in demand, even if they do sing."

I considered that. "You never told me Raven and Stubbs had been married."

"Everybody knows that!" She gave me a pitying look. "Besides, I don't see what it has to do with the thefts."

"You're supposed to tell me such things, Mary. Makes my job easier if I have all the facts." I watched her. "Instead, I had to learn from the sheriff that there was a previous death here."

Mary looked away. "Yale had no business telling you that," she muttered, rubbing a hand across her mouth and licking her lips.

Sometime between the morning and now she had combed and braided her hair and dressed in a dark blue sleeveless top and a long blue skirt. Still, she looked like a woman carrying a burden.

"It was Honey Miller," Mary said, so low I barely heard. "She committed suicide."

"She came to Midwest Music Madness?" I asked, establishing the facts. "When?"

Mary shook her head.

No? That made no sense. "Honey Miller wasn't at your festival?"

"No," said Mary. "It had nothing to do with Madness.

Which is why Yale had no business telling you." She looked directly at me. "I don't want you pursuing this, Frank. I'm not paying you for something from the past."

"You never know," I answered. "Who was she?"

Mary spread her hands out, palms up. "Nobody knows. An orphan. Yale never found any next-of-kin. I paid to bury her."

That — Mary paying for anything — struck me as unusual. "How did you know her? What was she doing here?"

Another sad sigh. "She was a folk singer, or rather she wanted to be. She was young, maybe nineteen or twenty. Edric sent her."

"What do you mean, *sent her?*"

Mary pulled the web strap out of her center drawer and toyed with one of the swivel-hook ends. "She was somebody he met at a festival, he said. She had no job, no family, she needed some place to stay. Edric had been here for the first Madness and he knew I had all these empty rooms during the winter. He called and asked if she could spend a couple of months with me."

"How could you afford it?" I asked, knowing how she felt about money.

"The rooms were already there, I didn't have to pay extra. Heat, either. She didn't eat much, I was always urging her to eat more."

Mary couldn't seem to get comfortable in her chair. She moved back and forth, left and right.

I remained silent.

"Edric sent me money to kind of pay for her room and board," she finally admitted.

"Did you consider that unusual?"

A calculating look. "Which: that he asked me to give Honey a place to stay, or that he sent me some money?"

"Either."

She toyed with the swivel before replying. "It's not unusual for folk musicians to ask one another for help or favors, especially to house and feed a friend for a while."

"What about paying?"

"That's not so usual. I never pay somebody to house friends of mine," Mary answered.

I believed that.

"What about the funeral: you said you paid for it. Did Edric offer to pay?"

Mary shook her head. "No. And I didn't want to ask him. I felt . . . not exactly responsible, but . . . Honey was . . . she was a good musician. I tried to help her," she said defensively, "but you can't cheer up someone who's depressed. I gave her the south bedroom, the one Raven always wants because it's the most cheerful."

I was bothered by Mary paying for the funeral. There was more to the story than she was telling.

And something else was bothering me. Edric had been at her first festival, and here he was at the third. "Was Edric at your second festival?"

"What?" she asked in a distracted manner. "No, just the first. He taught guitar. And this festival. But not the second." Out of nowhere a tear trickled down her cheek. "Honey died by putting her head in the oven. I found her one cold day in February when I got home from . . . from a late night."

"Was anybody else here?"

"No." She gave me a hard look, not liking the question. "I called Yale as soon as I found her. I was lucky the gas didn't blow up the house." She wiped her eyes, then waved her hand in the air as if to whisk away bad thoughts. "She was a troubled young woman. I urged her to seek professional help, but she wouldn't." Pulling open her desk drawer, she stared at something inside, then stuffed the web strap back into the drawer. I wondered how many web straps she wore out each year. "Honey would have been good," she added. "Very good. It makes me sad to think about it. I wish you hadn't brought this up."

I wondered why Davis had mentioned this death to me. I also wondered what Mary had been so upset about at dinner last night. And what she and the sheriff had said to one another in the parking lot.

She pulled open the drawer again and stared inside. After hesitating, she took out a thick blue rubber band.

"How's Bliss?" I asked.

"Better," she said. "Poor kid. She should really go back to Virginia, but Yale won't let her leave. She can't stay holed up in my room all day, she has to come out and face facts. I asked her to come to lunch, start to mingle." She leaned forward. "Yale says she can't leave until he's done questioning her. She asked me about making funeral arrangements — poor kid, she doesn't know about such things, she had to ask somebody. It's awkward. I don't think she can make funeral arrangements until the coroner releases the body — isn't that right?"

"Mary," I said, watching her closely, "the sheriff did tell you that Stubbs was murdered, didn't he?"

She nodded, looked away.

"Is that something you want me to investigate?" I asked. "Who killed him?"

"No!" she shouted. "Yale will take care of it. I'm not paying you—"

"— to find who murdered Stubbs," I finished. "Even though knowing somebody was murdered on the camping grounds might turn a lot of people off," I said. "They might not return to your festival."

Mary pulled her desk drawer open, looked down, closed the door. "Yale will take care of it. That's his job."

"What about Stubbs' fiddle?" I asked. "Did you ask Bliss if she knew anything about it?"

The old desk chair creaked as Mary adjusted herself in it. "I did. She doesn't know. I don't think she's going to hold it against me and make me pay the $30,000. I hope not." Looping the rubber band between a thumb and forefinger, she stretched it taut and plucked it. "I want you to find that fiddle," she ordered — more like the Mary Ployd I had grown accustomed to.

"Yesterday," I said, "when we were searching for Guy's hurdy-gurdy, Raven wouldn't let Suzanne into her room." That caught Mary's attention. "Did you by any chance search her room later?"

"I like to see you thinking like that." She nodded enthusiastically. "I've told you Raven is the thief, I'm certain of it. This morning," she whispered, leaning toward me, "after I saw Raven start her class, I asked Cindy to take over my class for a few minutes. Then I went up the back stairs to my room and crept down the front stairs to the second floor." She relished the telling of this. "But — her door was locked." Mary leaned back in her chair. "She has something to hide, and I'll bet it's Shelby's fiddle!"

"Don't you have a spare key?" I asked.

"No. I've been meaning to have them made, but there's been no need. Nobody else ever locks their doors, only Raven."

I had a set of door picks in the trunk of my car.

"Is Raven a good autoharp player?" I asked.

Plucking her rubber band, Mary nodded. "She's quite good. I draw more students by hiring her, she has a real following."

"What about Lafayette?"

Mary frowned, tossed the rubber band into a wastebasket and looked around for something else to pluck. "What about him?"

"Why doesn't he play the fiddle at these festivals?"

She blinked. "Well, I don't know, maybe he figures mediocre fiddle players are a dime a dozen."

"He's a mediocre fiddle player?"

"Yes."

"Wouldn't he be more popular as a mediocre fiddle player than as a bowed psaltry player?"

"You bet," she answered. "But with the bowed psaltry, he's, let's not say unique, let's say distinct. I've always thought Lafayette craves attention."

I nodded and sat there wondering about Honey Miller. But nowhere near as much as I wondered what was in Mary's desk drawer and on her mind. "When you work with another musician, Mary — perform on stage — do the two of you have the same set list?"

"Well, of course we do! And if only one has the set list, she tells the other musician what's next."

I knew that. "So clue me in on your set list, Mary. You can start with what's in your desk drawer."

What I didn't expect was the copious tears, even more than she had shed for Honey Miller. I moved to her side of the desk and pulled open the drawer. She didn't try to stop me.

A plain white envelope lay inside. I opened it.

You Stole It.

Clipped from a newspaper, the words were pasted on yellow tablet paper.

My first thought was that Mary had cut and pasted the letter herself, with the intention of slipping the note under Raven's door. Sanity returned: she would hardly be crying so heavily if that were the case. "Where did you get this?" I asked, looking around for some tissues to hand her. Spotting a box on the bookshelf, I plunked it down in front of her and watched as she snatched a large handful.

"Under my bedroom door," she heaved, blowing her nose and drying her eyes. "Yesterday. Just before dinner," she explained, recovering slowly, "I went upstairs to change clothes and maybe shower before the dance." She choked back a sob. "It was under the door."

I sat down with a sinking feeling in my gut. Mary shouldn't be crying, she should be fighting mad. Somebody at her own festival was accusing her of stealing. She should be marching up and down the stairs and through the fields threatening to expose the accuser. Unless . . . .

"Mary — did you steal the hurdy-gurdy?"

Her facial expression baffled me. Horror? Confusion? Relief? The next thing I knew, she was weeping again, head in her hands.

"Jesus Christ, Mary! Tell me you didn't take the *fiddle!"*

She shook her head. "No," she mumbled.

"Do you know who did?"

"No!" she said with more fire. But her head was still hidden in her hands: I couldn't see her eyes.

"What about Raven's autoharp last year — did you steal that?"

She denied stealing any of the instruments.

"Then why are you so upset?"

"I— I . . . . " She reached for the note, but I grabbed it out of her way. "That's mine!" she complained.

"Why are you so upset?" I repeated.

She thought for a moment. Composed herself. "Because. How would you feel knowing that somebody you've sheltered at your own festival would turn around and accuse you of something like this?"

Plausible, I'd give her that.

But hardly worth buckets of tears.

"Have you told the sheriff about this?"

"No!" she wailed, leaping to her feet, stretching an arm across the desk toward me.

I held the note out of her grasp. "I think you should. This looks like a prelude to blackmail."

Mary took a deep breath. "Frank Dragovic, you are working for *me*. I absolutely *forbid* you to show that letter to Yale Davis."

I studied Mary as she wiped her hands against her skirt and then smoothed the material out. "Please," she begged, "please don't discuss this with Yale, *please*! I couldn't bear it if you did."

I tried to get at the truth with more questions, but Mary was adamant. Finally I returned the letter to her, but only after she promised she wouldn't destroy it. On my way out the door, I delivered a parting shot. "I know you want your guitar stolen, Mary — I just can't figure out why."

She had the grace to blush.

11

After lunch I went off to drum. Not going would offend Kofi, I rationalized. Not going would single me out as strange in a gathering where everybody played music. Admit the truth: I was here because I couldn't resist the drums.

I caressed the goatskin drum head, savoring its gritty texture. All of us stroked our drums in one way or another, practicing the patterns. I tried a few of the deep, satisfying booms. *Left right left right.* The volume filled my chest, the reverberations thrummed through my veins. Fingers flattened, I slapped the skin just past the outer edge, producing a higher pitched sound that wakened my brain.

Attuned to life, and in this case death, Kofi taught us a pattern played during Ewe funerals. Only part of the pattern, he explained: the whole pattern was very long and complex. The mourning seemed appropriate, the pattern healing. We had been drumming for maybe fifteen minutes when I noticed Bliss. Like a barefoot waif she stood in the doorway of the pole barn, one foot curled over the toes of the other. Kofi signaled *Stop* on the drum. We all stopped except Lafayette, who did so only when he realized nobody else was playing.

"Come in." Kofi motioned to Bliss. "We are playing a song of mourning. You will feel better. Come."

Bliss hesitated, then selected a drum and sat near Cody. The drumming resumed.

Yesterday I'd left the class feeling invigorated. Today it took prime energy to drag my ass out of the pole barn and up toward the main complex. I was tired and bad-tempered. My head hurt, I could barely keep my eyes open. I sniffed under my armpits. I stank. At the pigpen I stopped, leaned over the rail, and rested. I squinted up at the sun. If I tried to nap, I'd probably steam to death in the tent.

Suzanne was standing outside the kitchen, talking to Aja Freeman. After a couple of minutes, she left Aja and marched my way, practicing her bones, a pair in each hand. *One-TWO-three-FOUR, one-TWO-three-FOUR.*

"What's wrong?" she asked, imitating my posture by leaning on the rail. She held the bones in front of her, clicking them softly.

"What makes you think something's wrong?"

"Easy. You're hanging with the pig instead of with me."

I didn't reply.

"What's with all these cupolas?" she frowned, studying the one on the pig shed.

"Ventilation."

"Over-decoration, if you ask me. I'm glad the barn doesn't have one." She did something quick with the bones, a series of fast clicks.

"What's that you're doing?"

"Triplets." She smiled in satisfaction. "Not bad, huh?"

"Yeah, I guess Best Bones West of the Mississippi would approve."

The triplets stopped a moment, then started up again. "What's wrong with you?" she asked.

"Did you know that Raven had been married to Shelby Stubbs?"

She snapped the bones loud enough to register three counties away. "I don't like it when you talk to me in that tone, Frank."

"What tone?"

"As if I'm holding out on you, as if I'm a suspect you're trying to extract information from!" She scowled at me.

"I need that kind of information to do the job I was hired to do."

Silence.

"Did you know?" I persisted.

"No!" she snapped, "I didn't know. I don't know these people like you think I do. Mary's the only one I know. What do I *care* who's married to who — you know how I feel about marriage anyway."

Right. Suzanne didn't believe in marriage, only in living together.

Except that she still wasn't living with me.

"You need a shower." She walked away, her body stiff.

"No, I don't," I retorted out of pure orneriness.

She turned and threw a bone at me. I caught it in my right hand. She threw another, I caught it in my left, barely. I thought she was going to throw the last two bones, but she turned and marched toward the farmhouse.

I looked at the bones in my hands: gray corners and sky-blue streaks winked back at me.

Singing woke me up.

I'd walked down to the black walnut tree near the creek, flopped on the grass in its shade, and dropped into a sleep so deep that, when I awoke, I thought I was back on Uncle Rudy's farm.

My eyes opened, lids heavy. Dappled light shone through the leaves. The heat was a down-filled quilt smothering me. I'd never take a case in Iroquois County in the summertime again.

Who was singing? Propping myself on an elbow, I looked around.

Bliss sat cross-legged in front of the pole barn, strumming her mountain dulcimer, singing Mary's song, "Jealous Man." Something about the way she sang it evoked sadness and mourning.

I lay back down and listened, trying to summon the energy to get up. After a while, I realized that I'd never listened to the words closely before. "Jealous Man" wasn't from the point of view of an innocent woman tired of her lover's suspicions. The song wasn't about that kind of jealousy at all. It was about the other kind: envy.

I was proud of Mary Ployd right then, proud that she could write such a song, which appeared to be about one thing but turned out to be about another. She was, I realized, an artist, and the song's deeper meaning was what attracted so many cover artists. I sat up, shook my head clear, and stood.

Sheriff Yale Davis marched toward Bliss.

Make that me, not Bliss.

"Dragovic," he greeted.

"Sheriff."

"Thinking hard about the thefts?" he asked, studying the grass clinging to my T-shirt.

I ignored that. "Absolutely."

He nodded. "Found something interesting for you to consider."

A sheriff was giving me information? "Yeah?"

"Edric English. Served three years in the Virginia state pen."

"I figured he was an ex-con," I replied. Just to show him I was no slouch.

"Did you figure what he was in for?"

Even in the heat and humidity I concluded it had to be theft.

"Theft is right. Our friend Edric stole some very valuable recordings. One-of-a-kind, Library of Congress material, from a collector down in North Carolina."

"How long ago?"

"Theft was nearly twenty years ago. English got out of prison eighteen years ago."

"Any record since then?"

Davis frowned. "He hasn't been caught at anything."

I thanked the sheriff and asked him how the murder investigation was going. He reminded me the murder investigation was off limits to me. I assured him that only professional courtesy made me inquire.

"Coroner didn't like being rushed. But these people — all 200 of them — leave Saturday morning!" Davis scowled just thinking about it. "Coroner places the time of death between 2 and 3 A.M." He turned his head toward Bliss, who had stopped singing "Jealous Man" and was now strummed a tune I didn't recognize. I liked the sound of the drone string on the mountain dulcimer. Davis turned back to me. "What do you make of English and Ms. Beckins?"

"There's something between them," I replied.

"Yeah. Suspicious," he muttered, studying Bliss. "Making headway on who's stealing the instruments?"

"Thought I might be," I replied, "but the missing fiddle complicates things."

He nodded. "I can see that it does."

The sheriff's cell phone rang. "Davis," he answered. Listened. "Stay right there." He pocketed the phone. "Good luck on the thefts, Dragovic. Keep me informed."

I watched him walk to the parking lot and drive his car down the east-west frontage road about a hundred yards. He emerged, slammed the door, hitched up his belt, and disappeared into the cornfield.

Bliss approached me, mountain dulcimer in hand.

"How are you doing?" I asked.

"Okay, thank you." She looked at me. "I was thinking, you

know. I felt better in the drumming class."

"Yeah. So did I."

"I was thinking," she said, tugging at one of the diamond studs in her ear, "would people think it was wrong if I went to the appetizer class? Edric is leading it."

Over near the farmhouse the appetizer class gathered under the sycamore. Suzanne stood there talking to Vance Jurasek, who had his minidisc recorder in hand. I'd probably snoozed right through a chance to enter his tent. I wondered if Suzanne would throw more bones at me. "Come on," I said to Bliss, "we'll go together."

The group was smaller than yesterday's jaw harp session. "This class costs a small fee," Bliss informed me. "Ten dollars a person. Edric says it's because of the extra materials we need to build a washtub bass. He's the one we pay." Her sales spiel finished, she moved off to sit with Guy Dufour.

I'd seen washtub basses at impromptu gatherings on Uncle Rudy's farm. Essentially a washtub, a piece of rope, and a long dowel. The tub served as the soundbox, the dowel as the neck, and the rope as the string of the homemade musical instrument.

I handed Edric a ten as Suzanne studied the supplies: five galvanized washtubs and fifteen empty plastic "gut buckets," the kind construction sealant comes in. "We should pick different ones," I said to Suzanne. "You take the washtub and I'll take the plastic."

"Why?"

Her tone said, *Why should we make joint decisions?*

"Washtub will make a better sound, and you're the musician, so you take it."

"Washtub takes up more space," she said after a moment. "You have a bigger apartment, you take it."

I figured she really wanted the galvanized tub for its better sound. I would, if I were a musician. "I'm hoping we'll be in the same apartment," I countered.

Another pause. "Then we wouldn't need two basses."

"We could each make one, then give one to Peter." Peter was my seven-year-old nephew. My sister would kill me, of course.

"Come on, folks, we haven't got twenty-four hours here." Edric fidgeted.

Suzanne selected a plastic bucket. I guess she was still annoyed with me. I took a washtub. Guy had picked a washtub, too, and was already working on it. Edric frowned at him. Bliss followed Suzanne's choice, taking a plastic bucket back to her chair. Kim Oberfeld had once again left the vendor area to participate in the appetizer class. She chose a plastic tub, which surprised me. I thought that, being an instrument dealer, she'd build a washtub bass for $10 and sell it at her table for more.

"Take one," Edric told Cody, "and your mother can pay me tomorrow."

Cody chose the tub because it was bigger, then lugged it to the chair beside me. I moved my tool belt out of his way.

Booker Hayes positioned a chair under the tree and plucked his guitar. I didn't know if he had agreed to accompany the appetizer class each afternoon or if he was just a good sport. Edric gave him a nod and a count and they were off, Booker on the guitar, Edric on his homemade bass. Edric was good, and he smiled as he played. Either he didn't mind Stubbs being dead or he felt it was his responsibility to give the appetizer class a good show.

After the tune he showed us how to construct our own basses. Booker followed him, acting as assistant.

"Now, you can use a broom handle for the neck," Edric explained as he moved among us, "but in my opinion a broom handle isn't strong enough. I prefer a one-and-a-quarter-inch dowel, like I've given you here. I keep mine plain, but if any of you gentlemen out there enjoy carving, you can whittle yourselves a fine scroll on the dowel."

Suzanne scowled at the "gentlemen" but kept her knowledge of firmers, tangs, and carving knives to herself. I could see her looking at the dowel, though, imagining how she would shape it. A good piece of hardwood would serve even better. Hickory, maybe.

"Cotton rope like this is fine," explained Booker, coming along after Edric, tightening a knot here, correcting a length there. "But I've known washtub players to use old bass strings. The D string is your best bet. Man, I even know a player who uses an old brake cable as his string."

His rounds completed, Edric glanced at his watch. "How about a little 'Whiskey Before Breakfast'?" he asked. Booker nodded and they began. Suzanne and most of the others had no difficulty playing along. I watched where she placed her hands and followed along, hoping my notes blended in.

As we played, the sheriff's car pulled into the parking lot. Davis emerged and walked in our direction.

When the class ended, he motioned Edric aside. "Are these your shoes?" he asked, holding a pair of running shoes wrapped in a plastic bag.

"You can't pin it on me," Edric said. "I didn't kill him."

12

Even though Aja's barbecued pork, sweet corn, and coleslaw, with watermelon and a cobbler for dessert, went down well, dinner was a subdued affair.

"She has my vote for best cook," I whispered to Suzanne.

I'd apologized for interrogating her, she'd apologized for throwing bones at me. We had exchanged information on things, and when I told her that Vance and others were learning pig tunes to surprise Mary, Suzanne decided that she would carve a miniature pig for Mary, as a gift. She was studying the block of wood now, looking for its pig features.

"I heard that, man," Booker admonished me. "You still can't vote until Friday."

Knowing I'd be patrolling the festival grounds until the wee hours, I helped myself to more food.

The scheduled evening concert was replaced by a Shelby Stubbs tribute. Raven played "Frankie and Johnny," which struck me as strange to sing in somebody's memory, but considering that Raven chose it, maybe not so strange. As if she hadn't given the sheriff enough to ponder, she followed with "Come All Ye Fair and Tender Ladies," about a false-hearted lover. Mary played "The Water Is Wide," then she and Raven performed a duet, "Auld Lang Syne." Propped against the barn wall, I watched and listened.

About halfway through the remembrances Davis and his

deputy walked in with Edric, who shook them off like a hound shakes water. The sheriff must have thought Edric's answers on the shoes good enough for now. When lab results returned, he might feel different. After conferring with Mary, Edric took the stage to play a solo tune in tribute to Stubbs.

"That's Waydell's *tyoon,"* Lafayette informed me, appearing at my elbow so quietly I didn't know he was there until he spoke. "Shelby never had a good thing to say about Waydell." He rubbed his hands together as if cold. "Worked the other way, too."

"So you think Stubbs wouldn't have liked this tune being played?"

"He'd have hated it." Lafayette emitted a high, reedy sound something like an asthma attack. I concluded he was laughing.

"Edric and Shelby had a big argument after class yesterday."

I took my eyes off Edric and studied Lafayette. "What about?"

"The Europe tour. Shelby wasn't going to take Edric — he was going to get a new guitarist. Edric said, 'Over my dead body.'" Lafayette wheezed out a laugh again. "Looks like it was the other way around."

"They argued about that in front of everybody?" I wiped my face and neck with a kerchief, just like the regulars.

Lafayette moved his head slightly, left to right and right to left. "They were off in a corner, didn't see me standing there."

On stage Edric played with feeling. "Edric seems like a good musician to me: why wouldn't Stubbs take him?"

"He didn't like Edric and Bliss being together so much." Lafayette's eyes narrowed. "Shelby always wanted what somebody else had."

Edric finished and found a seat next to Bliss. The sheriff sat behind them. Guy Dufour, who had been sitting with Bliss, walked away. I watched him exit by the south doors. Kim Oberfeld took the stage with Cindy Ruffo, Kim on the mandolin, Cindy on the mountain dulcimer. Cindy's dulcimer had been stolen two years ago, now she had a new one. Had she bought it from Kim? The Kim-Cindy combo lacked sound on the bottom end: an African drum might have worked wonders. I'd have to get into Kim's truckbed camper. And Raven's room. Not now, though: Nola was still in the office. Vance was nowhere to be seen.

Suzanne sat between Fonnie Sheffler and Jeff Glover. I hoped she was paying lots of attention to Fonnie and none to Glover. Off to my right more than a hundred instruments rested in disorderly piles. I looked them over as I exited by the south door. Eight o'clock. In the midsummer evening, I couldn't tell if a light glowed in Nola's office. I walked through the tent area, nodding to Vance, who was playing a fiddle. Fonnie was right, the man owned a heap of instruments.

On the near side of the creek a campfire burned.

Guy stood in front of the flames, stirring a cauldron. An unpleasant odor drifted my way with the steam — a grayish smell of gristle, fat, and marrow.

"What are you doing?" I asked casually.

"Boiling down the thief who stole my hurdy-gurdy."

"Uh-huh."

"Not really," grinned Guy. "It is Lafayette and his bowed psaltry." He chuckled as he stirred with a big wooden pole.

"Uh-huh. As long as it's not Mary's pig."

"Le porc!! No, not the pig."

"So what is it really?"

"Bones."

"Bones?" I repeated. "The kind Jeff Glover sells?"

Guy laughed. "Woods. He sells woods, as do the other vendors. They are made to look like bones, of course, and they are played the same way. But the sound isn't the same. I am making real bones, out of cow rib bones."

I looked into the pot and Guy obliged by stirring vigorously. The steam prevented me from seeing what was inside, but a bony rattle convinced me of the contents.

"Where'd you get the ribs?" I asked, feeling uneasy.

"From the butcher. Tansy told me where to go, and I went and got all the bones."

"Uh-huh. Why?"

Guy looked at me. "For the appetizer, of course."

"Appetizer?"

"You know," he said impatiently. "The appetizer course. I mean, class."

It finally became clear. "You're teaching an appetizer class. On how to play the bones."

"*Oui*. Real bones. You will come? Hold out your hands," he commanded. I complied. "Good. Your hands are large, you will be able to hold and rattle the bones well. You will be there?" he asked again.

"What day?"

"Tomorrow. You will love it," he laughed. "It will impress the women — you will look masculine and sexy." He did a few flat-foot dance steps while stirring the kettle, moving his free hand around, making clicking sounds with his teeth.

Guy's carefree abandon was admirable, I guess. Not sure I'd react the same way if it was my hurdy-gurdy that had been stolen.

Cody ran toward us. "Frank! Hey, Frank! Hey, Guy, look what I found!" He thrust a small black plastic box at me.

I examined it. An electronic tuner.

"Cool, huh? You know how much one of these things costs? Almost sixty dollars! And I found it."

"Let me see that." Guy dropped his stirring stick and practically tore the tuner out of my hand. "This is *mine!* This is my tuner!" he shouted. "See the little, ah, *nick*? See the nick on this corner? Where did you find this?" he demanded of Cody.

I couldn't figure why Guy was so excited. Cody backed off a step but Guy advanced. I stepped in front of him. "Stay cool."

Guy shook the tuner in my face. "Don't you see? This was in my case! My hurdy-gurdy case!" He looked over my shoulder. "Where did you find this, Cody?"

I felt Cody retreat another step. "You never said your tuner was stolen," I argued.

"Aaahhhhh!" Guy turned his back and stomped around the cauldron a few times. *"Imbecile!* Of course I did not say my tuner was stolen, it was my hurdy-gurdy I was worried about! The tuner was merely in the case! A song book was in the case, too! I did not say my song book was stolen!"

Right.

I suggested to Guy that he check the dining hall, to see if his hurdy-gurdy had been returned. I promised I'd talk to Cody while he went to check. Guy took off instantly, his boots pounding the ground as he ran.

I turned to Cody. "How you doing?"

He shrugged.

"Guy's big and he's intense, but he's solid."

Cody watched Guy cover the ground between us and the dining hall. "What's *intense?"*

I explained, then asked him where he'd found the tuner.

Another shrug. "I forget."

I draped an arm over his shoulder and directed us toward the tents. "You'll remember. Somewhere up here, wasn't it?"

Reluctantly, Cody pointed to a spot on the ground. "It was under the flowers, see?" He moved aside some thistle and pointed to the spot — just outside Lafayette's bedraggled tent.

Guy returned crestfallen: no hurdy-gurdy. Before he could rampage through the tent, I reminded him that Lafayette had been in the drumming class when the hurdy-gurdy was stolen.

He sighed heavily. "Come," he said to Cody after a moment. "I will reward you for finding my tuner. I will make you the best pair of bones in all of Midwest Madness."

"Can I stir?" asked Cody as the two of them walked toward the cauldron.

Back at the barn, the tribute had ended and people stepped outdoors for fresh air, for cigarettes, maybe just to look at the stars. Inside, the evening's dance band was setting up. Swinging her blue guitar case over her shoulder, Mary informed me she had to get back to the office.

I fell in step beside her. "Well," she said, looking up at me, "that wasn't bad, all things considered." Her sandals kicked up small puffs of dust. "Are you getting anywhere?"

"I'm a little closer than I was this morning."

She looked at me. Waited. "I see," she grumbled, flinging her braid over a shoulder. "You don't want to tell me."

"It's minor, Mary. I don't want you jumping to conclusions."

"Fine," she retorted, "Why did Yale take Edric into town?"

I explained that Edric said his shoes had been stolen, that the sheriff's deputy had found Edric's shoes in a ditch, and the sheriff had questioned Edric about the shoes. At least I assumed that's what had happened.

Again I tried to convince Mary that the anonymous letter she received should be turned over to the sheriff. I followed her to the stoop and through the farmhouse door, noticing that for once she didn't leave her guitar out where anybody could take it. Nola sat at the desk, organizing papers into stacks. She looked up as we walked in, but said nothing. Mary walked into her office, closing the door in my face. The lock clicked.

I looked at Nola, who looked at me.

"She's worried," I offered. "About the thefts and Stubbs' death."

Nola looked dubious. "What did you say to her?"

"Not much."

She stood, fiddled with her earrings, then arranged papers

into precise stacks. Her nails, painted a seasick pewter today, matched her outfit. She turned off the light. "I'd like to talk to you. You may not know this," she said as we stepped outdoors, "but I'm an attorney."

That didn't strike her name off my list.

"As an attorney, I know Sheriff Davis professionally. And personally — everything's personal in a farming community." She stumbled in the dark but I caught her by the elbow. The contents of her purse spilled on the grass. I retrieved them. Keys, jaw harp, coin purse, Swiss Army knife, lipstick.

"Suzanne carries one of these, too," I said, examining the knife.

Nola removed it from my hand. "Thank you." She veered toward the vendor area, now empty, the instruments and other items packed into their respective boxes and put away for the night. Locked up, I hoped.

Nola sat in one of the empty chairs and indicated I should sit, also.

I obliged her. "What did you want to talk about?" I prodded when she remained silent.

"When you found Shelby's body . . . do you think he suffered much?"

I ducked my head down, running my hand through my hair. "I don't know," I mumbled. "I'd say he died quickly." I looked back up, but I couldn't read her expression.

Nola chewed on her upper lip a while. I waited.

"I was a fan," she said.

I didn't get it.

"Of Shelby Stubbs," she explained. "I had every recording he ever made. I could tell you which songs he recorded on which album, in which studio. I paid to have one of his CD covers blown up poster-size.

"Part of the reason I volunteered to help Mary was that I wanted her to bring the Shelby Stubbs Band to Iroquois

County." Nola looked into the sky. "Pretty moon, isn't it? Mary didn't want to. No matter what I said, did, or promised, she refused to even *call* Shelby, refused to even *ask* if he wanted to teach a week at Midwest Music Madness." She gazed at the moon a while longer, then turned to me. "I couldn't understand it."

"Maybe she preferred Waydell Ames."

Nola nodded. "She did. She and Waydell knew each other from a long time ago, I guess. He was from Texas, though, and here in Illinois somebody like Shelby, who's from Virginia, has a bigger following."

My sister's an attorney, and so is my brother-in-law, and I've encountered plenty of others in my line of work, so I know they often talk obliquely. I've been known to do it myself. But whatever it was Nola was trying to say, the angle wasn't blunt enough. "You weren't in Stubbs class," I observed. Two could play angles.

She smiled as if I'd scored a point. "I signed up for it."

"What happened?"

"You were there on the porch yesterday morning," she supplied.

"Yeah, but I— oh. You don't play guitar, fiddle, or banjo."

Extracting the jaw harp from her tiny purse, she placed it between her lips. *Twang!* Pulling it away from her mouth, she examined it. "No. The jaw harp can't *drive* the music. It could fill in, though — but you know Shelby wouldn't have allowed it."

"I didn't see you on the porch."

Again the enigmatic, sad smile. "I listened from the open window. That's when I told Mary I wouldn't take Shelby's class if he was the last music teacher on earth."

I nodded.

"Are you familiar with Robert Frost?" she asked.

After a second I realized she meant the poet. "'Stopping by Woods on a Snowy Evening,'" I offered.

"'A Minor Bird,'" she countered, "in which he says it is

wrong to silence anybody's song. I'm paraphrasing."

I waited a bit, to let her know I understood.

"Looks like rain tomorrow," she said, gazing at the sky.

In the dusk I stared at the full moon. Not a cloud in sight.

The sheriff marched out of the barn toward the parking lot. Going home at last?

Dance music bounced out of the barn. Nola stood. "Would you dance with me?"

"My pleasure."

We entered the barn just in time for me to see couples form squares. Suzanne paired with Glover, who was holding her hand even though the dancing hadn't begun. Lafayette was with Fonnie, and Cindy with Guy. Bliss and Edric left together. Nola and I joined Suzanne's square. Lead couples exchanged places. The caller had us do a walk through, and then the dance began. Nola wheezed as we danced and every time I gave her a courtesy turn I worried that she might drop from overexertion. But no matter the tempo, she danced along with a smile on her face.

As Nola and I danced down the line I frowned at Glover. His limp, slight to begin with, disappeared on the dance floor. "He's holding you much too tight," I said to Suzanne when she became my new corner.

"Who?"

"Cowboy Hat."

"He's a good dancer." She grinned. "I'm thinking of buying wooden spoons from him."

I kicked my footwork up a notch and twirled Suzanne with more style. When the dance ended twenty minutes later, Nola was ready for another.

I introduced her to Glover and whisked Suzanne away from him.

Around 11:00 the band called it a night. Suzanne and I walked back to the tent and crawled in. We sat face to face. I leaned forward and kissed her neck, savoring the slightly salty taste of her skin. She murmured and moved forward. One move led to another and we made love quietly. Afterward we curled together, surrounded by small outdoors noises.

I awoke later, aware that something remained undone. When I realized what — that I'd fallen asleep instead of doing my night patrol — I rolled away carefully, felt around for my wristwatch. Found it in a pile of clothes and clicked its light dial. 12:57 A.M.

For a few minutes I sat there, staring at the dark, listening to Suzanne breathe, wondering if it made sense to go out at this hour. Rubbing my face, I felt the two-day stubble. Macho. I groped for the set of black clothes I had ready, pulled them on, and crawled out of the tent.

A wisp of a breeze stirred the sullen air. I sniffed, trying to detect the rain that Nola had predicted. Faint notes of music led me to one of the RVs, where a dozen people sat singing religious music. Cindy finished "Just a Closer Walk with Thee," followed by a tune about knowing her name was written there. No other lanterns were on, no other jams. I walked among the darkened RVs. Stubbs' was sealed off with yellow crime-scene tape, a sure give away to anybody paying attention that his death wasn't natural. My route wound through the parking lot. In the moonlight I followed the path down to the creek, walking softly, listening and looking. A rustle stopped me in my tracks.

Fonnie Sheffler spun toward me. She had been standing in the umbra of the black walnut tree. "What are you doing here?" she demanded.

"Sorry," I said. "I didn't see you." Her guitar was propped against the tree.

"What do you want?" Her tone was hostile.

"Nothing. I'm just out walking."

She bit her lower lip, then sank slowly to a seated position, her back against the tree. "You're going to tell, aren't you?"

I lowered myself to the ground and sat across from her,

putting enough distance between us that she wouldn't feel threatened. "Tell what?"

She looked away. "You know. About the tree."

I tried to calculate quickly what she was talking about but came up with *nista*. Nothing. I remained silent.

"Christianity isn't the only religion." She hurled a twig toward the creek. "They've been singing those religious songs since the dance ended. Right next to my trailer. You don't hear them singing about trees, do you?"

What had seemed like a non sequitur was beginning to make sense. "You're a tree worshiper?" I asked.

She studied me, then gave a curt nod. "You won't tell, will you?"

"No." I cast about for something to say: Fonnie was a loner and difficult to talk to. "That's a nice guitar," I tried, nodding toward her instrument.

She picked it up and looked at it. "No, it's not. You're not a musician and you don't know instruments."

Silence was my best bet.

Hers, too.

I sat there thinking about how to introduce the subject of the stolen instruments. Compared to outright investigation — "Hello, I'm a private eye and I'd like to ask you a few questions" — undercover work requires far more tact and sensibility in introducing subjects, mainly because you don't want your fellow-whatever to wonder why you're asking all the questions.

Fonnie tossed something, a chunk of dirt or pebble or bark, toward the creek. "I could teach you about the sacred spirit of trees," she offered. "The moon is full."

"Your guitar is made of wood," I commented.

She didn't seem to get it at first. When she did, she brooded. "It's old and beat up and I bought it used before I learned about the sacred spirit of trees. We can talk about trees if you want."

"Some other time," I replied, getting to my feet.

On the far side of the creek I turned north, toward the frontage road and the cornfields: the same path that Cindy had walked last evening. I didn't find it particularly strange that Fonnie was out at 1 A.M. Just because we were in Auralee didn't mean everybody went to bed with the chickens.

Somebody hummed a Beatles' tune. "Getting Better All the Time."

"Howdy," Glover said at my approach. He sat on a rock alongside the creek.

"You have to hide out here to sing rock songs?"

"Could be. Fact is, though, I'm on Mountain Time." He finished humming the tune. "Find your hammer?"

"Not yet."

"Suzanne like those bones she bought?"

I conceded that she did.

He started humming "I'm Looking Through You." I adjusted the bill of my baseball cap and continued on my way, across the road and into the cornfields. Half-expecting the sounds of a bowed psaltry, I trod on, hearing bullfrogs and cicadas, a few splashes that could have been raccoons.

By the time I had walked through the cornfield and along the frontage road and down along the creek again, Glover was gone. Perhaps he'd sung every Beatles song he knew and had wandered off to laminate more bones. Fonnie was gone, too. The black walnut tree remained.

Something odd about the pigpen. Its door stood wide open. Somebody had lifted the whittled block of wood that served to hold the door closed. I doubted that the pig was asleep in its shed: Richard impressed me as a pig who sought adventure. In any case, I wasn't about to traipse through the pigpen and stick my head inside the shelter. Mary could find her six-hundred-pound pet in the morning.

The tents were quiet, the gospel group gone.

Behind the farmhouse, a dim rectangle of light shone through the screened-in porch. Inside, somebody sobbed.

I'd heard that sobbing before.

"Mary?" I called softly.

A series of louder sobs, a hiccup, and a grunt. "Go 'way."

Pushing the door open, I stepped into the room. The floor was bare cement, the walls paneled, the screened windows bare. A beat-up turquoise couch leaned against the far wall. Mary sat on the floor in a dark corner, a woven blanket on her lap and a bottle in one hand. Her other arm draped around the pig, which lay there in comfort.

A half-chewed-through rattan chair occupied space between two windows. I tested it to be sure it wouldn't collapse under me, pulled it close to Mary, and sat. The pig followed me with its eyes. One lower tooth projected over its upper lip in a snaggletooth smile. The glow from a single lamp cast a yellow hue over its pink skin. "Want to tell me about it?" I asked.

"Go 'way." She raised the bottle to her lips and took a smack of its contents. Maker's Mark. "You're a man."

I didn't deny it.

She began singing, her words slurred. Something about a man to blame. The pig bobbed its head up and down in time to the music. Mary leaned down and kissed the top of Richard's head. The pig closed its eyes. Ecstasy, probably.

"There's something you aren't telling me," I said.

Mary and Richard snorted in unison.

"I'm sad, Frank. Sad."

"Why?"

She took another swig of bourbon. The bottle was almost half empty. "Shelby is dead, Frank. Dead."

From the cadence of her speech, I figured she might be writing the lyrics to a song. "Dead, Mary. Dead," I agreed, keeping to the rhythm. "Somebody killed him."

She sat forward, leaning on the pig. "He thinks I did.

Diddy-diddy-did, Diddy-diddy-dead." She waved the bottle at me.

I removed it from her hand and set it aside, trying to make sense of her words. "Somebody thinks you killed Stubbs?"

Mary nodded and the pig followed suit. "All because I asked him to ma- ma- marry me. I wouldn't marry him if he were the last — *hic!*" Her eyes were bleary. "What was I saying?"

Marry? "Did you propose to the sheriff, Mary?"

Laying her head against the pig's, she closed her eyes.

"Are you saying the sheriff suspects you of murdering Stubbs?" I asked.

Her eyes popped open. She rubbed them with both hands, brought her fingertips together at chest height, and thrust each hand outward to her side as if to say, *Finished.* "You're the detective."

I ignored the sarcasm. "Why?"

She shrugged. "It's what you wanted to be, I guess."

"I mean, why would the sheriff suspect you of murdering Shelby Stubbs?"

That brought another burst of tears and a series of grunts from the pig. "Help me," she begged, rubbing her forehead.

"Why would somebody kill Stubbs?" I asked.

"Puh!" It rolled off her lips with vibrato.

"Elaborate," I said.

"Puh — puh — puh ... begins with a *p*."

"The reason begins with a *p?"* I asked.

Mary nodded.

I looked at Richard. "Patrimony? Patricide?"

She shook her head. "Puh — pur — pur-something."

"Purse? Parsimonious?" Nothing. "Percussion," I threw in, grasping at anything.

Back and forth went her head. "Purserve. That's it, perserve."

The hour was late and I didn't get it.

"Whatever somebody wanted, Shelby wanted them to not have it. He was perserve. A hammered dulcimer player wants to play old-time music, Shelby goes out of his way to prevent it. Perserve."

Perverse. "You're saying Shelby was killed because he thwarted somebody?"

Mary closed her eyes and slumped against the pig.

Out cold.

I capped the Maker's Mark and was about to turn off the light when I noticed a piece of paper jutting out of Mary's pocket.

Reaching down, I extracted it.

An envelope with another anonymous note: one that chilled the temperature around me.

You will pay.

13 Wednesday

Fewer than half the festival goers attended Wednesday's breakfast. Most were still sleeping in their tents and campers. Stifling a yawn, I sat down beside Suzanne and waited for some wide-awake person to push the food my way.

Juice, pancakes, and a big bowl of cold cereal cleared some of the rust off my strings. More coffee helped.

"Mind if I join you?" Sheriff Yale Davis, resplendent in uniform, stood stiffly alongside our table. Vance and Guy rose as one to leave; Suzanne looked at me and followed Kim out the door.

Davis sat on the other side of the table and watched them depart. "I made a few calls, Dragovic. Word is you're okay."

Abundant praise from the law. I inclined my head a fraction of an inch.

The sheriff stared past me. I twisted to see what he was looking at. Raven and Booker? Nola and Mary? He didn't really suspect Mary of murder, did he? When I turned back, the edge of his jaw stood out white against the rest of his face. So did his scar. Looked like a knife cut, but it could have been made by a sharp rock. I sipped my coffee and thought about the second note: *You will pay.* I had an edgy feeling Mary's life might be in danger. When I'd spoken to her before breakfast, she held me to my promise: do not mention the notes to Davis. I wasn't ready to break the promise, but realized I might have to.

"Suppose you had a will," the sheriff said, moving his eyes toward me, "and in it you left everything to your wife."

"Yeah?"

"How would you word it?"

"Word it? You mean something like, 'I leave all my earthly possessions to my loving wife'?"

Davis wasn't satisfied with my answer. "That isn't what you'd say. Suppose you were Shelby Stubbs. How would you say it?"

I took a deep breath. "I, Shelby Stubbs, being of sound mind and body, do hereby bequeath all my earthly possessions — my home, my bank account, the residuals from all my recording contracts, my fiddles which drive the music, my RV, my dog and my cat — to my loving wife, Bliss Beckins."

Davis scowled at my attitude, but nodded in satisfaction at the conclusion. "Exactly," he said. "Exactly."

"I take it you already know the content of Stubbs' will."

"His attorney was cooperative."

"Um-hmm." I stretched and shifted my position on the bench, straddling it.

Davis studied me. "Mind if I bounce something off you? In strictest confidence."

"Your tune."

He rubbed his jaw. "Stubbs changed his will four months ago. The previous will left everything to, and I quote, 'my wife, Bliss Beckins.' The new will left everything to, and I quote, 'my first and only wife.'"

I frowned, imaging how Stubbs' lawyer must have argued with him. Lawyers are trained to write wills that can't be contested. Thus even though you know your wife is Bliss Beckins and the whole world may know it, you still have to say "my wife, Bliss Beckins." If it's a brother or sister or cousin or aunt or uncle or friend you're leaving something to, you provide an address, "last residing at blah-blah-blah."

"How do you read that?" Davis asked.

Why was he giving me this information? The law never shares with private eyes. Or anybody else, for that matter. "I read it that he doesn't want Bliss to inherit."

"I can't see his wanting Raven to inherit," the sheriff countered.

I remembered something. "Monday morning he was goading her — Raven, that is. When she stomped off, he commented that she has beauty and brains."

Davis studied the group at the coffee urn. "Hard to believe he'd want to leave it to Raven," he muttered.

"You don't like Raven?" I asked.

"Don't trust her," he answered.

"I've been told that Stubbs was the kind of person who got pleasure out of denying people what they wanted," I said. By now the sheriff should have heard the same thing.

"Meaning?" he asked.

"Meaning that if he knew Bliss really wanted his money, he might word the will in a way that would deny her what she wanted."

"Same applies to Raven," Davis argued. "If he knew she really wanted the money, he'd word the will in such a way she couldn't get it. Not that she could get it in the first place, unless she was still his wife. You know what bugs me?" he asked. "It's the 'my first and only wife.' Raven might have been his first wife, but she obviously wasn't his only wife." He glanced my way. "Unless the divorce wasn't legal and Stubbs learned that."

I thought that would give Raven a strong motive if she knew. Mary was walking toward the sheriff and me. I wondered if Raven and Stubbs had been considering remarriage. Where would that leave Bliss?

"Hello, Frank, how are you this morning?" Mary dropped a hand on my shoulder and forced out a stiff smile. She had already said hello to me earlier, when we'd argued about the second note. Although she wore a red jumper and yellow top and her hair was neatly braided, her face was still troubled.

"Good morning, Mary," said Davis.

She avoided looking at the sheriff and didn't reply. "Anything you want, Frank, you be sure to ask," she said, her hand still on my shoulder. "I've got to get to class now."

"Just a minute, Mary."

She turned slowly and gave Davis a cold look.

"I want to know what's wrong with you."

"Wrong?" she managed.

"Something's bothering you."

"Well, of course something's bothering me, Yale!" She lowered her voice, "Somebody was murdered right here at Midwest Music Madness, and you haven't found out who did it!"

"That's not it," he said, studying her. "Something else is bothering you."

"Nothing else is bothering me, Yale."

A lie at least as blue as her nylon guitar case, but I said nothing.

With a rueful smile the sheriff stood. "I'd like you to loan me a room. I need to interview people about Stubbs' death."

"You can use the chicken coop," she snapped.

"No."

"Then use the cornfields."

"I was thinking more along the lines of your office."

"You can't have my office," she said.

His jaw muscles jumped. "I'll use the dining room, then."

"Just be out by lunch." Mary stomped away.

I stood, strapped on my tool belt, and offered to fetch the sheriff some coffee before I left. He nodded, still fuming.

Raven was still guarding the coffee urn.

"Morning, Raven."

She stepped close, touching my arm. "Does the sheriff suspect you of something, Frank?"

"Not a thing. Why do you ask?" I focused on the coffee but watched her expression.

"You have a hammer and other tools," she said, dropping her hand to dead center on my tool belt.

She knew how to throw me off balance.

"Hammer?" I asked after a moment. "What do you mean?" I kept thinking that the blunt instrument used to kill Stubbs could have been a hammer. My hammer. Did Raven know something?

"Nothing, nothing," she backtracked. "Just conversation."

I looked down at her hand, sensed the sheriff's eyes boring into my back.

"Why don't you come back and talk to the sheriff," I suggested.

Would I go talk to the sheriff if somebody invited me to?

Hell no.

But to my surprise, Raven followed me back to the table.

Davis greeted her. "Good morning, Miss Hook."

"You called me Raven last year, Sheriff."

I handed him a mug of coffee and he took his eyes off Raven long enough to accept it. "I talked to your husband's attorney last night," he told her.

She smiled tightly. "Let's don't go down that road, Sheriff. I don't have a husband."

"Your ex-husband."

Settling her mug on the table , Raven stepped across the attached bench, stretching sinuously. "It's a shame about Mary's festival, isn't it." She sat across from Davis.

Davis studied her a moment. "In what way?"

He didn't tell me to leave, so I walked around him, removed my tool belt, and sat at the far end of the table, where I could observe both Raven and Davis.

"Well, nobody will want to teach here again." She blew on her coffee.

"Nobody?" asked Davis. "Mary's a very good organizer and a great singer. Her festival is gaining in reputation. She could get the Critten Hollow String Band, the Freight Hoppers, the Volo Bog Trotters, Cathy Barton and Dave Para, you name it."

Raven blinked.

Apparently the sheriff was an old-time music fan. And damned good at leading on a suspect.

"Well," Raven recovered, "there are the thefts, then the fact that Shelby was murdered — who would want to come to such a place again?"

I steadied myself. Davis kept his face expressionless. "How did you know Shelby was murdered?"

Raven turned pale. Stuttered. Finally got out that it must be, else why would the sheriff and his deputy be there day and night.

Me, I'd have mentioned the yellow crime-scene tape.

Now was the time for Davis to ask me to leave.

The fact that he didn't puzzled me.

"I think you should tell me everything you know about your ex-husband's murder, Miss Hook."

"Nothing. I know nothing," she protested.

This was the first time I'd seen Raven when she wasn't on the attack. She was genuinely worried, and as sure as *mi* follows *do* and *re,* she knew something about the murder. Time for the sheriff to press.

"What do you stand to inherit from your husband's will?" Davis inquired.

"*Ex*-husband, Sheriff. Surely you know the status of ex-wives: we inherit nothing," she said bitterly. "Which is pretty much what I got from the divorce settlement: nothing. Well, no, I correct myself: I did get the Super Duty Ford truck." She smiled at that.

Davis went at her in a bunch of different ways, trying to determine whether she knew about the will. From where I was sitting, Raven knew Stubbs was murdered, and if I were the sheriff that's the row I'd plow. I didn't think she knew anything about the will, but that's what Davis appeared interested in.

"I have a class," Raven informed Davis, beginning to extract herself from the bench.

"Sit down." His words sliced through the air.

She sat, her hands trembling.

"Yesterday you took Shelby Stubbs to your room here in the farmhouse."

Raven said nothing.

"You also brought his fiddle with you." He waited, but she remained silent. "Where's the fiddle?" he asked.

I watched Raven as she said that Stubbs took it back to the RV when he left her room. The sheriff asked her what time he left and she replied it was around dinner time. He asked her where she was all Monday evening and she claimed she was driving around, looking at the countryside. Hard to credit: the countryside was corn and more corn. A person like Raven, who has hidden motives for just about everything, always looks like she's lying. I didn't know whether to believe that Stubbs had in fact taken the fiddle with him, or that it was upstairs locked in Raven's room.

"Sheriff," she complained, looking at her watch pointedly, "I really do have to teach my class."

He let her scramble out of the attached bench seats, waited until she picked up her coffee mug. The vulnerable moment: she thought it was over.

"Shelby Stubbs' will leaves everything to you," he told her.

The mug crashed to the floor, spraying coffee in all directions. *"What?!"* she gasped, a hand to her chest.

Davis repeated his words, but Raven rejected them. "Shelby? Leave me something in his will? I don't believe you."

"Why wouldn't he, Miss Hook, seeing as how you were his first wife and he was married to you for a dozen years?"

"Because," answered Raven, "he was a son of a bitch and I

wasn't his first wife anyway."

I rubbed my eyes.

Davis blinked, then recovered. "Who was his first wife?"

"Why, Opal Jackson, everybody knows that, even though it lasted barely from winter to summer to fall and I can't say I blame her."

"Who is Opal Jackson?" asked Davis, still dazed.

Raven looked down at him. "Well, that's a good question, Sheriff." She stretched again. "She was a singer once, and after she left Shelby she played for a while in some other bands, but nobody's heard of her in years. Why don't you ask Edric, maybe he knows." She walked off without looking back. I studied Davis as he studied Raven's retreating form.

After a while I gave up on that and stared out the open window at the shagbark hickory and listened to a tune somebody was playing on a fiddle. "What's that tune?" I asked.

"'Soldier's Joy,'" Davis answered, looking at me as if I'd asked what crop was growing in the field across the road. "Best-known fiddle tune in the world."

"You play the fiddle?"

"Mandolin. Same fingering." He turned in my direction. "What do you think?"

What I thought was, if Yale liked Mary and Mary liked Yale, where was the problem? He wasn't wearing a wedding band. "You married?" I asked.

He frowned. "No."

"You think Raven's autoharp was really stolen last year?" I asked.

"Don't know. She seemed genuinely upset."

"Sheriff!" Tansy Thompson approached. "Somebody told me you were here, and you didn't even come back to say hello!" She was carrying two plates of something chocolate. "Hello, Frank. Those tables you built for Aja are *won*derful! Of course, they're for the rest of us, too, but you know what I mean. Here,

Yale, have some of my chocolate cake with cherry Jello filling and Cool Whip frosting."

Plunking a plate in front of each of us, Tansy slapped down napkins and forks, then beamed at the quivering pieces of cake. "I hope you enjoy my cooking, Frank," she said, looking me directly in the eye.

You don't have to be from Chicago, the city of "vote early and vote often," to know when somebody's soliciting your vote. In the City of the Big Shoulders they stuff ballot boxes: in Auralee they stuff voters. "Delicious," I volunteered.

"I'll just refresh your coffee cups." She smiled, walking away with our mugs.

"Tansy's cooking twice this week?" I asked Davis.

"Yep." He swallowed a chunk of cake the size of a hammered dulcimer. "Ummmm."

Tansy hurried back with two fresh cups of coffee. "Sheriff," she said tentatively, "Toby tells me that Shelby Stubbs was *murdered*, right here at the festival." She looked over at me. "Appreciate how you helped Cody out on that tuner he found. I think that guy from Maine scares him."

I nodded, my mouth full of the cold Jello cake and creamy topping.

"It's true, Tansy," replied Davis, "but I don't want you talking about it."

Right thing to say, but if he believed she wouldn't, his brain and the cake were filled with the same substance.

Grabbing my tool belt, I excused myself, telling them both I had work to do. As I was leaving, Bliss entered with Nola at her side.

"Good morning, Frank. If the sheriff has been questioning you and you'd like me present the next time he does, I'll be happy to sit in. You have the right to have an attorney present when questioned by the police." Nola was, as always, professional.

I thanked her and said I had carpentry work to do.

The sky held no clouds, but the temperature was dropping. I looked northwest toward Chicago, but Iroquois County was too far south for me to spot the skyscrapers. Strapping on my tools bag, I hoped to hell nobody asked me to repair anything today: I'd probably smash my thumb with Mary's curved claw hammer.

14

I spent the morning walking the grounds, looking and thinking. At noon I waited outside Mary's office door, chatting with Nola.

"Doesn't seem to me you'll have that much to report today, Frank," she chided. "You spent most of your time with Yale." Nola didn't fish with subtlety, but what could you expect from somebody who twanged a jaw harp. "I enjoyed dancing with you last night."

"You're a good dancer," I returned.

"You're not bad yourself, though Jeff could dance circles around both of us. Those cowboys know how to kick up their heels." She paused. "I danced with Vance, too. Ever since Edric asked him to play fiddle for the Shelby Stubbs Band, I've never seen him so happy."

"I thought Vance's main instrument was the mandolin."

"I guess he's a closet fiddler," she replied. "Same fingering as for the violin."

Somebody else had told me that. The sheriff.

"Vance has always wanted to play with a group," she continued, "but somehow he could never get one together. Or get into one. Actually," she confided, "I think Vance wants to form a duo with Booker."

Nola was pretty good at supplying me with information — or maybe it was misinformation. Time to reciprocate. "I heard

Edric say he was going to Europe with the Shelby Stubbs Band. He hinted that Vance and Booker could join him."

"Hmmphhh!" she pooh-poohed. "I'd say that's up to the people who offered the contract. They might not want the Shelby Stubbs Band without Shelby Stubbs. Anyway, I think Booker has bigger fish to fry."

I looked at her. "Such as?"

The phone rang and she answered it, turning her back on me and settling in for what looked like a long conversation. I used the opportunity to look for Mary upstairs. On the second floor, Raven's door was locked. The third floor — Mary's quarters — was empty. A queen-sized bed, unmade, on one end of the twenty-by-thirty room. A pair of bunks along the other wall, one of them covered with Bliss's clothes. No stolen instruments that I could spot.

Outdoors I looked for Suzanne and found her sitting under the sycamore, carving the dowel of her gut-bucket bass. Six or seven people stood around her, admiring the work. I stepped closer to observe her motif: pines and ferns. Lots of pines and ferns on Madeline Island, Wisconsin, where she grew up. Which reminded me: Suzanne had promised to call her mother and ask some questions about Mary Ployd. Suzanne would have been too young to know when Mary arrived on Madeline Island and where she came from and what gossip attended her arrival, but her mother might remember.

Over on the barn a shutter swayed. The weather vane had stopped fishtailing and indicated a steady west wind. Nola had been right: rain tonight for sure. Crops could use it, as Uncle Rudy always said. I walked to the pigpen, where Richard paced restlessly. Probably plotting tonight's adventure. Deputy Toby Thompson emerged from the woods, the sheriff close behind him. As they walked toward the trailers, I began to tighten rain flys on tents and make certain stakes and guy ropes were secure.

Cindy Ruffo's tent was tight: she was an experienced

camper. Lafayette's couldn't have withstood a mild breeze, so I used my borrowed hammer to pound in his stakes, tightening the ropes. Four or five other tents were sloppily set up, so I battened them down, too. If I couldn't discover who was stealing instruments from Mary's festival, I could always get a job as a campground manager.

Theft and murder occupied my mind. Were the fiddle theft and the murder connected? Had the thief seized on an opportune moment — Shelby sleeping, door open, fiddle case in sight — only this time the moment went bad, Stubbs awakening just as the thief was leaving? Rather than risk discovery, the thief bludgeons Stubbs to death. With what? It had to be something nearby. If so, then it wasn't premeditated murder. But if it was premeditated, what was the motive?

If the theft and murder weren't connected, when were the fiddle and bow stolen? Before the murder — or after? If, in fact, the fiddle and bow had even been there with Stubbs.

My brain moved to the hurdy-gurdy. Lafayette couldn't have stolen it: he was in Kofi's drumming class at the time. Vance could have; Cindy could have, too. Raven wasn't teaching a class that afternoon, she was supposedly in her room with Shelby. Fonnie was taking a class but said she left early. Nola and Mary were in the farmhouse, or so they said. Booker couldn't have taken the hurdy-gurdy because he was teaching the Old Time Songs in Black and White, and Suzanne said he was there the entire time, and I had no reason to suspect Booker anyway.

My ramblings, literal and figurative, led me to the dining hall, where lunch was a large assortment of farm-made cheeses with home-made bread and home-grown melons of various kinds. Suzanne and I sat with Kofi, Fonnie, Cindy Russo and Jeff Glover. Picking suspects and sitting with them was easy. Not, I thought as I chose some of each cheese (marked Farmer's, Goat, Sheep, and Cheddar with little autoharp-shaped signs), that sitting with these people three times a day had revealed all I needed to know.

Vance stood at our table, talking to Jeff. "I love the voracious sounds I get out of your fiddle. I think I'm going to buy it. I want to buy Booker's guitar, too."

Glover encouraged Vance to buy the fiddle.

At the table to my left Lafayette laughed in a high pitch and Cody giggled. On the other side of the same table Bliss sat with Guy. Vance, seeing no space at our table, sat on the other side of Bliss.

"How do you like those bones?" Glover asked Suzanne.

"I really like them. I love the way they're curved, and the smooth way they feel in my hand. The woodwork is wonderful."

Her description of Jeff's bones sounded a bit sensual to me, but Suzanne was sensual about wood. I glanced at Glover to see how he was reacting, but couldn't tell by his expression.

Suzanne reached into her backpack and pulled out a pair of bones. Bone bones. "Guy gave me these," she said, clicking them to her standard four beats.

"Excellent! *Bon! Bon!*" cried Guy from the other table. He wore another bright blue T-shirt with a drawing of several hurdy gurdies and the word *Blowzabella* coming out of the wheel of one of them. Lafayette had informed me that *Blowzabella* was an entire band of hurdy gurdies. I imagine the sound would be like swarms of mutant locusts attacking the crops.

"I like the sound of bone bones a little bit better than wood bones," Suzanne confided. "But I love the idea of making wood bones."

Across the aisle Bliss was talking to Guy. "When I hear people play it, it sounds kind of syncopated," she said. "I can't quite get that into my playing."

"What tune?" asked Lafayette who, as always, appeared a bit out of things.

"'Big Scioty,'" Bliss replied, unzipping her case and pulling out her mountain dulcimer. "Listen." She scooted around so her back was to the table, laid the dulcimer across her lap, and strapped it around her waist. She plunked away at the tune in what I'd come to recognize as the mountain dulcimer style: steady finger work on the frets with one hand, rapid strumming with a pick with the other hand

"She's not in the morning lap dulcimer class," Cindy said.

"She's part of the old-time ensemble," I replied.

Cindy extricated herself from the table and watched Bliss play.

"That is good," Guy told Bliss. "I can show you how to syncopate."

"Really?"

"Yes," he nodded. "And you know what? The tune is in G, and so is one of my favorites, 'Mouth of the Tobique.' Perhaps we could learn them as a medley."

Bliss smiled.

Guy smiled.

"That's my Blue Lion," Cindy said in a loud voice. "That's my dulcimer!"

Confused, Bliss looked up. "What?"

"That's my Blue Lion," repeated Cindy firmly. "It was stolen two years ago."

Bliss shook her head. "No, this is my dulcimer. I bought it."

"It's *my* dulcimer, custom built." Cindy stretched a hand out. Bliss leaned backward. "Give it to me."

The tables around us grew silent, all eyes turned toward Cindy and Bliss.

"You're wrong. How can you be sure it's yours?" Bliss argued.

"How can you be sure it's your golden retriever, your Volkswagen, your Mackinaw?" Cindy demanded, towering over her. "They look pretty much the same, don't they? But you know which is yours right away, you don't go around confusing it with the others, do you? Give me back my dulcimer."

"No." Bliss clutched the Blue Lion to her lap. Guy stood and put a hand on her shoulder.

"Everybody calm down," announced Kim Oberfeld, pushing herself between the opponents. "First let's determine whether this is Cindy's Blue Lion."

I moved behind Kim, expecting an explosion from either Cindy or Guy. Or both. Kofi and Glover continued to sit; Suzanne and Fonnie joined the standing crowd. Cody sat on his hands and stared. Vance helped himself to more cheese and fruit. Lafayette stared off into space, his lips moving silently.

Shouldering her way into the crowd, Mary demanded to know what the commotion was. Cindy told her. Mary looked at the dulcimer, then at Bliss.

"Bliss, honey, where did you get this dulcimer?" Mary asked.

"I bought it at the Houston Folk Festival last year."

"I believe you," Mary assured her. "Do you remember who sold it to you?"

Bliss nodded. "I bought it from Booker."

In the dead silence, cutlery in the kitchen clanged like tuning forks dropping on concrete.

Mary turned to call Booker, but he was already there. "That's right," he said. "I sold her that dulcimer in Houston."

Mary's head bobbed up and down. I could see she wanted to believe him. "Good," she said, putting a positive spin on things. "You weren't here the year this dulcimer was stolen, Booker, so you wouldn't know."

"That's right," he answered quickly.

"That's right," she repeated.

We waited.

"Well, Booker," she asked at last, "where did you get the dulcimer?"

"Barter. Put a new clutch in somebody's car, person couldn't pay me cash, gave me the dulcimer instead."

"Booker." Mary elevated herself onto her toes, leaning toward him. "Who was it?"

He paused, as if waiting for somebody or something in particular: something he expected. When nothing came, his reply was sad. "I don't finger people, Mary."

"Well, but — a thief, Booker! A thief!"

He shook his head. "You don't know that."

"Is that somebody—" Mary would have continued, but I stepped on her foot, silencing her. She gave me a baffled look, which I pretended I didn't see. She started to speak again, but I pressed down harder on her instep. She took the hint.

"I'll have to report this to the sheriff," she said at last.

Booker turned his back on her and walked up to the food window. Two helpings of coconut cake, and he ate them down to the last flake.

Kim removed the dulcimer from Bliss's grip and asked Cindy to describe it in detail: which she did, right down to the seven inlaid roses, three pink for her girls, four blue for the boys. She even described the scratch on the side, just under the third rose. "Where the baby knocked it off my lap," she explained, reaching for her instrument.

"No!" wailed Bliss. "No! It's mine, I paid for it!"

All the tears Bliss hadn't shed for Stubbs burst forth as she rocked back and forth, head down. Guy stood there awkwardly. Kim led Bliss away. "Come on," she said, "I have three lovely Blue Lions here at Madness. Why don't you borrow one?"

Cindy sat and stroked her dulcimer.

I lifted my shoe off Mary's foot.

"Booker's protecting somebody who's here!" she hissed. "The thief is *here!*"

"He's protecting somebody who's here," I agreed. "But that somebody isn't necessarily the thief."

She thought about it. "Well, why didn't you want me to say the person is here?"

"Because, thief or not, he might pick up and leave."

"So? Why not?" she demanded. "People would feel better!"

"Well, for one thing, the sheriff wouldn't want him to go."

"Why not?"

I stared at her. "Murder, Mary. Davis is going to want everybody here as long as he can legitimately keep them, so he can check out their motive and movements."

"Oh."

"I'll watch Booker," I explained. "He expected the person he got the dulcimer from to speak up."

I paused. "Let's see who Booker's pissed at."

15

I stood under the shagbark hickory and whistled. "African rhythms, Cody. Time to drum."

A branch rustled. Cody climbed down, grinning.

With the more bearable temperature, students begged to drum outdoors. Kofi hesitated, explaining that the booming might disturb other classes in progress. When Bliss softly said that she always pictured African drumming outdoors, he agreed to move into the open, so we each chose our drums and walked in a straggly line toward the black walnut.

Loud crunching of tires on gravel was followed by the squeal of brakes and the slamming of a car door. The sheriff's car was making a bee line toward the RVs and trailers.

Under the shade of the tree we looked to Kofi and followed his lead. I surrendered to the patterns of sound, the deep booms and sharp raps over and over and over until the pulse of the drum pounded through my blood.

The sheriff's car squealed down the frontage road and up to the pole barn. I lost my place in the pattern.

"Listen," Kofi instructed. "If you are lost, listen to the others and you will find your place."

I found it, but not for long.

Pig manure is the wasabi mustard of manures: the smell assailed me even before the shadow fell over me. The drumming stopped. I realize somebody was talking to me.

"Dragovic," commanded Davis, rigid in front of me, "you'd better have some answers." His face was beet red, his jaw tight. The stench came from his deputy, Toby Thompson, covered in dirt and what I surmised was pig shit.

I had no idea why the sheriff was pissed at me, but pissed he was.

Which made me retaliate. "I'm playing," I snapped back.

"The hell you are!"

"Yes," agreed Kofi, approaching us, "he is learning how to drum. You are interrupting my class, Sheriff Davis. It is a rude thing to do. You do not interrupt a drum master when he is teaching. You wait until he is finished. Even in the United States, here at Midwest Music Madness, you should respect a teacher and his students."

Turning an even deeper shade of red, Davis clenched his jaw so tight I thought it might crack. "I'll wait here." He moved a few feet outside the circle.

Kofi stood waiting for an apology, but Davis gave none. Those who weren't staring at Davis were staring at me. I brushed the skin of my drum with my fingertips, back and forth, trying to calm myself. Kofi returned to his seat, pulled his drum into position, and all eyes turned toward him. All except Davis's, which I felt boring into my back.

I tried to forget the sheriff behind me, and at some points in the drumming actually did, but for the most part I was aware of the law breathing down my neck. When the class ended Bliss whispered, "I hope you aren't in trouble, Frank." She glanced furtively at the sheriff. I shook my head, thanked Kofi, and approached Davis.

"What the hell do you mean, coming up to me like that?"

"Down to the patrol car," he ordered.

"Mind giving me a reason?"

"Just go to the patrol car." His teeth were clenched.

I took my time getting there, flanked by Davis and

Thompson. I stopped outside the car. Davis opened the rear passenger-side door and motioned me in. I refused. He told me it was an order, I told him I wasn't under arrest.

"You lied to me," Davis said. It came out final, as if his suspicions were fact.

I didn't reply, which pissed him off even more. Was he talking about the blackmail notes to Mary? My senses told me that somehow or other, the pigpen was involved.

The sheriff planted himself in front of me. "Don't play games with me, Dragovic!" Thompson stood behind me.

"You're the one playing games. I have half a mind to call Nola in on this."

"No!"

His tone contained far more horror than authority. I wondered what power Nola Grayson had, that the mere mention of her name elicited such a response. Davis turned his back to me. His neck muscle twitched. After a long couple of minutes, he faced me and spoke. "Where were you Monday night?"

"I've already answered that question. In detail."

He ground his teeth a while. Not to any discernible beat that I could tell. "What were you wearing Monday night?"

I thought back. "A black *Good Guys Wear Black* T-shirt, black Levis, black running shoes."

"I don't think so," he barked.

I remained silent.

He glared at me in what he thought was a menacing manner. He was a pussycat compared to Chicago cops. "Answer the question!"

"What's the question?" I asked.

Davis whipped off his cap and slapped it at the passenger-side window. "Don't jerk me around, Dragovic! You were wearing a white White Sox T-shirt and denim shorts."

The sudden realization hit me: he saw it on my face and read it as guilt. Behind me, the pig stench move closer. Davis opened the front passenger door and pulled out a plastic evidence bag. "Recognize these?"

I nodded. My formerly white White Sox T-shirt was splattered with dried blood. "Yeah, I do."

"They're yours, aren't they?"

"They look like the clothes I was wearing Monday morning, before I fixed the pigpen."

"And then you wore them Monday night, when you entered Stubbs trailer, didn't you?"

I followed the beat of this tune without trouble. "I assume somebody wore those clothes. But it wasn't me."

"You deny these are your clothes?"

"I said they look like mine."

He clenched his jaw. "I suppose you've got some bullshit story ready?"

If Nola were here, she'd tell me that was a leading question, one I shouldn't answer. I looked across the field to the black walnut. One drum remained, upright in the grass where I had been sitting. Lafayette trudged out of the pole barn and made his bowlegged way to the tree.

After Davis asked the question a better way, I reminded him what had happened with me, the pigpen, the drumming class, my shower, and my laying clothes out to dry.

"You forgot to mention that you laid your clothes out to dry and that they weren't there that night," he interrupted.

True. I had forgotten about the clothes: thought Suzanne had moved them into the tent. That sounded so weak, though, that I didn't lay it on Davis. Instead I told him that everybody in the drumming class would remember my appearing in pig-sty-scented clothing that afternoon, and that Cindy Ruffo or Fonnie Sheffler might remember my laying out the freshly washed T-shirt, shorts, and socks on the grass outside my tent.

"You're saying somebody took your clothes and wore them to kill Stubbs."

"Somebody took English's shoes."

"He says they did," replied Davis. "Just like you."

I couldn't fault his reasoning.

"Why would somebody want to frame you?"

"Maybe they don't want to frame me," I returned. "Maybe they just didn't want blood on their own clothes and shoes."

Davis scowled, but I could see he'd had the same thoughts. "Toby found these inside the pigpen," he said, "wedged up into the cupola."

I'd been against the cupolas from the beginning.

"Why do you think the shoes were in the cornfield and the clothes in the pigpen?" I asked. "Why weren't they together?"

"Forget the cornfield, you're the one hanging around the pigpen all the time," Thompson growled from behind me.

"And you're the husband of Tansy Thompson," I countered. "Mountain dulcimer, guitar, autoharp, hurdy-gurdy, maybe a fiddle — she's been on the grounds each time an instrument was stolen."

Davis got in my face so fast I thought he'd plow on through me. "Don't ever impugn my deputy again, Dragovic."

"Batima ima dva kraja," I replied.

"What's that supposed to mean?"

"A stick has two ends."

Across the field Lafayette picked up my drum and carried it back to the pole barn. Every twenty feet or so, he stopped to rest as the instrument slipped out of his hands. In a face-to-face encounter with Stubbs, Lafayette couldn't hold his own. But if Stubbs was asleep . . . . .

"You and English take about the same shoe size," Davis continued. "You could wear his shoes because they're bigger, but I doubt he could wear yours."

I couldn't believe he was still pursuing his half-assed theory. Me, I was saying goodbye to the possibility that the murder was spur-of-the-moment, that the thief saw an opportunity to steal the fiddle, stepped in to take it, accidentally woke up Stubbs, then killed him rather than be exposed. Now everything — English's stolen shoes, my stolen clothes and, worst of all, I suspected, my stolen hammer — pointed to premeditated murder.

Was it necessary to point this out to the sheriff?

Maybe. "The killing looks planned."

"That's right, Dragovic. And who better to confuse the scene with stolen shoes and stolen clothes than a private eye who's been around murder scenes before?"

"I didn't kill Stubbs," I said. "Your theory is full of holes. Motive, for example."

"You were hired to do it."

I snorted. Then I looked at him straight. Did he mean what I thought he did?

He nodded, as if my silence confirmed his suspicions. "You were hired, weren't you?" he asked bitterly.

Mary may have been drunk last night, but she was right: Davis suspected her of murder. "I was hired to find the instrument thief, you know that."

"A cover." The bitterness was still in his voice.

"Look, Davis, nobody hired me to commit murder, and I didn't kill anybody. You're way off base."

"I don't think so, Dragovic. I think you did it."

"Then charge me with it," I challenged, walking away.

"Come back here!" Davis shouted.

I kept on walking, out toward the pigsty. Richard, at least, had a clean mind.

It didn't take a roomful of brains to see where this was going. Mary was in serious trouble. What did Davis know that I didn't? Could it have anything to do with the blackmail notes?

Davis shouted one more time. I heard the slam of his car door and the sound of the engine in low gear. By the time I reached the pigpen, the sheriff had wheeled into an empty spot of ground near the campers. Hitching up his gun belt, he walked toward one of the campers. Fonnie's, from what I could make out. Maybe if he walked at least as often as he drove, he'd deliver more oxygen to his brain and think more clearly.

Foot propped on the new rail I had built, I stewed over the fact that Davis considered me a hired gun. I have no love of the law, law and justice being no closer than kissing cousins, but I'd thought Davis more capable than that. My mistake.

It was obvious to me that Sheriff Yale Davis wasn't going to solve the murder case. Either he couldn't, or he didn't want to.

But if Mary's festival was to continue, somebody had to.

Under the sycamore Suzanne carved a long pole: somebody's bass. She put down the pole, put something — the carver, probably — in the leather kit she wore strapped to her waist, and walked toward me. The wind, coming from behind her, blew her hair forward.

"We've got to stop meeting like this," she said, slipping an arm around my waist.

"Here at the pigpen, you mean?"

She sniffed. "Not exactly the most romantic place on the grounds."

I didn't reply.

"You looked angry walking to the pigpen. Tell me what's wrong," she said.

Richard rose from his wallow and trotted over to us. Suzanne reached through the rail and scratched behind his ears.

"Mary," I muttered.

Suzanne looked at me.

"Do you think the sheriff's in love with Mary?" I asked.

Her turn to ponder. "I don't know," she said at last. "I'd have to have seen them before the murder."

"Meaning?"

"His eyes don't leave her. When she's in the room, he's always aware of her."

I breathed in the scent of her hair, a mixture of shampoo, sweat, and grass.

"He looks at her as if he loves her, but also as if she disappointed him." Suzanne studied the railing. "Big time disappointment. He treats her like a suspect." She looked at me.

Was that a warning about how I treated her? "We're not having much time together, are we?" I said.

Suzanne looked up at the sky. "On top of that, it's going to pour." A big sigh. "I talked to my mother today. About Mary."

The gist of what her mother had to say was threefold.

First, that Mary had arrived on Madeleine Island about thirty years ago, nobody knew from where. Second, rumor had been that Mary was suffering from a broken heart, that she had come to the island to get over the rejection. Third, everybody agreed that Mary Ployd had a beautiful singing voice and a pleasing way of singing folk songs. When Mary left the island later to make her way in the world as a singer, everybody hated to see her leave, but everybody wished her well.

Suzanne finished relaying her information, then frowned. Across the way, walking from the direction of the tents, strode Sheriff Yale Davis — like a bad player who shows up at every jam.

"You haven't asked me whether I think Mary loves the sheriff," she whispered. "I think she does."

Davis reached the pigsty, chose a side that intersected ours, selected a rail, and honored it with the toe of his shoe. "Afternoon, Miss Quering."

I didn't like it that he knew Suzanne's name so readily, though I had to admit that in the course of investigating a murder he'd want to know who each of us was. If he was here to question her about my clothes, he was late: by now the two of us could have concocted any story we wanted.

Suzanne's eyes were a clear gray, a lighter shade when she was tranquil, darker when stirred by emotion. They darkened perceptibly as she stared at Davis.

"I'd like to talk to Dragovic now," the sheriff informed her.

A frown wrinkled Suzanne's forehead. Then she got it. She looked at me as if to ask whether she should stay around to protect me. I indicated she could go. "Don't forget Guy's bones class," she called as she walked away.

"I'll be there," I said.

I kept my foot on the rail, Davis did likewise. We stood there like two characters at the OK Corral. "I talked to Fonnie," he said across the top of the pigsty. He studied the railing. "She remembers you spreading wet clothes on the grass outside your tent Monday afternoon. She even described the clothes."

I saw no need to reply.

"Then I talked to Cindy Ruffo."

He went quiet. I looked at him. "Cindy says you were on the grounds all night, walking along the creek and through the parking area and around the campers. She says you were wearing all black Monday night. She couldn't say for sure what the writing on your shirt said."

"I'm surprised she noticed that much. She looked unaware."

"She figured you might be the devil."

He was serious.

"Because I was walking around at night?"

He shook his head. "Because you were dressed in black."

The pig grunted loudly and we both looked at it.

"She tell you what she was doing walking around that late?" I asked.

Davis nodded. "Praying."

I couldn't think of any motive Cindy Ruffo had to kill Shelby Stubbs. Opportunity, though, I suppose she had that. I considered Davis. In the way of lawmen (forget the law part, Suzanne would say, make it just *men*), he was offering me an apology for his earlier behavior.

I just wasn't ready to accept it.

Clearing his throat, he looked at the sky. I looked up, too. Dark clouds were rolling in from the west, no blue sky in sight beyond them.

"Rain coming soon," he commented. "Gonna be a hard one." After a minute or so of lifting his hat, wiping his brow, and studying the weather patterns, he shook his head. "You don't know this," he said, "but I asked Mary to marry me. Sounds funny, doesn't it, 'Mary to marry.'"

I waited.

"Fool that I am, I've asked her three times: two years ago, one year ago, and six months ago."

"Mary's a good woman," I offered. Stubborn. Conniving. Penny-pinching. But basically good. "The festival crowd loves her."

The sheriff nodded. "She said she loved me, but she didn't believe in marriage. She suggested the two of us live together. Here in the farmhouse or in my house in town."

"Doesn't sound bad to me," I admitted, thinking of Suzanne and me.

The snort came from Davis, not the pig. "This is a small town, Dragovic, not like Chicago. And I'm the sheriff, I have to live right."

The first drop of rain bounced off the pig. The second hit the rail in front of me. I sensed the sheriff still had something in his craw.

"I met her at a folk festival out in Nebraska," he told me. "Five, six years ago. We met again at another festival in Texas. One thing led to another, and she bought land down here in Iroquois County. To be close to me, she said." He peeled splinters of wood off the top rail. "When Mary first moved here, she and Nola and I would go out together. Every once in a while we'd tie one on. It was one of those times that Mary told me about Stubbs."

I waited for whatever was coming.

"You know how it is when you're involved with crime," he

explained, making us brothers in arms. "People ask, Have you ever wanted to kill anybody? Or, If you wanted to commit the perfect crime, how would you do it? That sort of thing."

I acknowledged the experience.

"It was one of those times," he said. "I remember Nola said the perfect crime was one nobody could tie you to because they don't know the motive. Mary said — and I'll never forget it — said the perfect crime wasn't how, it was *who,* and that the only person she thought worthy of murdering was Shelby Stubbs."

The raindrops tickled as they fell, evaporating almost immediately. "You can't take things like that literally," I argued.

He removed his hat and turned his face up to the rain. "I know that," he admitted after he'd had enough of the raindrops. "But the minute I showed up on Mary's doorstep to investigate the murder of Shelby Stubbs, she asked me to marry her. If that's not suspicious," he informed me, "I don't know what is."

16

"Of course I'll give you a private lesson, and now is fine." Raven led the student by the shoulder into the corn crib. "How are you today, Frank?" she asked in passing.

I allowed I was fine, then marched straight to my Camry, opened the trunk, and grabbed my lock picks. I lucked out in the farmhouse: Nola wasn't at her desk. I took the stairs quickly. Three doors stood ajar. One was closed. And locked. Raven's.

Extracting a pick, I knelt in front of her door. A whiff of something chemical made me cough. I listened. No other sound. The tumblers and I barely had time to execute a courtesy turn before the downstairs door opened and closed. The footsteps sounded like Nola's. I breathed quietly. For long seconds, somebody stood there, at the foot of the stairs. What the hell was she doing? Finally I heard shuffling papers and the sound of a drawer being pulled open. I went back to work. Sweat trickled down my face, but not from the heat.

"Raven! My goodness, you look positively upset!" Nola spoke in a loud voice, much louder usual. Pick in hand, I jumped to my feet and backed into the nearest open bedroom, closing the door. Raven's footsteps pounded up the stairs, her key clinked in the lock and the door closed behind her.

The room I was in faced north, with a view of the barn, the frontage road, and the cornfields. I checked the closet for stolen instruments but found only a banjo, which I recognized as the one

Booker had been playing Monday morning. No guitar, which meant he had his guitar with him. I looked under the bed, in the humidity-swollen, hard-to-open drawers, and through his canvas suitcase. Felt the mattress. Firm, not old and sunken. That spoke well of the way Mary treated her instructors. I ran my hands underneath the mattress. Nothing.

No sound yet of Raven leaving.

The dresser was old, dark mahogany with a few water stains. Its mirror stood upright on two curved posts, one of them sporting brass hooks for shaving straps. In a Chicago antique store the piece would fetch a lot more than I was fetching from Mary.

Between the mirror and dresser top the corner of a key protruded. Using the pressure of a fingertip I dragged the key out and examined it. The numeral *6* was stamped into it.

I'd seen such keys before. Many times before. But most recently Sunday night, when I had checked out the bus depot in downtown (if you could call it that) Auralee, thinking a locker would be a good place to store a stolen instrument.

Just as I pocketed the key, I heard Raven close her door, then lock it. I waited until the downstairs door opened and closed. Then I stepped out of Booker's room, walked softly up the stairs to Mary's floor, down the back stairs where Nola couldn't see me, into the dining hall, and out.

I sprinted to my car. Buzzing through the raindrops, the key and I made it to the bus depot in six minutes.

The depot housed a drugstore and eight-chair soda fountain as well as two cracked shoe-shine chairs and a dust-covered phone booth. Bus tickets were sold from a small booth just to the side of the food counter. Hamburgers, hot dogs, cheese, chicken- and tuna-salad sandwiches constituted the entire menu, along with soft drinks, coffee, tea, and ice cream concoctions.

When the counterman went into the kitchen, I inserted the key into locker number six.

Inside was a black metal fiddle case. Using my kerchief, I

lifted the case out and snapped it open. Shelby Stubbs' fiddle and two bows nestled inside the red cloth liner. I recognized one of them as the bow he had used Monday morning. After a moment I closed the case, returned it to the locker, and pocketed the key.

I had to think but couldn't do it inside the stuffy, dust-covered depot. That left the rain and the sidewalks of Auralee. I walked up and down the four blocks of town, enjoying the rain, noting the oak-lined streets, the public drinking fountain in the square, the post office, and the two bars, one red brick, one aluminum sided. The sky was darker than before, the wind stronger. Something big was heading toward Auralee.

I should report the fiddle to the sheriff.

But I wasn't going to.

For one thing, Davis wasn't thinking clearly about the murder. For another, I could stretch the point and say I was in charge of solving the thefts, and the fiddle was part of the thefts.

The point about not telling Davis settled, the next question was, what should I do with the fiddle? If I removed it from the locker, the counterman would be sure to remember me when Davis and his deputy came around asking questions. I assumed they were checking the depot every day, though I couldn't be sure. If I left the fiddle in the locker, it was safe as long as I kept the key.

Except that I wasn't going to keep the key — I was going to return it to Booker's room, exactly where I found it.

That decided, I reentered the depot, sat at the counter, said howdy to the man behind it, and ordered a two-scoop chocolate sundae. I told him I was attending Midwest Music Madness. We yakked about Madness, Mary, Tansy Thompson's cooking, Chicago, the White Sox, the Cubs, and the Cardinals. I told him I was thinking of storing my guitar in a locker for a few days and asked if any other festival goers did that. He said he hadn't seen anybody here except me. And the sheriff, he added. Eventually I got around to asking about depot hours and learned the place was closed from midnight until 6 A.M. I figured that meant two countermen, each with a nine-hour shift. I paid for the sundae and drove back to Madness.

The rain seemed to intensify with every minute that passed. Punching the Search button on the radio, I found a station playing folk music — Mary Ployd singing "Jealous Man."

Did Booker steal Stubbs' fiddle? Did he murder Stubbs? Or did he just steal the fiddle and somebody else was the murderer? And if Booker did neither, then who put the key in his room, and why? Raven was right across the hall. Nola was downstairs and had easy access to his room. So did Mary. And so did Bliss, who was staying in Mary's room. But judging from the ease with which I'd gone up and down the stairs, just about anybody could have slipped that key under the mirror. Including, of course, Booker.

I headed straight for Mary's office. Sprawled in her chair, she frowned at the rain. "This weather is terrible for the instruments," she muttered. "People will be spending all their time tuning."

I sat in what I'd come to think of as my chair. "I found Stubbs' fiddle."

"What?" Her mouth fell open.

"I found Stubbs' fiddle and bow."

"Where?"

I told her. She asked if the fiddle and bow were in good shape. I assured her they were. She wanted to know if I thought Booker was the instrument thief. I reminded her he couldn't have stolen the hurdy-gurdy — he was in class with Suzanne and a dozen others. Nor was Booker at the two previous festivals. In addition to which, the hurdy-gurdy wasn't in the locker with the fiddle.

Mary looked genuinely pleased, to say nothing of relieved. But I was still convinced she was hiding something.

Rain pelted the window, rattling the panes. I told her my plan to return the locker key and not inform the sheriff yet. She thought about this, then nodded. "Yale was up there, he should have found the key. He didn't, you did. Thank you, Frank. You've saved me from ruin."

Ruin was perhaps exaggerated, but I had saved Mary from shucking out $30,000 or handing over a piece of the farm. "When was the sheriff upstairs?" I asked.

"Yesterday morning."

If somebody was framing Booker, they could have slipped the key under the mirror yesterday afternoon or evening, or this morning. Maybe they weren't framing Booker, maybe they were just hiding the key in a room that wasn't theirs, so they'd never be caught with it. Maybe Davis himself slipped the key under the mirror.

"Are you and the sheriff lovers?" I asked.

Mary frowned. "That's a very blunt question."

"Davis told me he asked you to marry him. Three times."

Her face, neck, and arms turned scarlet. "Why would he tell you a thing like that?" She squirmed on the chair. "That's so personal. I'm disappointed in Yale."

"Mary — he thought you hired me to kill Stubbs. For all I know, he still thinks that. Why would he think that?"

Staring out the window, she said nothing. Apparently it didn't bother her that the sheriff considered me a murder suspect.

I answered my own question. "He thinks that because yesterday morning you asked him to marry you. Is that true?"

"It was a mistake." She planted her hands on the desktop. "These questions are out of order, Frank. It's none of your business what my relationship with Yale is. Or was. It's over now."

I stood and stared out at the rain, hands in my pockets. "I'm going to find who murdered Stubbs."

"No! Absolutely not!" she protested. "I hired you to find the instrument thief, that's what you should work on. I'm not paying you to solve a murder."

"I don't expect to get paid, Mary. I want to *know*." I told her about the murderer wearing my clothes.

She waved a hand dismissively. "You can't take this personally, Frank."

"I can. I do. Besides," I added, "*you* need to know. Everybody needs to know."

"Why?"

"So that it won't happen again. So people will know who it was and won't suspect one another. So they'll keep coming to your festival, Mary."

She shook her head. "If you just find the thief, people will be happy. The thefts have kept happening, murder isn't going to keep happening."

"You don't know that," I said.

"I think I do," she murmured.

I jumped on that. "What do you mean?"

"Nothing, nothing," she replied. A glare from me caused her to pull open her drawer and pull out the now-I'm-nervous web strap with the swivels. "Just a hunch, that's all," she assured me.

"You know something about the murder, Mary."

"No. I swear I don't know who killed Shelby."

I listened to what she had said. "You don't know who killed him — but you know something about it."

When she wouldn't cooperate, I walked out. And bumped into Nola, who looked as if she'd been listening at the door, but who claimed she was on her way to the appetizer class.

"Did you know Honey Miller?" I asked her as we walked to the porch.

"How do you know Honey?" Nola countered.

"When the sheriff was questioning me, he mentioned there had been a previous death at Midwest Music Madness. I asked Mary about it, and she told me about Honey Miller."

We stood on the porch, watching the downpour.

"I'm surprised Mary told you," Nola murmured. "I don't see what that has to do with carpentry and drumming."

"Mary was feeling sad."

Nola nodded.

I could see she wasn't going to say anything about Honey Miller, so together we ran toward the barn.

17

Just about everybody was in the barn, vendors as well as students. People who this morning had been wearing tank tops now wore long-sleeved T-shirts or light rain jackets. I spotted Suzanne, who was wearing my Chicago Architecture sweatshirt. I sat next to her and shook off some water.

A dozen of us dripped dry as Guy distributed his home-boiled bones. Bliss sat alone. As far away from her as possible sat Cindy, settling her recovered dulcimer protectively under her chair. Edric, thoroughly drenched, found Bliss and sat beside her. I looked around for Lafayette, but he wasn't there. Neither were Vance or Fonnie. Nola wasn't around, even though she had come in with me. Thunder rumbled in the distance.

The bones that Guy distributed weren't as long as the wooden ones Glover sold. Say six-and-a-half inches long compared to eight. The real bones weren't as smooth as the wood, either, though Guy told us we should wait a month and then polish them. I studied the visible cells at either end of my pair.

Vance hurried in, shook himself, and set up a folding chair. Kofi strolled into the barn at a leisurely pace, as if it weren't raining hard enough for even a home-crowd umpire to call the game. "Now we are both pupils," he declared, sitting next to me.

Basking in the attention, Guy asked Booker and Cody to play "Gaspe Reel" and "La Bastringue." Booker flat-picked the melody and Cody played rhythm. Tansy Thompson stood well inside the doorway and beamed at her son. The clicking and clinking of bones in the barn sounded like a ghostly echo of the hammers that had built the structure long ago. Davis came in and stood next to Tansy.

Demonstration over, Guy got down to the serious business of bones. First he showed us how to hold them. I stretched my right hand straight out, palm down, fingers apart. I slipped one bone between my index finger and middle finger, the other between my middle and ring finger. Then I closed my hand into a fist, my fingers curved tightly around the bones. Tighter around the first bone, which Guy called the anvil bone because it never moved. The second bone was held a bit more loosely.

"Now, snap the wrist outward," Guy instructed, demonstrating. His snap caused the loose bone to hit the anvil bone, producing an authoritative click.

The rest of us snapped with lesser degrees of efficiency. One of Vance's bones went flying off toward the sheriff. Cindy's bones emitted a *snick-snick.* sound. I managed a click or two. Suzanne, who had been practicing for three days, produced solid clicks. Guy smiled as he walked around observing each of us. "The most difficult thing," he explained, "is to hold the bones correctly. If you master that, you can master the bones. Now, we will do 'Road to Boston,' an old-time tune in two-four time. I want you to hit only the one and two in each beat."

"*Only* the one and two," muttered Vance.

Guy nodded to Booker and Cody, and we were off.

When we finished, Guy grinned. "The road to Boston was rough, no? But not bad. Let me see how each of you clicks the bones. Booker, 'Hand Me Down My Walking Cane.'"

As we played Guy corrected us. "Good, Frank. Keep the anvil bone straight, like you kept my elbow. That was very good." I couldn't tell if he was referring to my snap and click or my locking his elbow. Time flew by, mostly to a four-four count, and when the dinner bell rang we were disappointed to leave.

"Good class, Guy," I told him.

"Wonderful!" beamed Suzanne.

"Tomorrow," said Guy, "I will teach you to play the hurdy-gurdy."

"Really?" asked Cindy.

"No, no, it is a joke. Remember," he announced to the assembly, "if my hurdy-gurdy is returned to the dining hall, there will be no questions asked!"

As one, we made a mad dash through the drenching rain for the dining hall. All except Davis, who stepped into his car.

Dinner was what Tansy called an Auralee speciality, a one-pound pork chop. Kofi, who had gone up to the food window with me, frowned. "One person eats each of these?"

"That's the idea," I replied.

"One is enough for a village. You carry them," he said, dismissing the pork chops. "I will take the potatoes and the spinach salad."

Edric brought the cornbread, Kim the iced tea. Bliss and Guy rounded out the table. Not having Kofi's sensibilities, the rest of us each tackled a pork chop, chewing to the sound of thunder and lightning. The dining room lights flickered, went out, came back on.

Bliss left first, taking the back stairs to Mary's room. Kofi left next. Kim ran toward the barn, presumably to tend to her goods.

Suzanne leaned my way. "Mary looks miserable," she observed, nodding toward where Mary sat alone at one of the tables. "I'll go talk to her." She extricated herself from the bench.

That left me with Edric. "More coffee?" I asked, studying the tattoo on his forearm. It looked like a chain, but might have been a snake.

"Wouldn't mind," he answered, staring out at the rain. "Cadillac version." He eyed me. "Man, you get some strong rain in Illinois."

"This is nothing," I informed him. "You haven't seen a real Midwestern thunderstorm."

"Hope I never do. Radio says I might, though."

I brought a black coffee for myself, a heavy cream-and-sugar for English. Then I sat and stared out at the weather.

Edric sat like a con, elbows on the table, arms protecting his food. Coffee, in this case. He seemed on edge, his eyes jumping sideways, looking for someone to come at him. After a while, he spoke. "Bliss says the badge was questioning you this morning."

I grunted in the affirmative.

"What about?"

I wasn't going to tell him about the will, that was in confidence. "Same questions he asked me yesterday. When did I hear Bliss moaning, what did I see, that kind of stuff."

A loud slurp indicated Edric was enjoying the coffee. He fingered his sideburns. "That was this morning. What about this afternoon? Either you and the badge are tight, or there's a lot more to why he's questioning you."

He seemed a bit too interested in the sheriff's movements. Maybe with good reason. Giving him information seemed the best way to trade for information, so I told him about my T-shirt and shorts being found in the pigpen cupola.

"The same peckerhead that lifted my shoes!" he growled. Coffee sloshed out of the mug and onto the table. He glanced at me, away, then back at me. "I hear somebody stole your hammer."

"It's missing," I agreed.

"Shelby's head was bashed in," he said in a low voice. "I saw it when I stepped into the trailer."

I nodded and watched him. I could see him putting two and one together: that the murderer had used his shoes, my clothes, and probably my hammer. He reached for a cigarette, looked around, saw the same No Smoking sign he'd seen after every meal, put the cigarette away. "You think it's the same hound dog who heisted the hurdy-gurdy?"

The lights went off again as lightning flashed. After about twenty seconds, the lights came back on.

"Stubbs' fiddle is missing, too," I said.

Edric could have lied about his shoes being stolen. In which case, he probably took my clothes and hammer. I left the whole thing open for grabs, wondering which way he would strum it.

"The sheriff asked me when I last saw Shelby alive," he informed me. "I told him it was right before the dance. Say 7:30."

"Where?" I asked.

"His trailer," Edric answered.

"What'd Stubbs have to say?"

"Nothing." Edric shook his head. "I knocked, not loud. I didn't know if Shelby was there or if he was still with Raven. Bliss let me in, motioned I should be quiet. Shelby was asleep on the couch."

"That was the last you saw of him?"

"Right." He looked out at the storm. "Right as rain."

"You didn't happen to notice if the fiddle case was there, did you?"

"Sheriff asked me that. I didn't notice one way or the other." He shrugged. "Bliss and I went to the barn, I played for an hour, danced afterwards . . . . "

"How long have you known Bliss?"

He touched the pack of cigarettes in his pocket. "He should have left her alone." His eyes stared at something not present. "Shelby saw me with her a couple of years ago, wanted an introduction. I could tell he was gonna move in on her, I warned her." He sighed. "She's not the first one whose head he turned. Shelby could lay down a tune, I'll give him that."

I didn't know if Edric would be sitting here talking to me if he hadn't seen the sheriff question me. Or if it weren't pouring pig troughs of rain. "The sheriff mentioned somebody named Honey Miller."

The cup was halfway to his lips. He lowered it without drinking. "What about her?"

"Don't know," I confided truthfully. "Mary told me you asked her to give Honey Miller room and board."

No response.

"Who was she?"

This time he lit the cigarette. Inhaled. "Kids need a father to show them the temptations that are gonna try 'n trip them up. When I was in the pen — sheriff probably told you that, didn't he?" I nodded and Edric continued."My daughter was born. Wife divorced me a couple of months later. Then she remarried, my daughter was adopted." A puff of smoke obscured his face. "They moved away. I got out . . . married . . . divorced . . . ."

I waited, sorting the information.

Edric stubbed out the cigarette, pocketed it. "Honey had no mother, no father. She played clean guitar, sorta in my style. Her real strength was songwriting. We played one of her songs Monday morning, 'Orphan Blues.' She could have made it as a songwriter, all she needed was a little support. Room and board, encouragement." He looked me in the eye. "I thought being here with Mary would help her. I was wrong."

"You regret sending her here?"

"No." He considered it. "No, I think Mary was good to her. What happened . . . would probably have happened anywhere."

Over at the other end of the hall, Suzanne had an arm around Mary's shoulder, consoling her. "I can't be sure," I threw in, changing direction, "but the sheriff seemed to be talking about the motive for murder being close to home."

"It wasn't Bliss." He gulped his coffee. "Hell she couldn't kill a flea if it was biting her favorite hound to death. Anyway, she was with me."

Before I could say anything, Edric continued. "Bliss says the badge wanted to know if she was legally married to Shelby. Now what the hell do you make of that?" he asked.

"I'd have to guess the sheriff's thinking she wasn't."

"He treated her rotten. He treated all his wives rotten. Bliss was his wife, she deserves what he had."

"Raven was his wife, too."

"Yeah, well." He studied the rain. "I suppose Raven deserves some of whatever Shelby left."

"What about his first wife?"

A sharp look. "Opal Jackson? I don't think so, she was married to Shelby less than a year."

"What happened to her?"

"Don't know." He shook his head. "Haven't heard of Opal in years."

"Sheriff might be looking for her," I suggested.

"What for?" Edric guffawed. "He can't think she came back after all these years and did the bastard in!" Looking me up and down, he cleared his throat. "I had you pegged for a badge, but now I'm not sure."

"Not a badge," I said. "Just trying to help Mary find who's been stealing instruments."

"Private?" he asked. "A beagle?"

"Right."

He nodded, satisfied. "I won't finger you." He stared out at the rain. "Opal was lucky, you know."

"How's that?"

"She saw what Shelby was and got out of the situation fast. Not like Raven."

I conceded that Raven was a bitter woman.

Edric leaped to her defense. "She wasn't always like that. Before she met Shelby she was the sweetest thing. Happy. Not making all those barbed remarks like she does now. Pricklier than a porcupine." He thrummed his fingers on the table.

"Getting back to the money," I said. "Is there a lot of it?"

"What?" he asked. "Shelby's money? Hell, I don't know. A hundred-fifty thousand maybe, if you include the house."

"I heard you were angry over Stubbs not taking you to France."

The curve caught him unaware. He flinched, then turned red. "I said a few things, but they didn't amount to a hill of beans. It was the insult I minded, that the peckerhead would do this behind my back. Like telling the world he doesn't think I'm good enough."

"If Stubbs was such a bastard, why'd you stay with him?"

Edric looked at me. "You're not a musician, are you?"

I shook my head.

"When we were on, we were tight. We made good music, laid down good grooves."

I guess I looked skeptical, because he shrugged and shook his head.

"What about Booker Hayes?" I asked. "It looked as if he and Shelby had run-ins before."

"Here and there," he conceded. "What you saw Monday was due mostly to the soundtrack."

"Come again?"

"The soundtrack. Big film company's making a movie something like *O Brother Where Art Thou,* you know, old-time music stuff?"

"Yeah?"

"So they're looking for somebody to do the background music. Not somebody big and beyond their budget — somebody known but not so famous. They narrowed it down to Booker or the Shelby Stubbs Band."

"And now they've chosen Booker?"

"Yeah," he grinned, "but Booker and me are gonna do it together. Joint billing: Booker Hayes and Edric English."

18

When Vance leapt to a table top, the few of us remaining in the dining hall looked up. "Listen everybody," he shouted, holding a radio in one hand for veracity, "the National Weather Service has issued a severe thunderstorm watch for Iroquois County. And a tornado has been spotted. It's heading our way and we need to do something."

An emergency was just what Mary needed to galvanize her into action. She too climbed to a table top and stood facing Vance halfway across the room. "Midwest Music Madness has a plan," she announced loudly.

Mary then assigned us into squads: emergency food, bottled water, flashlights and batteries, first-aid-kits. She instructed Tansy to turn off the water, gas, and electricity to the farmhouse and dining room. Then she lined us up in two's and marched us and our supplies toward the barn. All she needed to complete the picture was a guitar: she could tilt the neck forward and yell "Charge!"

Vance's radio warned of 40-mile-an-hour gusts, but what greeted us as we stepped out the door was stronger than that — enough to blow our column off-path and some off their feet as we fought our way toward the barn.

Inside the barn Mary grabbed the microphone and issued instructions for dealing with a severe thunderstorm — potential tornado. First she assigned everyone to their morning session group in order to make certain each class member was present. "That way, we'll be sure everybody's here in the barn," she said.

Thunder drowned out half her words. Bolts of lightning ripped through the sky. The woman from Kansas City waved a hand. "What about people like me," she asked, "who don't have a morning class?"

"You all meet in that corner," Mary directed, "and report to Nola. She knows everybody and everybody's schedule."

A melee of voices shouted that Nola couldn't be found. Then Mary remembered that Nola had gone home to secure her own house against the storm. "All right," she shouted, "all unassigned morning people report to Frank Dragovic, the carpenter. Put your heads together and try to account for everyone you know who wasn't taking a morning class."

The woman from Kansas and I counted up the others, ten in all. I felt reasonably confident that everyone without a morning class was present and accounted for.

"Attention, attention!" Mary was calm. "Cody Thompson has not reported to his morning group." Somebody went up to the stage and spoke to Mary. She announced that two people had seen Cody go home with his mother minutes earlier.

"Attention, attention!" she continued. "Fonnie Sheffler is missing from the old-time ensemble group."

There was a general shuffling, people looking left and right and all around, as if the missing person had simply failed to report to the right group. During these few seconds of confusion Fonnie herself staggered in through the southern doors. "Where were you?" demanded Vance. "We were worried about you."

"Sorry," she gasped. "I wanted to secure my camper." She struggled for more breath. "It's really bad out there."

"Fonnie has been found!" shouted Mary. "Lafayette Wafer is also missing from the old-time ensemble group. Has anybody seen Lafayette?"

We looked around again, and then we looked toward the

south door, as if Lafayette would repeat Fonnie's trick of appearing out of the blue. In this case the black.

Once it was clear that Lafayette wasn't there, Mary asked if anybody knew where he was. Voices offered facts, opinions, judgments.

"I saw him around four o'clock," Cindy called out. "He said a tune was calling him."

"That's right," shouted Vance. "He was heading toward the big tree by the creek."

"But it was already starting to rain," Cindy yelled. "He might have gone to the pole barn."

Mary repeated these remarks to all over the microphone and asked if any of us had seen Lafayette after that time. Hearing her was becoming more and more difficult in the thunder. I walked over to Suzanne and took the flashlight and first-aid kit from her backpack. She had packed our rain jackets and I pulled mine on.

"Where are you going?" she asked, a note of panic in her voice.

"The pole barn."

"No!" She grabbed my arm. "Frank, don't go."

I shook my head. "I've got to."

"For who?" demanded Booker, watching me. "Lafayette?"

I stuffed the first-aid kit in a pocket and gripped the flashlight.

"Don't do it, man." Booker placed a hand on my shoulder. "It's too dangerous."

I moved to leave but Booker pushed me back. "No! Let the little rat drown! He doesn't deserve saving."

Guy spoke up. "I will help."

"Thanks," I said, "but there's no sense in two of us going out."

"You're both crazy!" Booker was agitated. "Lafayette's not worth it!"

"I could carry him back," offered Guy.

I didn't doubt he could, probably with a hammered dulcimer strapped to his back.

Booker stepped in front of me again and placed a hand on my chest, pushing me back. "I'm telling you," he warned, "you're being stupid. I've seen people die in this kind of weather. You go out there, you might not come back."

"Lafayette's the one who traded you Cindy's mountain dulcimer, isn't he?" I said.

Booker clenched his teeth. "I ain't sayin.'"

Guy stepped back, reconsidering.

"What are you doing?" Mary asked, hurrying toward us.

"He is going to find Lafayette," replied Guy. "Lafayette is the one from whom Booker got the stolen mountain dulcimer."

"I didn't say that," muttered Booker.

Mary hesitated. "It's dangerous, Frank. The creek floods."

Suzanne gripped my arm but said nothing.

I tested the flashlight and walked to the barn's eastern door. Suzanne, Guy, Booker, and Mary followed me. "Every five minutes," I instructed them, "open this door as wide as it'll go. Hold it that way for a minute if you can, then close it. I'll use the light as a guide. If the electricity goes, light the battery-operated stuff."

Suzanne squeezed my hand. "I'll be back," I assured her. Then Guy rolled the door open a notch and I slipped out.

The first four steps weren't that bad. Like stepping into a pugnacious, overweight waterfall. After that the wind whipped around the corner of the barn and bulldozed me in directions I didn't want to go. But mostly it came from the west and I was heading east, so for a while it simply impelled me forward.

Coming back would be the problem.

Even with the powerful flashlight in my hand, the path wasn't visible. Walls of water poured down, obscuring everything. I tried to run but couldn't, the wind shoving me everywhere. I fell, got up, was blown back down a couple of times. Being blown off my feet didn't bother me too much, at least not yet. What made my heart race harder was the fear of lightning. It crackled in the sky behind me as if deciding where to aim next.

Uncle Rudy's thunderstorm advice filled my brain. When out in the fields during a thunderstorm, never go near a tall tree that could attract lightning. Never stand upright. Never lie flat. Instead, crouch: present the smallest surface possible to the bolts from above. My sister and cousins and I would go around pretending we were running from lighting, our backs curved, our arms hanging loosely at our sides. We'd sway back and forth and huff-huff like apes.

Back then, it was funny.

Now it was damned awkward to run all hunched over, as close to the ground as possible.

The one-pound pork chop I had eaten cramped my stomach, making progress even more difficult. If I survived, I would not vote for Tansy Thompson as best cook.

The wind knocked me over again and I fought my way back up, trying to remember which direction I'd been heading. I chose what I thought was the right one, then looked back over my shoulder. At that moment Guy must have rolled the barn door open — a huge rectangle of light shown through the darkness. I turned my back on it, confident of my bearing.

Several minutes later I sensed something massive, as if it were sending out vibrations. I looked up. The black walnut tree loomed, its branches whipsawing in the wind, its trunk swaying. The pole barn, then, was to my left.

I veered in that direction. I sloshed through the swift creek, forgetting to crouch as I hurried against the rising water, which had already reached the pole barn. I clicked the flashlight button: a long beam of light picked up the barn wall. The door wouldn't slide open. I pulled and pushed and at last squeezed through an opening.

"Lafayette!" I shouted.

He stood in the far corner . . . on the little ladder nailed to the wall, his bowed psaltry case clutched to his chest.

I slogged my way to him. "Come down! I'll get you to the big barn."

He shook his head back and forth. Took a step up the ladder.

I took a step up, too, grabbed him by the belt, and pulled. The three of us — him, me, and the psaltry — tumbled off the ladder and splashed into the cold creek water. The psaltry case bobbed up first. I snatched it, struggled to my feet, crossed the strap over my chest, and pulled Lafayette upright.

"Let's go!" I had a strong grip on his wrist.

He resisted with more force than I thought he had. I turned and clipped him on the jaw, caught him as he fell, and struggled to heave him across my shoulders. Finally I stood upright, more or less, with Lafayette draped over a shoulder. More or less.

The flashlight was gone. I found the door because that's where the wind blasted through. I shouldered it open a bit more and squeezed out, my steps elephantine.

If we survived the rising creek I would worry about the lightning. The creek water raged, halfway up my thighs. I managed to cross. Lightning lit up the sky and I saw the black walnut to my left. I labored up the small slope of land toward higher ground.

The psaltry dug into my back and Lafayette slumped on my shoulders. He must weigh only 140 pounds. It felt like 340.

Watch for lightning. Don't lose the way.

I tried to crouch but Lafayette and the psaltry prevented it.

Every few seconds the sky lit up in fuzzy electric gray.

I toiled onward. Finite distance, finite, I could do it. Where was the barn? I'd been peering for the light until my eyeballs burned from not blinking, and still I hadn't seen the rectangle. Where was I? Shouldn't it be ahead of me? Had they forgotten they were supposed to open the door every five minutes and leave it open for a full minute? Had I missed it?

And then I smelled the pigpen. I was way off course, the barn in another direction. Lafayette moaned. I shifted his weight, my back burning. There, far off to my right — a huge rectangle of light. I stumbled, crashing against the pigpen railing.

Richard's squeal rode over the wind and thunder. He raced back and forth inside the shed, butting his head and haunches against the wood.

I slipped Lafayette off my back and shook him. "Wake up!" I shouted. But he didn't. I was about to dump him on the ground but at the last minute I realized how difficult it would be for me to lift him, so I draped him over the rail. Then I opened the pigpen door and kicked the side of the shed.

Stubborn at even the best moments, Richard went silent.

And didn't come out.

I kicked again. Heard nothing.

"Sooooo-eeeeeeeeee!" I called, trying to imitate Uncle Rudy's call to the sows and boars at feeding time. *"Sooooo-eeeeeeeee!"*

Richard rocketed out of his shed and through the open gate, knocking me off my feet. I fell forward.

Shit!

Pig shit.

I pushed myself up and again tried waking Lafayette. When he didn't respond, I worried: he'd been unconscious longer than one punch could account for. Then I smelled the alcohol on his breath and hoped he was more drunk than hurt. I hefted him across my shoulders again. Not as well as before.

The light was gone, but I focused on an imaginary line from the pigpen to the barn's east door. All of a sudden something sharp and hard hit me.

Again.

And again.

Hail.

I staggered in circles, lowering my head against the pelting. Minor hail is annoying, pinging off car windows and inflicting nicks on paint jobs. This hail was major. Dozens of crystals sliced into my arms, my neck. "Goddamn!" I shouted as one hit above my eye and ricocheted off. Something dark blurred my vision.

I forgot all about the hail when a ferocious *Boom* split the air and shook the ground. An immense bolt of lightning hovered over the barn, three thinner but no less deadly bolts radiating from it to the barn's three lightning rods. For what seemed like hours the bolts pulsated and the barn appeared as if with photographic backlighting. Then the lightning gave one last shudder and disappeared from the sky. My feet tingled. The ground buzzed.

There would be no further rectangles of light to guide me: the barn had taken a direct hit. But the eerie picture fixed its location in my mind.

I lurched on, Lafayette gaining weight with every step I took. The wind spun me around. Shouldn't I be there by now?

I squinted into the storm, only one eye functioning.

Despite the energy I was expending, which should have kept my body stoked, I felt a deep chill. Goose bumps stood out on my skin. I was running on empty.

Then I knew. I felt it. Close, very close. A reassuring solid bulk. A warmth.

The barn.

I hit it shoulder first, lost my footing, went down, rolling to the ground with Lafayette. Something wet prodded me in the shoulder. It grunted. Placing a hand on Richard's back for support, I pulled myself up. More hail sliced me. My ability to lift Lafayette onto my shoulders vanished. I pulled him into a sitting position, laced my hands under his armpits, and walked backward, dragging him with me. I kept my shoulder against the barn, so that with every step I took, I felt its side against my skin.

Shivering and shaking, I counted my steps.

The barn disappeared. I fell sideways and landed on somebody's feet.

"He is here!" shouted Guy, pulling me into the barn. "And Lafayette is with him!"

Somebody held a lantern. Suzanne helped me to my feet. Others took charge. Somehow or other I got out of my wet clothes and put on dry ones, a hodgepodge of somebody else's shoes and socks and shorts, but my own Chicago Architecture sweatshirt. Mary swabbed the cuts on my arms and neck and patched the big one above my eye. Lafayette came to and screamed for his psaltry. Cindy, who was wiping off the case, handed it to him. Somebody gave him dry clothes. A butane stove burned nearby. Somebody thrust a hot mug of instant chicken broth into my hands. I sat between several bales of straw in a dark corner — of course, the corners were all dark with the power out. Suzanne sat on one side of me, Lafayette on the other. Mary hovered a while. She whispered something about Lafayette and Richard, I wasn't sure what. Mary seemed twitchy. After a while she disappeared from the small circle of lantern light.

"Frank." Lafayette whispered so softly I could barely hear him.

"Ummmm?" I was falling asleep.

"You saved my . . . my bowed psaltry."

"No problem, Lafayette."

The straw creaked as his head waggled back and forth against it. "I owe you," he whispered.

Suzanne sat absolutely still beside me.

"You want to know things. That's why I tell you things, because you want to know."

A thank-you seemed wise. I mumbled it through dry lips.

"I did it," he said in a voice so soft I had to tilt to hear him.

I waited. "Did what?"

"Strangled Shelby's fiddle."

"The red one?"

"Yes. He insulted me. I cut the strings and wrapped them around the fiddle's neck." In the glow of the lantern his hands were shadows strangling something.

"What time was it when you did that?"

"When everybody was at dinner."

Lafayette hadn't been to dinner Monday night, I remembered that clearly. "Where was Stubbs when you did that?"

"Sound asleep." His thin reedy laugh floated my way.

I paused, wondering exactly how to formulate the next question. "Why the red fiddle?" I asked. "Why not his best fiddle, the one he performed with?"

"The red fiddle was out on the table, just sitting there. The black one was in its case." His voice was full of regret. "I was afraid if I snapped the case open, Shelby might wake up."

I took a slow breath. "You're sure his performing fiddle was there?"

"Of course I'm sure, Frank. The case was on the bed beside him."

"What about the case for the red fiddle?" I asked. "Was it there?"

"Yes," he answered. "It was there on the table, alongside the red fiddle."

I thought about that for a while. "Lafayette, did you steal Cindy's mountain dulcimer two years ago?"

"No," he answered. "I don't play the mountain dulcimer."

"You traded one to Booker."

"Because I don't play it."

"How did you get that dulcimer," I asked.

"I don't remember," he said, and within a few seconds started to snore.

I closed my eyes and slept.

What woke me was the guitar and Booker's tenor voice singing about the deep river blues. I recognized it as a Doc Watson song. Lafayette moaned in his sleep, but I could sense Suzanne smiling. Her voice joined Booker's, and from the darkness of the barn more voices rose up in song.

The singing continued for a long time. Whenever it stopped, we were aware of the rain pounding on the barn roof. Even muted by the upper story, the drumming was still there, the storm a presence no one could ignore. I drifted off again, hearing other songs about water and rivers and oceans.

"Let's hear it for acoustic!" shouted Kim at one point. "Electric instruments couldn't do this!" Her voice sounded both triumphant and frightened. Her laugh turned into a sob.

The storm lessened, or so it seemed, and we were all getting a bit loose and cocky, the way people do when they've survived a danger they didn't expect to survive. But the thunder returned with a vengeance, deeper and louder; the lightning bolts blazed longer and wider, casting the entire barn in their pale glow. The barn swayed with the wind. It felt as if the whole building would be lifted and blown away. If we were in the path of a tornado, little could save us. Except possibly the banked earth of the western wall, where we all huddled.

A blast shook the earth: it sounded like a bomb going off. I was on my feet, my hand around Suzanne's wrist, ready to run. The lantern jittered on the floor. Everybody I could see was poised for flight — with nowhere to go. I looked up, sniffed the air, worried about fire. Had the barn taken another direct hit?

No.

My brain interpreted the sound.

"A tree," I said to nobody in particular.

A few gasps, some nervous titters, some crying. I paced in a narrow row, too charged up to sit down again.

For a second time, the thunder and lightning abated. Eventually people settled down, myself included. Except for somebody still crying.

"It's Mary," whispered Suzanne.

We followed the sobs to where Mary, looking spooked, clenched her fists. "Stop it!" she whispered between coughing sobs. "Stop it!"

"Mary, what's wrong?" Suzanne patted her shoulder.

"Stop it! Stop it!"

"Stop what?" I asked.

"Listen! Can't you hear?"

Suzanne and I looked at each other. All I heard was the wind and the rain.

And then, a thin wail of a voice. Maybe singing, maybe crying. I strained to make out the words. Something about one sister drowning another out of jealousy, then somebody making a fiddle out of the drowned sister's bones. Every other line seemed to be, *"Oh the wind and rain."*

"You mean the song, Mary?" I asked.

She nodded tearfully. "Stop it. Stop it."

To me it was just another rain song, like we'd been hearing all night long. Perhaps more morbid than the others, but I was learning that folk music recorded a lot of violence.

"The only tune the fiddle would play / Was oh the wind and rain."

"He's bowing double stops," whispered Mary. "Hear? Hear the double stops?"

"Why are you upset?" Suzanne asked, probably as perplexed as I was.

Was it the song itself? The singing? The double stops — whatever the hell they were?

"And one sister floated down / Oh the wind and rain."

Mary gave a small shriek. Suzanne gripped her around the shoulders and shook her.

Hysteria is the last thing any group under stress needs, and for the hysteria to come from the head of the festival would be utterly demoralizing. "I'll stop it," I told Mary. "Just keep calm. Everybody here needs you calm."

She nodded, and underneath the trembling I think she understood that much.

In the dark of the barn I followed the sound, which wasn't audible a great distance. I crept closer to the source.

Jeff Glover, minus his cowboy hat, sat on a bale of hay, rocking back and forth as if in pain, playing his fiddle, singing *"Oh the wind and rain."*

"Jeff," I said, "Mary's really upset by that song."

He didn't look up. I wasn't even sure he heard me. Back and forth he rocked, fiddling and singing.

I touched his shoulder.

He jumped a mile, stood facing me with his fiddle behind him, his bow thrust forward like a sword. The whites of his eyes glinted in what little light there was. I caught the odor of sweat and fear. "Mary's upset," I said, keeping my voice soft and low. "All the songs about wind and rain are upsetting her."

I waited, watching to see if it would register. I could see him trying to gain control. He took a deep breath and shuddered, brought the fiddle and bow down to his knees. I still waited. Finally, he put the fiddle and bow on a bale of hay and sat down with his back to them.

That was as much of a response as I was going to get, so I turned and walked away, still not knowing why this particular song upset Mary so much. Or Glover, for that matter.

She and Suzanne were sitting pretty much the same way Glover sat: on the floor, with their backs to a bale of hay. I lowered myself beside them and kept an eye on Mary.

After a quarter of an hour her breathing was normal, she seemed alert, and every once in a while she'd look up toward the roof, as if wondering when the rain would stop.

I heard a grunt and a shuffle. Somewhere nearby, the pig was bedded down for the night.

"Mary," I said, "tell me about you and Waydell and Stubbs."

Her intake of breath was sharp. She exhaled. "We knew each other a long time ago. When I was young, trying to make it as a folk singer. Shelby and Waydell were playing in a small band down in Amarillo, where I met them. They asked me on as a singer. We played one-night stands in seedy bars in Texas, New Mexico, Arizona, Colorado, even Utah and Nebraska." She sighed, as if remembering. "We called ourselves the Boot Jacks, don't ask me why, I can't remember. It was always Waydell and Shelby and me, and we picked up a bass player or mandolin player here and there. We even had a washboard player once and a hammered dulcimer player. Shelby wasn't so righteous back then."

She went silent and Suzanne asked her what happened.

"I wanted to be a folk singer," she replied. "Not old-time, like Shelby and Waydell wanted me to be. I wanted to be more like Joan Baez and Odetta." She seemed to think about that a long time.

After a while she continued. "Whatever people wanted, Shelby tried to stop. I'm not the only one he stopped. I was in love with Waydell, you know."

I wanted more information, but Mary clammed up. "I hated Shelby," she said. "Hated him."

19 Thursday

Raven's soprano voice, singing about the great storm being over, penetrated even the grayest corners of the barn as daylight poured through the chinks. One bright beam warmed the spot where she stood strumming her autoharp and singing. A sleepy-eyed Booker joined her. Not to be outdone, Mary scrambled to her feet, brushed off broken stalks of hay and straw, and made it a trio. Within minutes we were all gathered round, two-hundred-some worn survivors. Some knew all the words, some only the chorus. Even I sang the chorus.

"It's a modern folk song," Suzanne whispered to me, "written by Bob Franke."

From here and there banjos, guitars, fiddles, and dulcimers joined in. I wondered if all the musicians had brought their instruments into the barn. The distinctive sound of a hand drum boomed out. Kofi sat on a bale, a drum between his knees. He told me he had carried all of his drums into the barn before dinner.

The music sounded good. Better than that, downright appropriate.

Raven led us into the last refrain, which we sang with drama and gusto, and then Guy and Vance stepped forward from the circle, walked to the southern doors and swung them open. A wet but tranquil world greeted us, the temperature in the mid-sixties. The sycamore and shagbark hickory gleamed in the morning light and beyond them the farmhouse stood undamaged, its windows glinting. The circle of day lilies at the back door lay flattened.

Mary stepped out the door and onto the grass. "Midwest Music Madness continues," she announced, turning to face us. "Everybody to your tents and campers, see what damage has been done. There's an emergency generator in the kitchen — we'll meet in the dining hall for breakfast at eight o'clock sharp."

Suzanne and I walked toward the tent area, which looked blown to kingdom come. Ahead of us Mary stopped in her tracks.

Down by the creek, the black walnut tree sprawled uprooted. Beneath it the pole barn lay splintered. The creek swirled in eddies around them both.

Mary, Suzanne, and I sloshed across the soaked field to the fallen giant. A few others followed us, but most merely glanced in the direction of the creek, then continued toward the tents.

The tree had fallen almost due north, its trunk imposed on what had been the ridge of the pole barn. Most of the black walnut's branches lay flattened to the east and west. Other branches sprouted upward, unharmed by the fall.

Kofi nodded as he gazed at the tree, most certainly congratulating himself on having moved the drums. Fonnie and Lafayette looked horrified, Cindy fascinated. Vance remained expressionless.

"This is terrible," said Raven into the long silence.

I stared at her in surprise.

"Mary, you can't have this tree lying around like this," she continued, "it's too depressing. I can call some friends of mine and have them haul it away, clean up the grounds."

Mary snorted. "The lumber's worth ten thousand, Raven, though you probably don't recognize good wood when you see it."

"What's that supposed to mean?"snipped Raven.

"It means you probably won't want to buy any of this black walnut when I offer it to every musician who's here."

"*Magnifique*!" cried Guy. "I want to buy some! With the black walnut I will make the best hurdy-gurdy in the world. You will offer it to us at a discount, no, Mary? Because it is a very expensive wood."

Raven stood, lips tight.

"So this is a big Midwestern thunderstorm," observed Edric. "Take me back to Ol' Virginny." Standing beside him, Bliss shivered.

I walked parallel to the tree, or at least that part of it on this side of the creek. Something caught my eye. I looked for it again, letting my peripheral vision do the work. Not green like the silvery-green underside of leaves, but emerald green, the green of an artificial substance.

There.

Keeping my eye on it, I moved forward.

A large emerald-green instrument case hung from one of the sturdy inner branches of the tree. Stepping into the water, which had receded considerably, I hoisted myself onto the trunk. I walked up the trunk slowly, pushing branches aside, making my way through the sticky black walnut resin.

"What are you doing?" asked Mary.

"Emerald green," I replied, "hanging from a branch. Where is it?"

She and everybody else peered into the swirl of leaves and branches.

"Look for a different color," I suggested. "Let your eyes slide over the tree."

"There it is!" shouted Suzanne, pointing. "To your left." She guided me until I saw the case swinging above me. Somebody had attached it to one of the thick middle branches by unclipping its strap, double-looping the strap around the branch, then clipping it back to the case: a secure arrangement.

I undid the rigging, slipped the strap over my chest, and walked back down the tree trunk with the soft-sided green case.

"It's a hammered dulcimer case," said Mary. "How in the world did it get there!"

It was more than a dulcimer case: it was where the stolen instruments had been stored. Three years in a row, I'd be willing to bet. If just Mary, Suzanne, and I were present, I'd explain it. But a host of suspects looked up at me. "There's something in it," I said.

Raven and Edric stared. Fonnie trust her hands into her pockets and frowned. Lafayette covered his mouth with a hand. Vance stepped forward, as if he didn't want to miss anything, but Guy pushed him aside. "My hurdy-gurdy?" he asked.

I unzipped the case and pulled out what was inside: a charcoal gray instrument case, and it wasn't empty, either.

"Ma vielle!" Guy grabbed the charcoal gray case that had been inside the green dulcimer case and clutched it to his chest. After a moment, he opened it. Everybody watched Guy. Everybody except me: I kept my eye on the people around me, trying to read their expressions.

Carefully Guy lifted the instrument from its case, absentmindedly thrusting the case at Mary. Turning the hurdy-gurdy this way and that, he examined it: ran his fingers over the wood, checked out the joinery, studied for dents or scratches. Guy moved through the group toward the vendor tables. We followed. He found a chair and sat. Placing the hurdy-gurdy on his lap, he turned the handle, activating the drone. A tear fell on the soundboard. Guy wiped it away.

He fiddled with the keys and checked the tuning pegs while the rest of us waited in silence.

"It is fine." He laughed nervously. "Fine! I cannot believe it, it should be broken."

"Whose dulcimer case is it?" asked Fonnie.

"Does anybody know?" I asked. "Mary?"

Before Mary could speak, Raven answered the question. "Anybody's! Hammered dulcimer cases look pretty much alike,

Frank. The two most common colors are burgundy and green. This one's green." She shrugged her shoulders as if to say that accounted for nothing.

"Maybe there's identification inside," Cindy suggested. She leaned forward on her toes, trying to see inside the case.

I doubted it, but looked in the zippered compartments. No ID, and as far as I could tell, no identifying marks of any kind on the outside.

Mary looked at her watch. "Guy, I'm so happy your hurdy-gurdy has been found. Your dulcimer, too, Cindy," she added, stressing the positive. "Frank, I'd like you to take the hammered dulcimer case and give it to Nola. She can turn it over to the sheriff as evidence. I'm going to check out the barn before breakfast, make certain it gets tidied up before class." Mary stared at Raven. "Midwest Music Madness will prevail," she said firmly. And then she headed for the barn.

Suzanne put her hand on my arm and squeezed. I looked at her and she smiled. "I'm going to help Mary," she said.

I nodded and watched the two of them march to the barn. Everyone else who had been standing around started for the tents, campers, or the farmhouse. Bliss and Edric walked side by side toward the tents. Observing Raven, I fell in beside her. "I promised I'd do some repair work on the kitchen cabinets for Aja," I lied. "I'd better hurry."

Raven paid almost no attention to me. I increased my speed, entered the dining hall, and hurried up the back stairs as quietly as I could.

Halfway up, I stopped. Parked behind the farmhouse, out of sight of the barn, stood Sheriff Yale Davis's vehicle. I had no idea how long it had been there. Or why it was parked on the lawn. Or where the sheriff was.

My last question was answered quickly: Davis sat on Mary's bed, staring at the door. His uniform was rumpled.

"What are you doing here?" he demanded, leaping to his

feet. "What happened to your eye?"

The real question was, What was he doing here?

I put a finger to my lips, warning him to be silent. Without making a sound, I closed Mary's door, then positioned myself against the wall.

Davis stood there for a minute or two, watching me as if he expected something. When it didn't come, he lowered himself to the bed again and sat there in disapproval. After seven or eight minutes, I began to think I'd made a mistake. I glanced at my watch: I'd give it another ten minutes.

But I didn't have to wait that long. The stealthy footsteps moved up the front stairs. As the envelope shot under the door, I jerked it open.

"Let me go!" Raven shouted as I pulled her into Mary's bedroom. "What are you— Yale, what — Yale, make him let go!" I pushed her toward the sheriff, stooped and retrieved the envelope. The name MARY was pasted onto the outside, the letters cut from a magazine.

As soon as she saw what I'd done, Raven lunged for the envelope. I held it out of her grasp. "Give me that, that's personal! You have no right! Yale, that is my property, make him give it back."

Davis reached for the envelope. I hesitated, then handed it to him.

As I kept Raven from bolting, he tore it open.

Studied it.

Showed it to me.

The same cut-and-pasted-words technique as previously.

Pay me $50,000 or I will tell.

20

Davis waved the envelope in front of Mary's nose. He had personally gone to fetch her, ordering Raven and me to remain in the room.

"What's she blackmailing you about?" he demanded.

"Nothing." Mary's face burned bright red. "It's Raven's idea of a joke."

I noticed that Mary avoided eye contact with Raven. Davis noticed it, too. "How many of these notes have you received?" he asked.

When she didn't reply, I did. "Two others that I know of."

That earned me a dark look from the sheriff.

"What did they say?" he asked Mary.

Mary remained silent, so I supplied the information. "First one said, *You stole it*. Second one said, *You will pay*." I gave him the rundown on when I thought they'd been delivered.

Without giving me his full attention, he nodded. His eyes were on Mary. "What did you steal?"

"I did not steal anything," she declared. But her words lacked conviction.

"Yes, you did," smirked Raven.

"You stay out of this!" Davis barked. "You talk when I tell you to."

The sheriff went at Mary in a few different ways, but the result was always the same. Then he turned on me, demanding I tell him what Mary had stolen. I explained I had no idea. I don't know if my words rang true to Davis, because just as I was uttering them, the answer flashed through my brain.

"Don't give me that, Dragovic. You came bounding up those stairs, barged into the bedroom, and waited for this note to be delivered."

"That's right. I figured Raven was the blackmailer and that she would slip another note under Mary's door."

"How'd you figure that?" he demanded.

"We were down by the black walnut. Raven offered to have it hauled away, but Mary didn't fall for that, said it was worth $10,000. Guy and Vance and a few others said they'd buy the wood. After the thunderstorm there was a general bonding. People were talking up Mary's festival. Things were looking good. That made Raven jealous."

"I am not jealous!" Raven shouted.

"Shut up!" Davis ordered.

"I knew she couldn't have delivered a note last night: we were all in the barn. I figured she'd run upstairs and compose it, slip it under the door while Mary was still working in the barn."

The sheriff sighed. "How'd you know it was Raven?"

"Glue — I smelled it coming from her room yesterday, figured she used it to paste the words down on paper."

"I should have known!" Mary's anger showed.

Taking advantage of the anger, Davis again asked Mary what Raven was blackmailing her about. She replied it was nothing. "She's asking a lot of money for nothing," he retorted, removing the letter from its envelope. *"Pay me $50,000 or I will tell,"* he read.

"Fifty thousand dollars!" Mary gasped, sitting heavily on the bed. "Raven Hook, you are a conniving, money-grubbing, thief! I know you're stealing instruments from my festival, I just know it!"

"How dare you!" Raven jumped to her feet. "I've never

stolen an instrument in my life. And I've never stolen someone else's song, either, and called it my own!"

The silence was so total that muffled sounds drifted up from the dining hall: the plastic rattle of dishes, the metallic clang of silverware. Lafayette's high-pitched laugh. Somebody strumming a guitar. I even smelled pancakes cooking.

Mary hung her head.

"Exactly what are you saying?" the sheriff asked.

But Davis was stalling. We all knew "Jealous Man" was the song in question.

When Raven made the accusation specific, the sheriff asked whether she had any proof. Raven replied she did — that words to the song were traced into the nightstand in the south bedroom. "Honey Miller wrote that song, I know she did," Raven argued. "She sat there night after night, composing tunes. On this one, the pen pressed through the paper and indented the tabletop."

When Davis demanded the room key from Raven, she reluctantly forked it over. Ordering us to stay put, he walked down the front stairs. I heard a lock click. The three of us said nothing until he returned, carrying a small table with him.

"Looks right at home," he announced as he settled it between two wicker chairs. "Just the kind of table Mary writes on when she's composing."

"You bastard!" Raven was on her feet. "I'll tell what I saw, you can't stop me!"

"Yes I can," he answered, unlooping handcuffs from his belt. "Raven Hook, I'm placing you under arrest for attempted blackmail. Mary composed 'Jealous Man' and there is no evidence to the contrary." He slipped a cuff on one of her wrists, reaching for the other.

I stood there wishing I'd never come to Auralee. Mary had stolen a song and claimed it as her own. I had no idea if she stole it after Honey Miller died, or whether her stealing it was the cause of Honey's suicide. And Davis, who represented the law, compromised evidence and called the truth a lie. Him I was even more disappointed in: him I didn't trust. I could understand his hatred of blackmail and blackmailers, but he was ready to swear that the table belonged in Mary's room.

Mary sat in shock. Or relief.

"No!" Raven struggled. "Don't! If you arrest me, nobody will believe me!"

That was the point, all right. Davis was determined to protect Mary.

"Wait." Raven went rigid. "I know something you need."

One cuff still in his hand, Davis stopped. "What do you mean?"

"Shelby's murder. I know something."

A sharp intake of breath from Mary.

Davis thought about it quite a while. "Tell me what you know and I might go easy on you," he said at last.

Raven shook her head. "No. You promise you won't arrest me for blackmail and then I'll tell you."

They stood there a time, each trying to best the other. Davis clearly had the upper hand, even threatening to book Raven on both blackmail charges and withholding evidence of a crime. The most she got from him was that if he considered what she had to say important enough, he wouldn't charge her with blackmail — under the condition that she never breathe a word of her *false suspicions* about Mary and "Jealous Man" to anybody.

"Is that acceptable to you, Mary?" he asked. "Or do you want me to proceed on the blackmail charges?"

"No, that's good," Mary answered miserably.

"Okay, Raven, Let's hear it."

"Can you uncuff me first?"

He did. She rubbed her wrist. Sat in the wicker chair again. "Now, Yale, there's just one little problem."

Silence. Then, "What might that be, Miss Hook?"

"What I know, uh . . . well . . . that is, I did something that wasn't quite legal. In fact, you won't be happy with it, but I can explain. But I don't want you arresting me for what I did."

"That won't work. You tell me and I'll decide the severity of what you did."

They wrestled back and forth, but Davis was a heavyweight and Raven a featherweight: pesky but squashable.

She gave in. "I may have been the first person to see Shelby dead."

Davis asked for elucidation. She explained that around 1:00 A.M., she had knocked on Shelby's RV door and, getting no answ.er, walked in. Why? Because he was behind in his alimony payments and she wanted her money. Hadn't they discussed alimony when Shelby was resting in her farmhouse room? No, they hadn't because she wanted to let him rest in air conditioned comfort, hoping to get him in a better mood. Didn't Shelby's RV have air conditioning? Yes, but only Raven's room had seclusion. So why didn't she discuss alimony with her ex-husband when he woke up refreshed, asked the sheriff. Raven frowned and said that Shelby woke up in a foul mood.

Raven looked at Mary. "Shelby said he was going to leave your festival the next morning," she said vindictively, "go home to Virginia and leave the teaching to Edric."

Mary looked dumbfounded.

"Did he say why?" asked the sheriff.

Raven claimed he didn't say, just left her room without giving her satisfaction about the alimony, so she decided to confront him again that evening. Why so late, asked the sheriff. Raven said Shelby was a night owl. When she entered the trailer, Raven saw him lying there, blood-spattered and dead.

I found it interesting that Raven had the presence of mind to not scream.

She continued her narrative to Davis. On the bed alongside the body was a blood-covered hammer. Raven took the hammer, put it in the case that belonged to the red fiddle — because the case was sitting open on the dinette — and carried it away with her.

Hearing this, Davis exploded. She had removed evidence from the scene of a crime. Not just any evidence, but the murder weapon! He paced, he thundered, he threatened her with every charge he could think of. He accused her of murdering her ex-husband and hiding the murder weapon. No reason not to believe she did it, he roared.

"That's just what I thought you'd think," she wailed. "That's why I took it!"

After more of Davis's bellowing, Raven explained that when she saw the hammer, she panicked — because she'd been using a hammer on the corn crib door that very morning, and she was afraid that very hammer was the murder weapon, and that it had her prints on it.

"No," I spoke up. "The hammer you were using ended up in Mary's shed. It's on my tool belt right now." I removed the curved claw Craftsman hammer and showed it to the sheriff.

"But, it looks just like the one I found," Raven said.

"No," I said. "I'll bet it looks different."

Raven stared uncomprehending.

"Are you trying to say what I think you're trying to say?" demanded Davis.

I shrugged. "It's the logical conclusion. Has been all along."

"You mean?—" Raven stood, hand to her chest, "it was *your* hammer?" She backed away.

"Where is it?" demanded the sheriff.

"I hid it in the crawl space behind Mary's bed," she answered.

At which point Mary rushed her.

21

Davis locked Raven into the back of his car. He didn't want me sharing the back seat with her: I guess he thought we might cook up something or discuss the bloody hammer which, when retrieved from the crawl space, turned out to be mine.

Nola Grayson volunteered to accompany me to town. "He'll want consul, Yale, and it's best I represent Mary's interests anyway, so I'll bring him in."

But when we got to the parking lot, Nola informed me her car was low on gas and we should take mine. So I drove, Nola beside me.

Little sleep, no shower, no breakfast. I didn't think my hammer, the one my father had given me, would ever be returned now that it was a murder weapon. My client turned out to be a thief and the law was fine with that. The same law was taking me in for questioning. *Sullen* was too upbeat to describe the mood I was in as I followed the sheriff's car down the county road. The patch above my eye dangled into my lid: I ripped the patch off and threw it into the back seat.

Nola's chirpy attitude annoyed me even more. I ground my teeth in order to keep from snapping at her as she pointed out the Iroquois County sights, including the bridge over the creek. Creek hell — the surging muddy water had overflowed its banks and tangled an uprooted willow through the bridge structure. Traffic was reduced to one lane as a work crew studied the tree.

Puddles of water filled the road. I made sure to hit every one.

"Water's high, Frank, haven't seen it like that since the flood of '93. It's a shame about the black walnut, isn't it, but in a way it will help Mary's festival."

Nola pointed out the Possum Patch Bar, a two-story flat-roofed, aluminum-sided building with a cupola on top. I accelerated as I drove by.

"That's where the three of us got drunk the night Mary said if she killed anybody it would be Shelby Stubbs," Nola informed me. "From which statement it does not logically follow that if Shelby Stubbs was killed, Mary did it. Are you familiar with converse and obverse, Frank?"

Most of my brain was working on whether Raven had truly walked in and found Stubbs dead or whether she had bashed his brains in herself, then come up with a plausible story. She was wily enough. But a small part of my cerebellum was paying attention. That part wondered why Nola was feeding me this information. That part also sent a short sharp buzz to the center, telling me a carpenter interested in folk music probably wouldn't know about obverse and converse. "I'm more an oblong and acute kind of guy," I answered.

"That's clever," she said. "Pull over. I want to show you my house. We won't be late," she explained. "Yale will take Raven's statement first. This will take just a minute."

I pulled over on Main Street. Nola's house was a dark green three-story structure, probably built in the 1890s. She lived next to a drugstore and across the street from a bank, in the heart of town, "town" being all of four blocks long. Two blocks ahead, the sheriff's car pulled into a diagonal parking place.

"Nice," I managed to say. "Those old houses take a lot of upkeep."

"Yes, they do."

"Any storm damage from last night?" I asked.

"The red cedar in the back yard came crashing down.

Missed the house by two feet." She shuddered. "I used the berries in cooking, they give a nice spicy flavor to venison. All kinds of birds would flock around to eat the berries. I'll miss the tree." Nola glanced at me, then away.

I watched the sheriff lead Raven out of the car.

"Cody Thompson found out about the tree," she continued. "Gossip travels fast in a small town. He said his father was willing to section out the tree and pay to have it transported to a sawmill. Cody is always scouting out trees that might fall down, asking the owner's permission to cut them up for firewood. Before they fall down, mind you — he's like the tree ghoul of Iroquois County."

"They wouldn't burn red cedar," I argued.

"Of course not. They'd sell it for fence posts."

I asked Nola how the Thompsons felt about not getting the land that was now Mary's farm. She said they were still hoping to get it. I asked how they expected to do that and she said they figured Mary would get tired of farming. I wanted to ask her if Tansy knew that Mary had guaranteed the safety of Shelby Stubbs' fiddle and bow, and was out $30,000 if they were damaged or stolen. But I didn't see how a carpenter had any legitimate reason for asking the question.

"Of course," Nola said as if our brains were on the same wavelength, "if Shelby's fiddle and bow aren't recovered, Mary could end up losing the farm. Then again, Bliss might not insist on the money, she's such an innocent." She pursed her lips. "Mary doesn't seem worried about the fiddle any more. I wonder where it is."

About two blocks away.

I drove the short distance to the police station, parked, and the two of us entered. Trimmed in limestone, the jail of course sported a cupola.

The sheriff must have gotten right down to business with Raven: the two of them were out of sight. Deputy Toby Thompson waited for Nola and me.

For the next two hours I sat alongside Nola while Thompson asked me the same old questions in the same old way, most of them about my hammer. I could tell he was still irked by my statement that his wife was present when all the instruments were stolen. If Nola hadn't been there, Thompson would have tried to detain me for the duration of the festival. I wondered why the sheriff wasn't there. Didn't he want to question the person who owned the murder weapon?

About the time I was close to losing my temper, Thompson wrapped it up. I signed the statement he typed and offered Nola a ride back to Madness, but she said she wasn't through with Toby and could ride back with him, so I left on my own.

My hand was on the car door when I spotted a familiar figure up the street. Five-feet-four, rounded shoulders, slightly bowed legs. Fonnie Sheffler, and if I wasn't mistaken the gate she just closed behind her belonged to Nola's yard. I stepped back toward the jail and watched her walk my way. She looked upset, her brow furrowed.

Fonnie stopped in front of the pizza parlor, one of the few buildings in town without a cupola. After a moment, she entered. Last night's one-pound pork chop was ancient history: my stomach needed food. I followed her into the pizza parlor.

She sat at a table, wiping her eyes with a tissue.

"Hi, Fonnie."

She jumped a mile, then turned on me. "What are you doing here? Are you following me?!"

"I was at the sheriff's office. I was coming out the door and saw you walk in here. Is anything wrong?"

Her lips trembled. She seemed to steel herself to settle down. "The tree," she said through a sob in her throat.

I pulled out a chair and sat beside her. "Mushrooms and pepperoni okay with you?" I asked. "My treat."

"Just no anchovies."

I ordered the pizza and two colas. "The black walnut?" I asked.

A curt nod of the head. "And the one in Nola's yard."

"How did you know about that?"

She looked at me suspiciously. "Nola told me this morning."

Time spent leading up to a subject was wasted with Fonnie. "How well do you know Booker Hayes?" I asked.

She stared off toward the kitchen. "He gets privileges."

"What do you mean?"

"Playing on stage Monday night, that's not fair. Why should he get to play, he's not the main act."

Fonnie didn't impress me as the kind of person who valued fairness. The personal was all that mattered to her. A member of the staff played every evening, so what did she have against Booker?

She pointed a finger at me. "Why didn't Mary kick Booker out of the festival after he admitted to stealing the mountain dulcimer? You seem to be her friend, ask her that."

"Booker didn't admit to stealing the dulcimer," I said. "He said he received it in barter."

"Yeah, right. From Lafayette — why didn't he tell us that, huh? Then we'd know who's been stealing the instruments."

The pizza arrived. I pulled the bill to my side and dished slices to the two of us. "How do you know he got the dulcimer from Lafayette?" The pizza didn't live up to my Chicago deep-dish standards.

"I just know, that's all."

"Did Lafayette tell you he gave Booker the mountain dulcimer?"

She studied the pepperoni pieces on her slice, probably looking for a way to complain to the management that the distribution was unfair. "I was there, at the Texas festival. I saw Lafayette give the dulcimer to Booker."

"Uh-huh. How did you recognize it?"

"I—" She gave me a calculating look. "I didn't recognize it. Not until Cindy said it was her dulcimer. Then I remembered what I'd seen."

"So you're saying you think Lafayette is the thief. Do you have any proof of that?"

A long piece of mozzarella stretched from the pizza slice to Fonnie's mouth. She pulled the pizza away from herself, stretching the cheese further. "All I can say is, I'm keeping a close eye on my guitar."

I tried more questions, some oblique, others more direct, but Fonnie switched the subject to the sacred spirit of trees. A technique that was wearing thin. I stood and dropped a few bills on the counter. I was about to offer her a ride when a siren split the air.

Lights flashing, the deputy's cruiser sped down Main Street. Nola was in the passenger seat. I ran out the door, Fonnie right behind me.

22

The mess of Midwest Music Madness loomed large as I sped toward it: the fallen tree with two lumber mill trucks parked alongside; the crushed pole barn; power company trucks in the front yard; electrical crews working everywhere.

Siren screaming loud enough to curdle the day's milk supply, the deputy's car screeched to a stop, gravel flying. Thompson and Nola exited and ran toward the back of the barn. Fonnie and I jumped out of my car. I passed Nola on the run and followed the deputy.

A crowd gathered in a half-circle. Straw, loose and baled, was strewn about. Mary lay on the straw, Suzanne and Kim on either side of her, Sheriff Yale Davis kneeling with two fingers at her throat. Jeff Glover hovered near Suzanne. Best Bones West of the Mississippi was beginning to annoy me. Mary's eyes were closed, her body limp, one arm twisted. Her face was badly scratched, a crisscross pattern of blood seeping through. The crowd was hushed, as if keeping vigil.

"What happened?" I asked, kneeling next to Suzanne.

"We were eating lunch when we heard a loud scream, and then a thunk." She lowered her voice. "We ran out and Kim was running this way. We followed her and found Mary like this."

The sheriff looked at Kim, who nodded at everything Suzanne said. "Tell me again what happened, Ms. Oberfeld" he said quietly, watching Mary.

"I was in the barn," said Kim, "looking for a guitar case. I thought I might have left it here yesterday, when we moved indoors. Or maybe last night."

"A new case?" he asked sharply.

Kim nodded.

"Are you saying it was stolen?" he demanded.

"I — uh — no, I probably just misplaced it." Kim looked down at Mary.

Siren wailing, the ambulance arrived.

"She was pushed," announced Davis as he stood.

Mary opened one eye and stared at him. "Yale Davis, I was not pushed. I *slipped*, that's all."

The paramedics elbowed Suzanne, Kim, me, and even the sheriff aside as they knelt beside Mary. "What is your name?" asked the first one.

"My name is Mary Ployd and today is Thursday," she answered, giving him a steely look. "Hold up your fingers and I'll count them."

"Yes, Ma'am." He smiled, holding up three fingers.

"You can call me Mary or you can call me Ms, but do *not* call me Ma'am. Three."

"Yes Ma'am, I mean Mary. Now, can you tell me what happened," asked the second paramedic.

Mary lifted an elbow and winced. Gingerly, she pointed a finger. We all turned to stare at the wide-open hayloft door forty feet up. "I fell," she said. "Find Frank Dragovic."

"I'm here." I moved to the front, between the medics, so she could see me.

Mary lifted the elbow again, winced even harder, and pointed to the open door once more. "I want you to build a gate across that opening so nobody else falls out. Something that lets air in when we want the doors open."

One medic probed Mary for broken bones while the other strapped a neck brace on her.

An order to continue the carpentry seemed irrelevant in the face of all that had happened. I considered my options, among them announcing I wasn't here to do carpentry work. Finally I replied. "Okay. I'll start on it now."

Mary gave a short shake of her head and turned so white I thought she was going to pass out. "No," she breathed. "You came here. For music lessons. Take them." She spoke with effort. "Go to your. African drumming class. Build gate immediately afterwards." She rested a moment. "Everybody," she commanded, "go to your afternoon classes."

I liked the word *immediately*. I'll bet Mary had never measured or sawn lumber.

I wondered if she was trying to tell me something.

The medics slipped her onto the stretcher with such professional skill that she barely gasped from the pain. Lifting it, they moved toward the ambulance.

From the stretcher Mary held up a hand. "Listen. Everybody," she declared. "I'm not badly hurt. I'll be back. Meanwhile. Vance and Kim in charge."

"Sure, Mary," said Vance, pushing his way toward the front.

"We'll take care of everything," Kim assured her.

The sheriff listened to all of this with a hard look on his face.

I was scowling, too, though maybe for a different reason. Why was Mary putting Vance, who was high on the theft suspect list, in charge of the festival? Kim was on the list, too.

"Nola," whispered Mary, "come with me."

Nola walked alongside the stretcher as the paramedics proceeded. Mary let one arm fall. It hung off the edge in a dramatic fashion: Caesar's body borne out of the Forum.

Davis waited until the crew closed the doors and drove away, siren screaming, lights flashing. Then he strode into the barn. The crowd murmured, then began to drift.

"What happened?" I asked Suzanne.

She shrugged. "Pretty much what I said. We were eating lunch and heard the scream. We ran out and found Mary on the ground." She looked up at the hayloft door. She looked down and kicked the bales and sections of straw with the toe of her shoe. "The straw saved her life, didn't it?"

"Where'd all this straw come from?" I asked. "It wasn't here before."

"Morning classes were canceled — everybody was spending time putting their tents back in order, clearing the emergency supplies out of the barn, watching the lumber companies bid on the tree. A lot of people just went to sleep. So Mary asked Guy and Vance and a couple of others to scatter the straw here. She said the ground was too wet and muddy." Suzanne looked concerned.

"The ground is wet and muddy in lots of places," I said, looking around. "I don't see straw anywhere else."

Suzanne stepped back. "What do you mean?"

I studied the general sogginess. "I don't know," I said. "But Mary has a flair for drama."

"Frank!" She sounded outraged. "She wouldn't jump out the hayloft door just to gain attention! She could have been *killed!*"

We stood there, neither of us looking at the other.

"Where were you?" she asked after a while.

I told her. Suzanne wanted to know if I knew who took my hammer, but I wanted to concentrate on Mary's fall. I asked her what details she could recall as she and the others ran out of the dining hall. Who was at the vendor area? Who was still in the dining hall?

Eyes closed, she concentrated on remembering. Raven and Bliss were in the dining hall when Mary screamed. Lafayette and Vance weren't there for lunch at all. She thought Cindy wasn't in the dining hall, but couldn't swear to it. Fonnie wasn't there, she told me. That I knew.

"I saw Tansy walking toward the barn earlier, but I don't know if she came back." Suzanne sounded perplexed. "I don't remember seeing her after we heard the scream."

"What's Tansy doing here? She isn't cooking today."

"She wanted to talk to Mary," Suzanne replied, "but Mary was going around canceling the classes, organizing the cleaning of the barn, talking to the lumber mill and the electric company. Tansy said she'd stick around."

I walked around the straw, tried to determine the trajectory of Mary's fall. I started toward the barn itself.

"I'll come with you," Suzanne said.

I shook my head. "The sheriff's up there. He'll talk more readily if it's just him and me."

"Frank — don't let anything happen to Mary." She gave me a hug, then said she was going to practice singing before Booker's Old-Time Songs in Black and White.

I walked around to the west side of the barn and up the earthen ramp to the second floor. Bales of hay were stacked nearly to the ceiling for half the depth of the barn. Alongside the hay was the straw, similar from a distance, different up close. The sheriff was in silhouette, lit by the hayloft door.

Finely milled particles of hay seed and dust covered the century-old floor, imparting a slippery quality to it. I suppose if you weren't careful, you could slide right out the door and forty feet down to the ground. Uncle Rudy had told me stories of people falling out of hayloft doors to their deaths or to a crippled existence. He also told me stories of the lucky cases who landed on the hay below and survived without a scratch.

I stood beside Davis and looked down.

"What do you make of the straw down there?" he asked.

What it looked like was a rummage sale on straw: entire bales, sections of bales, and forked loose straw were all mixed up below. Lots and lots of straw. More straw than the normal person would scatter if asked to cover up a muddy area. "I'd say Vance and Guy enjoyed their work."

"Yeah," he replied, giving me a look. After a while, he spoke again. "I'd hate to think Mary staged this whole thing. I'd hate to think the two of you are trying to put something over on me."

I examined the floor, searching for scuff marks, footprints, signs of a struggle. The pine boards were worn through in layers. I worked a few splinters loose with the toe of my shoe. Looking for evidence of a scuffle here was like listening for one drum beat in a thousand.

"I'm an outsider," I said, "so I can see why you'd want it to be me." He glared at that, but I continued. "What I don't understand is why you want it to be Mary. Sure, she may have said she wanted to kill Stubbs, but that's not enough. Even proposing to you after he was dead isn't enough."

"It's suspicious."

I asked if there was something else, something he wasn't telling me. His response was to remind me to leave the murder investigation alone.

Right.

"You may not believe this, Dragovic, but I don't want it to be Mary."

Time to cut to the chase. "I agree with what you said out there. I think somebody pushed her."

"If that's true — who's she protecting?" demanded Davis. "And why, that's what I want to know."

We tossed it around. She fell. She jumped. She was pushed.

"Help me out here," he complained. The sheriff teetered on his toes, back and forth. A bit close to the edge. Maybe he intended to illustrate a point. "If she fell," he said, teetering forward, "then we have to accept it's just a coincidence." He teetered back onto his heels. "Hard to do."

I agreed with that one.

Footsteps sounded on the stairs leading up from the first

floor. We turned to see Guy approach, carrying both his dulcimer and hurdy-gurdy. Taking no chances.

"Just the man I wanted to see," said the sheriff, staring hard.

"What?!" demanded Guy, setting down his burden.

"Tell me about the straw down there."

"Mary asked Vance and me to scatter it. Frank was not here or she would have asked him, too. Lafayette tried to help but we sent him away, he almost fell out the door."

"Go on," urged Davis. "Did Mary tell you how she wanted it done?"

Guy shrugged. "She told me the straw and the pitchforks were up here. Lafayette was tired from all the pitchforking, so Vance and I told him to push bales out this door and then we would all go down and scatter them below. He almost went out with one of the bales: I pulled him back. Some of the bales broke open, others did not."

"Why did Mary want this spot covered with straw?"

"It is much frequented," answered Guy with a bored look. "Perhaps she did not want mud in the dining hall or the classrooms."

"How long did you work?" Davis asked.

"We quit at lunch time."

"Did everybody leave here together?"

"Lafayette was already gone," Guy replied. "Vance and I started to leave, but Edric came by to help, and Vance stayed with him. Oh, Cindy was here at the end. She said she would straighten up. Then the vendors came, one by one. I think business was slow after the rain." Looking at his hands, he held them out. "I have blisters already from the pitchfork. So does Vance."

"Why didn't you finish?" asked the sheriff.

"But we did finish!" Guy looked affronted. "We covered the ground. There is no mud. We did a good job." He looked to me for confirmation. I nodded.

"Why didn't you finish scattering the bales that are down there?" asked Davis.

"Oh. That. It would have been a waste," Guy explained. "Mary wouldn't want us to waste the straw." He stepped close to the floor's edge and looked down. "It was easier to get the bales down than it will be to bring them back up, *non?*"

Davis looked Guy up and down, maybe trying to fit him into Edric's shoes and my clothes. As the sheriff was contemplating, Vance Jurasek came walking up the earthen ramp.

"We're here to start working on the gate," Guy said to me. "You have an afternoon class, and Mary said you must take it."

"I thought you were busy running the festival," I commented to Vance.

He dismissed it. "The festival runs itself, except for the office. Kim's there now. The gate seemed important."

"There's wood in the storage shed," said Guy. "What kind of gate do you have in mind?" he asked me.

Davis stood there silently, listening.

I pointed in the direction of the pole barn. "I thought we'd save Mary some money by using timber from the pole barn."

"Good idea." Vance nodded in approval. "Mary loves saving money."

The sheriff snorted.

"*Bon!* We will rescue the wood from the pole barn. This is a magnificent festival," enthused Guy. "The black walnut, the pole barn, so much wood! Mary should have T-shirts made!"

I asked Guy if he wanted me to draw a sketch of the gate, but he assured me he could handle it. "My tool belt's in my car," I told them. "If you need it I'll give you my keys." I looked at my watch.

"I have my own tools," Guy reminded me, "and I still have Jeff's hammer. You'd better run."

Would any detective worth his salt run off to a drumming class instead of investigating?

I'd reserve judgment.

No pole barn to meet in, no black walnut to meet under. Kofi had claimed the high ground just upwind of the pigpen. From inside his pen, Richard watched.

I chose the same drum I'd had each day, recognizing it by a splotch of red paint on one of the ropes. Kofi proceeded with a review of the pattern we had been learning, then introduced the second half of the pattern: entirely new. We spent more time on that one, then he divided the class in half, left and right. Those on the left played the first pattern. Those of us on the right watched Kofi and came in with him on the second pattern, not imposing it on the first, but integrating the two patterns.

"Awesome!" Cody flailed away.

I noticed that Glover wasn't in class and I wondered why.

Somewhere around us things were happening. The pig rooted in its pen, Guy and Vance carried boards from the pole barn to the big barn, Aja Freeman was cooking fried chicken for dinner, the electric company trucks came and went, the lumber company trucks remained — but all of it was muted, in the background. What drove us was the drumming: keeping up the rhythm, holding onto the pattern, creating something complex and powerful and liberating.

Eventually Kofi gave the signal to stop. He smiled. "Now we will introduce new instruments. The bell. The shakere. Two stick drums."

We looked at the instruments as he picked them up. The bell was hand-forged iron. The shakere was a gourd covered with a web of plastic beads. A dual-purpose instrument, I surmised: you could thump it, or you could shake it. I found the tall, thin stick drums uninteresting.

The bell, it turned out, was more than a filler instrument: its rhythm was the clue for when others would come into the pattern. Kofi assigned the bell to Bliss while the rest of us took turns on the shakeres and stick drums. The two-part drumming that had seemed complex suddenly became simple in comparison to the combination of patterns created with the hand drums, bell, shakeres, and stick drums.

After a time we changed places, Kofi assigning the bell to me. It was a single bell: he had double bells, too, but I guess we weren't ready for them. I struck the iron with a soft wood dowel, enjoying the way the clear tones rode above the deep drum booms.

When Kofi said our time was up, we groaned, not wanting to stop.

"We can practice again tonight," he offered, "although we no longer have the pole barn. Perhaps we can meet upstairs in the big barn, after the dance." He looked at us critically. "Tomorrow night our class will perform on the open stage."

"What?" I said.

Cody laughed at me. "Don't worry, Frank, everybody gets nervous."

Back in the barn, a finished gate leaned against a wall. From below came the sounds of a dulcimer and fiddle and the lyrics to yet another pig song. When I started building a jamb for the door, Guy and Vance heard the hammering and came to help.

After that I headed toward the farmhouse to check things out. Just outside the corn crib Raven and Edric were having what looked like an argument. Raven saw me and turned her back my way.

At the appetizer class I came up behind Suzanne. "Who's pounding what today?" I asked.

"Wrong verb, wrong instrument, carpenter."

That gave me pause. She'd never called me carpenter before.

Booker was up front, tuning his guitar. Edric approached carrying a saw. I wondered what he had used it for. Cindy arrived carrying a pitchfork. "Was Cindy spreading straw this morning?" I asked, keeping my voice low.

Suzanne shook her head back and forth.

Cody came running up. "This is going to be good, Frank. Awesome!"

"Right, Cody." I hadn't a clue.

Edric took a chair next to Booker and called class to order. Suzanne sat next to Bliss, but I remained standing, knowing I had other things to do. When Edric introduced the saw as a musical instrument, I gave Suzanne a wry grin, understanding her humor.

Holding the saw between his legs, the blunt tip down, the handle up, the teeth pointing where they could do the most damage, Edric twanged out "In the Pines" with a rubber mallet. The moans of maimed ghosts filled the air. Next he abandoned the mallet and used a bow to play — I was using the verb loosely — "The Girl I Left Behind Me." Bliss accompanied him on that one, playing an ocarina. I recognized the instrument from my grade school days, where the music teacher had called it a sweet potato. Bliss and Edric had bloomed after Stubbs' death, dragging out instruments that would have Shelby stomping in his grave to the tune of "No sir!"

I was about to leave when Edric relinquished the spotlight to Cindy, who still held the pitchfork. Cody squirmed in his seat. Tansy came up behind me. "I'm hoping he'll turn to pitchfork playing rather than pitchfork throwing," she whispered.

"Is it good?" I asked skeptically.

Tansy shrugged.

Flanked by Edric, who now had a guitar, and Booker, who had switched to banjo, Cindy stepped back, behind the melody players. She planted the handle of the pitchfork on the ground and stood there like half of *American Gothic.* In her right hand she held a thin iron rod. The band lit into "Momma Don't Allow," with Cindy beating the tines of the pitchfork as if the whole season's crop depended on her. I caught Suzanne looking at my feet and realized I was tapping them.

The music was infectious.

"Isn't this a day off for you?" I asked Tansy.

"I came in to see Mary." She kept her eyes on Cody.

"Thinking of taking music classes yourself?"

"No, no. I heard there was a hammered dulcimer case somebody found and I was wondering if it was the one I lost two years ago."

I stepped away from the music, motioning Tansy with me. "I found the case," I said. "What did yours look like?"

"Green," she replied, "to fit a fifteen-fourteen."

"What's a fifteen-fourteen?"

She smiled, not at me, but at Cindy's pitchfork playing and Cody's hanging on every note. "The numbers refer to how many sets of strings there are. Guy has a sixteen-fifteen, which is bigger. Is the case you found green?"

"Yeah, it is. When did you say you lost it?"

"Two years ago, at the first Madness festival."

"How can you lose a case and not the instrument?" I asked.

She turned red and stammered. "I . . . well . . . ."

I waited, listening to the clanging of the pitchfork.

Tansy crooked a finger and motioned me further away from the music. "I thought it was stolen," she whispered. "That's why I never said anything, because that was when Cindy's mountain dulcimer was stolen and that was bad enough. I didn't want poor Mary to have any more problems."

"I didn't know you played the hammered dulcimer."

"Oh, yes," she nodded, "I love the sound. It was a Thursday night and there was a big jam going on and I wasn't cooking that day, so I brought my dulcimer in its case and left it in the barn, along with the other instruments. After the dance dozens of us sat around and jammed. It was wonderful. Then when it came time to go home, I couldn't find my case. I looked all around. I thought, you see, that somebody might have taken it by mistake, thinking it was their case."

I nodded, studying her face for any signs of lying.

"So I went home that night without my case. I thought the next day I'd ask around, see if anybody had taken it by accident, or see if maybe it just showed up back in the barn." She frowned. "But it didn't, and then Cindy's lap dulcimer was stolen and Mary was almost as upset as Cindy, so I didn't say anything." She looked me in the eyes. "Now, though, I don't know what to think."

"What do you mean?"

"Well, I thought the thief had taken my case. But if you found it down by the tree, maybe it was here on Mary's farm all along, accidentally put some place, and it took a major storm and big wind to bring my case out of hiding. You know what they say — it's an ill wind that blows nobody good." She waited for an answer.

"Could be," I said, remembering that I had dismissed Tansy to Suzanne, saying she didn't have time to steal instruments. "You don't have to see Mary personally to claim your case," I said. "You could tell Nola. Or Kim, who's in the office now." Either of them would soon enlighten Cindy, explaining that her case had housed the stolen instruments.

She looked over her shoulder, toward the office. "That's okay, I don't mind waiting for Mary. I hope she's okay. She could have been *killed*. You'd think Mary would know better than to fall out of a hayloft door, don't you?"

"Did you see it happen?"

"No, I was out back, checking to see what Aja was cooking."

Tansy moved back toward the music. I watched a while, wishing I could play a pitchfork, then headed toward the office.

Mary's guitar was still on the stoop, and I still didn't understand why she wanted it stolen. When I lifted the case my hand shot up past my chest, the way it does when you lift a milk carton that you think is full, only to discover it's empty.

I unzipped the case.

Sure enough.

Empty.

The sheriff's car pulled into the parking lot. I zipped the case closed and leaned it up against the siding.

I entered the office.

"Nola," I said.

She jumped a mile, dropping the large envelope she had been holding. She closed her center desk drawer swiftly. "You startled me," she said, patting her chest for emphasis. Lowering herself into the chair, she rolled it forward, placed her elbows on the desk, propped her chin on her hands, and blinked at me. "What did you want?"

What I wanted to know was what was in the envelope she had dropped into her desk drawer. "How's Mary?" I asked.

"Good," she said, looking relieved. "No fractures. They're going to release her tomorrow morning."

"Did she take her guitar with her?"

"No, I don't think she can play. Her right arm is badly sprained: wrist, elbow, and shoulder."

"Then where is it?" I asked.

She looked perplexed. "Where is what?"

"Her guitar. Where is it?"

Nola stood with a frown. "Isn't it on the stoop? I thought I saw it."

"The case is on the stoop. There's no guitar in the case."

"You're saying the guitar is stolen?" asked Nola, her voice quavering.

"I'm saying it's not in its case, Nola."

"Oh," she replied. "Oh." And then she held her head in her hands.

23

After a minute or so Nola recovered her composure.

She stood. "Come with me," she commanded, removing the large envelope from her desk drawer. In Mary's absence, Nola seemed to assume Mary's attitudes and demeanor.

I shrugged and followed.

We entered Mary's office and Nola locked the door behind us. Seating herself at Mary's desk, she motioned me to sit facing her. I did. The green dulcimer case caught my eye. I wondered why Tansy didn't simply come in and claim it.

"This is an envelope," pronounced Nola, annoyed that my eyes had wandered. She held the heavy manila envelope in her fingertips, tipping it toward me so I could read the writing. *Testimony of Mary Ployd.*

Confident that she had my attention, Nola turned the envelope over, still holding it with her fingertips. It was sealed, and across the seal were two signatures — hers and Mary's, and the date.

"The contents of the envelope are confidential. In the hospital this afternoon Mary asked for stationery. I provided it. She then asked for privacy while she wrote something of 'great importance,' to use her own words. It took her a long time."

I guess it would, since her shoulder and arm and hand were injured.

Nola continued. "When Mary finished, she called me back

into the room and asked for an envelope, which I also provided. She then inserted the document she had written and sealed the envelope. The two of us signed it, as you can see."

Certain that I had grasped the essentials, Nola put the envelope in her briefcase, which she zipped shut. "As I am Mary's attorney, she entrusted the envelope to me, though I stress that I do not know the contents. Nevertheless" — she paused to study me a while — "nevertheless, an educated person can make a good guess as to its contents."

"And your guess is?" I asked.

Nola smiled. "No. You are the educated person I'm referring to. What is your guess as to the content and importance of this envelope?"

"Why are you asking me?"

She frowned. "I had hoped you would confide in me, Frank. You're a private detective operating out of Chicago. You're down here working for Mary."

"Did she tell you this?"

A superior smile. "No. I figured it out myself. Then I checked the Chicago yellow pages and found you listed under Private Investigators."

I nodded, acknowledging her work.

"So," she summarized. "What conclusions do you draw?"

Evasion crossed my mind, but I dismissed it. "I think Mary didn't fall, I think she was pushed. I think her testimony gives the name of the person who pushed her."

"Yes. I think so too. Although it's a pretty thick document."

I had noticed the same thing. "Motive," I said. "I think Mary knows why she was pushed."

Nola nodded. "Either the thief pushed her, or the person who murdered Shelby Stubbs pushed her."

"You're thinking the thief and the murderer are two different people," I countered.

"Why, yes," she replied. "Aren't you?"

I nodded.

Nola's thoughtful look turned perplexed. "I don't understand why she wouldn't just go to Yale and tell him who pushed her and why."

"She doesn't want him to know why she was pushed."

Nola cleared her throat. "Mary explained to me about 'Jealous Man.' I can understand how she wouldn't want anybody to know what she had done." She studied me. "Do you think she's done something, uh . . . worse?"

I didn't speculate. "She might want to protect the person who pushed her," I suggested.

"Horsefeathers!"

"We're throwing out possibilities here, Nola — it pays to keep an open mind."

Her look told me she disagreed. We sat there speculating until we heard the dinner bell. "What about the stolen guitar?" I reminded her.

"The stolen guitar! I'd forgotten all about it!"

"Leave the case where it is," I said, "and don't say anything about the guitar until we've told Mary. It's her festival. Besides," I said, "I think she wanted somebody to steal the guitar."

Nola looked shocked. Even when I explained that Mary had been deliberately tempting fate, she refused to believe it. It flitted through my brain that the terrible trio — Davis, Nola, and Mary — were playing some sort of grand scheme, each covering for the other. I quickly dismissed it as the raving of a hungry mind.

When we exited Mary's office, Cindy Ruffo was waiting at Nola's desk, so I stepped outdoors alone. Suzanne was waiting there, and from the agitated way she grabbed the sleeve of my T-shirt and dragged me off the stoop, she was either starving or had something to tell me.

"Come with me, there's something you should hear. Hurry, before he quits," she whispered.

She led me to the barn and pressed a finger to her lips as we slipped inside. Vance paced the floor, fiddling as he listened to two small speakers wired to his minidisc recorder. Suzanne selected a bale of straw near him. We sat and listened.

What was I supposed to be listening to, the tune he was playing? Something about the fiddle? Vance played, stopped, punched a button on the recorder, listened, started again. Suzanne tapped her foot impatiently. It was when she poked me in the ribs that I understood — listen to the recording, not the playing.

"This is 'Quince Dillon's High D,'" said the voice of Shelby Stubbs. "Those of you who can't play up to speed, just listen."

"Right after he plays the A part, listen," whispered Suzanne.

I didn't know the A part from the B part, but I tried to get up to speed.

On the recorder, Stubbs stopped playing abruptly. "Goddamn it, Lafayette, stop scratchin' that miserable fiddle of yours! Didn't I say if you can't play up to speed, just listen?"

Lafayette said something I couldn't make out. Vance punched another button and started playing all over again. "I'm having trouble with the A part," he grimaced.

"I love that tune," Suzanne said. "Would you play it on the recorder all the way through?"

Vance complied by punching a button. Stubbs spoke again as Vance sat on a bale. We listened to the A part and the exchange again, then Stubbs began to fiddle again. Somewhere in the middle of what I surmised was the B part, Stubbs stopped again. "Lafayette," he intoned, "I cannot have you castrating a cat while I'm teaching a tune here, no sir! I want you —"

I couldn't hear the rest of Stubbs' comment because objects clattered on the tape. Chairs overturning? Then I heard Lafayette's quavering voice quite distinctly: "One of these days you'll get yours, Shelby!" he threatened. "Somebody will pound you into the ground, just like you deserve!"

More clattering noises, then Stubbs' voice. "Okay, we're rid of that nuisance. Let's take it from the top again."

"Quite a confrontation," I said, studying Vance.

"Who?" he asked, trying to carry off nonchalance. "Shelby and Lafayette?"

"Uh-huh. When did this take place?"

"Oh, just a few months ago. March."

"At a festival?"

"Yes, the Texas Music Festival."

I thought about it. "Did Lafayette ever come back to the class?"

Vance shook his head. "No. I think he took another class instead. Tell the truth, I think that's when he bought the bowed psaltry."

I rubbed the four-day growth on my chin. Game face. "You were in Stubbs' class down in Texas."

Vance gave me a *Duh* look.

"But he didn't seem to recognize you Monday morning on the porch — he asked you what you played."

Gripping his fiddle by the neck, Vance tried to contain his anger. "That's the kind of person Stubbs was. You could take a class from him and four or five months later he'd never recognize you. Not only that, he'd insult you."

I remembered the Monday morning porch incident, where Stubbs said in front of everybody that either Vance or his mandolin had been playing out of tune.

When the dinner bell rang out a second time, Vance packed up his fiddle and recorder and its little speakers. We followed him to dinner, but he made a point of not sitting with us.

"Makes you wonder about Lafayette, doesn't it?" asked Suzanne.

"Makes me wonder about Vance," I said. "He was using speakers instead of his headphones. He wanted somebody to hear."

Dinner was a strangely happy affair. You'd think that with a murder, stolen instruments, a thunderstorm that threatened our lives, and an organizer who fell out of her own barn and miraculously escaped death or maiming —you'd think that with all that, people would be glum.

Exactly opposite. Kim and Edric chatted away. Raven joined them, sitting next to Edric, and the trio found something to laugh about. Over at another table Guy and Vance regaled all with stories of their straw scattering and the building of the gate. Everybody talked of how wonderful the old-time music ensemble class was. Cindy had forgiven Bliss for having the misfortune to buy a stolen instrument and seemed to take her under wing, teaching her the ins and outs of living in a world full of deceit. I half-expected them to form a group, the Lost But Found Dulcimer Duo. Cody was entertaining everybody by playing the tines of his dinner fork.

Glover, still wearing his cowboy hat, looked happy. He informed us he had sold seven knives, three fiddles, two mandolins, and all of his Best Bones West of the Mississippi.

Booker was obviously happy. Who wouldn't be, with a lucrative movie soundtrack contract. If Booker stole Stubbs' fiddle, he might be happy thinking he'd gotten away with it. He dug into dinner — Aja Freeman's fried chicken, with sauteed okra, mashed potatoes, and homemade biscuits. Aja had my vote for best cook.

I was just digging into the sweet potato pie and coffee when Mary walked in the door.

The room went silent, then exploded in shouts of joy. Even Booker left his dessert to join the mob gently embracing Mary, welcoming her home. I watched, taking in who was where and what expressions their faces were wearing, what their body language was. Eventually the crowd parted so Mary could make her way to the microphone.

I had to hand it to her: she knew how to make a dramatic exit and she knew how to make a dramatic entrance. Maybe she coached the nurses on how to bandage her, maybe not, but limping up to the front of the room she reminded me of the fife player in *Spirit of '76*.

Coming in behind her, Yale Davis propped himself against the door jamb. His eyes searched for Nola, found her, stayed there.

"Friends!" called Mary, her voice radiating happiness, her one good arm raised in the air, the other confined to her side in a sling. "I have returned!" A roar of genuine approval filled the dining hall. Over by the door, Davis grimaced.

"No broken bones, no concussion!" Another roar.

"That's because I take my daily calcium supplements!" Laughter.

"And live for music!" The crowd rose to its feet, applauding.

Mary continued in that vein, promising that Midwest Music Madness would continue, that even though she couldn't play the guitar for a week, she could teach her history of folk music class, with Cindy leading tunes on the mountain dulcimer. She then announced she skipped her hospital dinner in order to taste some of Aja's cooking so that when it came time to vote for best cook, Mary's vote would be a fair one. More applause.

I watched as Mary took a seat at one of the front benches. Aja herself, smiling happily, brought her a plate of chicken, okra, and potatoes, and Cindy followed with bread and a glass of milk. After that I couldn't see Mary because one by one and in small groups most everybody at the festival stopped by the table to give her another hug, a pat, a handshake.

I had to face it: Mary Ployd was wildly popular. And Midwest Music Madness, instead of suffering from the thefts and the murder of Shelby Stubbs, had rebounded with a vengeance. Surviving the great storm had wiped out the fact of Stubbs' death and the previous years' thefts. Mary's fall and miraculous survival and her indomitable spirit inspired everybody. I wouldn't be surprised if next year's Madness attendance doubled.

Except that an unsolved murder eats away at those involved, corroding relationships, eroding trust.

In addition to which, Mary's life was in danger.

After the supper dishes were cleared and the tables and benches wiped down, people dispersed. When Nola left, the sheriff followed her. Only Mary and I remained in the dining hall.

Her back was to me. I watched as she sighed heavily, then held the mug of coffee to her forehead. Sensing she wasn't alone, she looked over her shoulder. Or tried to: she winced, stopped, and then turned her body fully in the seat.

"It's you," she said after a moment.

"It's me," I agreed.

"Come here," she said, patting the bench.

I sat down across from her rather than beside her.

"Did you build the gate like I asked you to?"

I told her the gate was built, the role Guy and Vance played in it, the recycling of the wood from the pole barn.

"Good. You can show it to me after I finish my pie. You don't think there's another piece somewhere, do you? I never did get lunch."

She might have been hungry, but she was also trying to misdirect me. I entered the kitchen, where Aja gladly cut a second piece of sweet potato pie for Mary. I placed it before Mary, brought her more coffee, and once again took my seat across from her.

Before I could say anything, she held up a hand. "Please don't ask me why I took 'Jealous Man' as my own. I know I shouldn't have."

"When did you take it, Mary?"

"*After,* Frank. After Honey committed suicide. I'm the one who cleaned out her room and tried to find somebody she was related to. Nola tried, too. There was nobody."

I didn't say anything.

"I want you to know — not that it makes much difference

— that I made changes to what she'd written. Improvements." Her skin was pale. The fork trembled in her hand. "It was wrong, I know. I have a some big decisions to make," she mumbled. "I don't know whether to confess publicly, or hope nobody believes Raven. You know she'll say something sooner or later."

I understood the dilemma, but that was Mary's problem, not mine. "Who pushed you?" I asked.

Her lips twitched. Maybe a smile, maybe a tic, maybe she was expecting the question. "Nobody pushed me, Frank. I fell, which is why I had you build the gate."

I nodded. "The gate's a good idea. Should have been built years earlier. Who pushed you?"

Her eyebrows formed a straight angry line across her brow. "Nobody pushed me. I fell." The arm that wasn't in a sling flashed across the table crosswise: The Subject Is Closed.

"I think you know something about Stubbs' murder, Mary."

She concentrated on the pie and coffee.

"Don't you want the murder solved?" I argued. "So that Lafayette isn't a suspect? So that Edric isn't?"

Silence.

"Apparently you don't mind being a suspect," I said. "Or having your guitar stolen."

"This is outstanding pie. As was the chicken dinner. I just don't know who to vote for tomorrow morning, do you?"

"It was, you know."

"What?" asked Mary.

"Stolen."

I don't know how I expected her to react, and I can't say the way she did came as a complete surprise. Still, it was unusual. She dropped the fork, sloshing coffee everywhere as she lifted the mug and slammed it on the table victoriously. Her eyes were bright, her face radiant. "My guitar has been stolen? Has it?! Has it really?!"

"It has," I said, annoyed.

Struggling out of the bench, Mary used her good arm to support herself. "This is wonderful, Frank," she whispered. "Wonderful! Now we'll know who the thief is! I can't wait to get my hands on her! I'll turn her over to Yale. I'll blacken her name throughout the world of folk music! She'll never attend another festival if I have anything to say about it, the dirty rotten little thief!" She scooped up her sweet potato pie and thrust it into the quilted purse she carried over her shoulder, hurried out the door, turning to make certain I followed, motioning for me to catch up to her.

"Keep this quiet," she warned. "Just you and me and Richard. It won't take long."

Richard?

We headed toward the pigpen, a sign that I hadn't heard wrong.

At the sound of our approach Richard trotted over to the gate, which Mary unlatched. "How's my pet?" she crooned, kissing the top of the pig's head. "How's my baby?"

The pig snorted that it was fine. Mary pulled out the pie and dropped it on the ground. The pig scarfed it down and looked up with one of its snaggle-toothed smiles. She scratched the top of its head. "Time to go to work, Richard," she said. "Work," she enunciated, looking into the pig's beady eyes. Reaching into her quilted sack, she pulled out a plastic bag, opened it, and unfolded a small square of cloth. She placed it in front of the pig's snout. Richard inhaled once and took off at a swift trot.

"Musk," Mary explained, hobbling after the pig. "I've been training Richard to hunt down musk all winter. I impregnated things with musk and hid them on the farm, then rewarded Richard whenever he found them. This is no reflection on you, Frank. You'll still get paid. I just wanted to catch Raven myself."

So that's how she saw me: a third-string catcher.

Before I could do anything about it, Richard stormed

straight into the tent area and through Vance's tent like a freight through match sticks.

"Oh god," groaned Mary. "Not Vance!"

"This is stupid," I grumbled as Richard rooted around in Vance's sleeping bag, leaving muddied, cloven prints everywhere. "If your guitar had been here, the pig would have smashed it to pieces. Call the pig off," I ordered.

Mary called and Richard came to her side.

"There's no stolen guitar here," I indicated. In the middle of the tent's bedroom stood a large wooden box with a chain wrapped around it and two heavy-duty padlocks on it. Jurasek was taking no chances with his instruments.

Mary looked around. "No. But . . . ?"

The scent of musk filled the tent. I picked up pieces of a bottle broken under the pig's weight and held the shard up to Mary. "Musk-scented aftershave lotion." I watched Richard, who ignored the wooden storage box. Before I could say another word, the pig grunted, jumped, and took off again.

"Wait!" I shouted, but Mary was already following her porcine detective.

At the farmhouse stoop the pig jabbed her guitar case with its snout and looked at Mary for approval.

Which didn't come.

Mary looked poleaxed. "But . . . but . . . I don't . . . you said . . . ."

"I said your guitar was stolen, Mary. Not the case."

"But it was the case I scented with musk oil!" she wailed. And then she collapsed on the stoop. "My guitar. My new Tippin! Somebody stole my guitar!"

The pig needed approval. I patted it on the head, then sat down beside Mary.

"It's worth six thousand dollars, Frank! It was made special for me! I'll never find another one like it! How will I sing? My career is gone! I'll never cut another album!" Her tears were copious. "I know it's Raven!" she said suddenly, struggling to rise. "I'm tearing down her door and getting my guitar. I'll skin her alive."

I pushed on her good shoulder, forcing her back down. "Raven didn't steal your guitar."

"What?"

"I said, Raven didn't steal your guitar."

Mary wiped a sleeve across her nose. "I'm ruined. The festival is destroyed."

The pig plopped down beside her.

"No," I said. "I have it under control."

She looked up at me. "You do?" she sniffed, wiping her nose.

"I do," I replied.

Mary looked at me with adoration. Pretty much the same way she had looked at the pig. Even when I wouldn't divulge the name of the thief, she accepted it, patting my hand and telling me I was a good man, a true professional. And a great carpenter, she added. Probably she wanted me to repair something else tonight.

"Will you explain to Vance that Richard got loose and destroyed his tent?" she asked as we walked toward the barn.

"Your pig," I countered, "your job."

She groaned, slowed her step, limped more pronouncedly, and crooned softly as she cradled her injured arm more closely to her body.

"That won't work, Mary."

"Then I'll have Nola tell him," she said.

Mary went off to find Nola and I headed for the showers.

24 Friday

"Guitar . . . stolen . . . Frank . . . guitar stolen."

Bad dream. I rolled over and covered my ears with my arms.

I jolted awake. Mary was in my tent, shaking my shoulder.

"Stop wasting *time,* Frank." She shook me again. "Booker's guitar has been stolen and I'm afraid he'll go berserk. I thought you said this was *under control!"*

If she looked at Richard the way she was looking at me, he'd be breakfast bacon.

I wore nothing but a pair of boxers with corncobs printed all over them. A gift from Suzanne. "Let me pull on some clothes." I mumbled. "I'll be right with you."

Mary backed out of the tent.

Suzanne sat up in her sleeping bag. "You didn't tell me you had the case solved."

"You were asleep," I evaded, scrambling out the tent. Mary was already halfway back to the farmhouse, striding that severe stride of hers. I overtook her at the stoop, noticing her guitar case was no longer there.

"Oh! Nola!" Mary exclaimed, startled. "What are you doing here so early?"

"Last day. Lots of work. What's wrong with Booker? He's in your office hitting the desk."

Mary flapped a hand at Nola. "Later," she promised,

motioning me into the office and closed the door firmly.

Booker looked wild and desperate. "Did you take my guitar, man?"

"No," I said. "Keep your voice down."

"Hell no! My guitar has been stolen, man! Stolen!"

"Booker, please sit down." Mary pulled out a chair. "Frank is here to help."

"Is he gonna get my guitar back? 'Cause if he's not, forget it, man, I'm searching everybody. Everybody. Nobody's getting out without my knowing they don't have my guitar." He paced the office, emphasizing each point by thrusting his neck forward.

"By now," I said, glancing at my watch, "your guitar's not on the premises, so any search for it is a waste of time."

Stunned, Booker fell into the chair. "What do you mean?" he asked at last. "You mean the thief's like a cattle rustler, swoops in, grabs a guitar, and disappears?"

"Not exactly," I said, leaning against the windowsill, "but if you'll tell me how your guitar was stolen, I can get it back."

I'd better be right.

Mary, who had been looking at me without much enthusiasm this morning, brightened at this. "If you get our guitars back today, Frank, I'll double your wages!"

"Guitars?" screeched Booker. "What's this *guitars* business, Mary?"

Reluctantly, Mary explained that her guitar had been stolen yesterday while she was in the hospital. She and Booker began to argue over whether or not she should have announced this information, Mary saying it would have harmed the festival, Booker saying it might have saved his guitar. I held up a hand to stop them. They ignored me. I kicked the side of the desk. Hard. They looked at me.

"When and how was your guitar stolen?" I asked again.

"Who are you, man? You a cop? Why should I tell you?"

Mary explained who I was.

"You're a sorry excuse for a private eye," Booker informed me. "Two guitars are gone."

I rubbed my face, ignored the insult, and asked the question again. He said he'd left his room around 5:00 A.M. to shower, closing his door behind him. His guitar was in its case, standing upright in the closet. The upstairs bathroom was occupied, so he proceeded to the outside men's showers.

"You're sure the guitar was in the closet when you left?"

"Sure I'm sure, man. I was playing it last night before goin' to sleep. I put it away. Nobody came in and took it in the middle of the night. I'd have heard."

I nodded. "How long were you in the shower?" I asked.

"Half an hour."

Mary frowned, probably at what she perceived as a waste of hot water.

"And then?"

"Then I strolled on back here, got a cup of coffee, walked up the stairs, walked into my room, opened my closet door, and my guitar was gone." He glowered at Mary, who looked down guiltily.

As I questioned him, I considered what had happened. It could be that we had a second thief: somebody who just went into action this morning. Raven had easy access to Booker's room. Possible, but I was betting we had only one thief. First she stole the hurdy-gurdy, then she stole Mary's guitar. Now, either because the hurdy-gurdy had been retrieved or because she was feeling greedy — but most likely because she saw an opportune moment — she stole another instrument.

"Don't forget Vance," offered Mary.

"What about him?" I asked.

"He slept on the sofa bed in the room off the office."

"That's right," Booker recollected. "He was there when I came down the stairs, but he was long gone by the time I returned." He frowned. "He kept asking questions about my guitar a few days ago, remember? Wanted to see it, hold it, strum it a little. Wanted to buy it, but I wouldn't sell." Suspicion settled on Booker's face as he remembered the exchange.

"Why was Vance sleeping here?" I asked Mary. "His tent was livable."

"He said the sleeping bag and everything else smelled like pig manure." She looked offended. "I gave him sheets and a blanket and let him sleep here."

"Was there a light on in any of the other rooms this morning?" I asked Booker. "Could you tell who was in the bathroom when you wanted to use it?"

He shook his head. "I think it was Raven, but I can't swear to it. There was light under her door."

"Who all did you see on your way to the shower?"

Booker closed his eyes and thought. "Like I said, Vance was here. Fonnie was sitting on top of her trailer. She looked like some sort of Buddha, starring east. Lafayette was standing outside his tent, looking all around like a mole that's come out by mistake. He had his psaltry with him." His eyes opened. "Cindy was leaving the women's showers, carrying her dulcimer." He looked at me. "If it's Lafayette, I'm going to wring his scrawny neck, and *then* I'm going to turn him over to the sheriff — and that's only if he hasn't put the hurt on my guitar."

"Cindy's dulcimer was in its case?" I asked.

He considered it. "Yeah. A quilted nylon case."

"Go on."

"Guy was in the shower, just finishing. He left a few minutes later." Booker closed his eyes and thought a while. "That's it. Nobody else."

"Booker came running up the stairs," Mary explained, "and knocked on my door. Thank you, Booker, for coming to me first. Not shouting it to the world like Guy Dufour did with his hurdy-gurdy. We came down to the office and I ran out to get you, Frank."

"Don't thank me," Booker said, his voice hard. "I might have to shout it to the world yet."

His eyes bore into mine. "That guitar is worth a lot of money, maybe four thousand dollars, but to me it's worth more than that, it was my daddy's and his daddy's before him. Leadbelly borrowed it more than once and Big Bill Broonzy played on it. Precious hands have held that guitar. You better not be wasting my time sitting here asking me questions."

Mary pleaded with Booker to play it my way.

When I promised Mary and Booker they'd have their guitars back tonight, after the concert, they looked at me with hope and doubt mingled across their faces.

"What am I going to do about a guitar?" Booker asked Mary. "That's the only one I brought."

I glanced at my watch. "Kim should be at her stand now. I bet she'll loan you one."

Mary nodded. "Kim's a good vendor, I'm sure she will."

When Booker and I walked out of the office, Lafayette jumped back as if he'd been standing by the door. I grabbed him and dragged him and his psaltry into Mary's office, Booker following.

"What are you doing here?" I demanded.

"Hi, Frank. I'm here to see Mary."

"What about?"

Thrusting back his shoulders, Lafayette tried for dignity. "You know, Frank. I've composed a tune in her honor."

"Forget that!" growled Booker. "Did you take my guitar?"

Lafayette blinked. "I don't have your guitar, Booker."

"That isn't what I asked. I said, did you *take* my guitar — this morning, from my bedroom?"

Shaking his head vehemently, Lafayette denied stealing Booker's guitar. I knew he hadn't, but Booker needed convincing. "Lafayette," I said, "Booker doesn't understand why you didn't admit you traded him the mountain dulcimer for fixing your car.

Down in Texas last year."

Lafayette readily admitted that he had traded a Blue Lion mountain dulcimer for getting his car repaired. Booker then demanded to know why Lafayette had sat there at lunch while he, Booker, was made to look like a thief. Lafayette claimed he remembered no such thing, that a *tyoon* was calling him and he was listening to it. When the accusations settled, Lafayette told us he got the mountain dulcimer from somebody he had never seen before and couldn't remember. Why? Because the man needed money to get home and was selling his dulcimer cheap. Lafayette bought it, figuring he could sell it for more money later on.

Mary was angry. "You should know better than that," she lectured. "A good instrument sold cheap by somebody who 'needs the cash to get home' is most likely a *stolen* instrument!"

"Get out of my way," snarled Booker, pushing Lafayette aside and striding out the door.

I followed Booker to the vendor walkway. Early morning, but all the merchants were at their tables doing last-day business. Vance stood talking to Jeff Glover, Guy was at Kim Oberfeld's table.

"Kim," asked Booker without preamble, "I wonder if you could loan me one of your guitars for today's class."

"Sure, Booker. What's wrong with yours?"

"I've got a problem with it."

Kim blinked. "Well, you see what I have, take whichever you want. The Martin HD-28 has a great sound."

Booker unerringly knew which model she meant, selected the guitar, touched the wood, attached a strap that Kim held out to him, plucked, started to tune.

"Ah," said Guy, who had been watching, "I have a problem with my hurdy-gurdy, Kim. Can you loan me one for today's classes?"

Booker glared at Guy, who took a step back.

"I don't carry hurdy-gurdies, Guy."

"Ah, but then you are losing sales, no? You tell me what kind of hurdy-gurdy you could sell at your store and I will build one and send it to you on six-month consignment. What do you say to that?"

Kim looked at me, trying to convey something, I didn't know what. "Give me your card, Guy, and I'll think about it and give you my decision at lunch."

"Bon!" Guy whipped out a card, handed it to Kim, and ambled over to Glover's stand, probably waiting to lay the same line on him.

Strumming the guitar, Booker moaned a bluesy tune way down in his chest as he rocked back and forth. I used the opportunity to return to the farmhouse and enter his room. His banjo was still in the closet.

And the rounded top of the locker key still projected from under the dresser mirror.

Back outside, I saw Suzanne coming out of the women's showers. "So," she said by way of greeting, "you've got the case solved."

"I know who the thief is, yeah." We walked in silence a while. I could see her studying me sideways.

I put an arm around her shoulder, she put an arm around my waist, and we walked to the tent, trusting each other. If we could do that, no reason we couldn't live together.

After a quick shower — why bother shaving at this point — I met Suzanne in the dining hall, where Mary and Nola smiled broadly as they walked among the tables, distributing ballots and pencils. "Vote for what you think was the best meal day," Mary instructed. "The cooks, the days, and the menus are listed on the ballot, to refresh your memory."

Booker stepped between Suzanne and me. "Sorry," he said to the people behind us, "they're saving me a place." To me, he whispered, "Stay with me, man."

I nodded. Booker was lucky: if I was right, he would get

his guitar back tonight. My hammer was another story. It would be years — if ever — before a murder weapon was released from evidence.

Friday was the day the two cooks worked together, and Tansy and Aja outdid themselves: fresh fruit compote, pancakes, eggs, bacon, cereal, rhubarb muffins, and sour cream coffee cake.

Mary stood up and reminded us to vote. "Remember — the person voted best cook wins free tuition to next year's Midwest Music Madness for herself or somebody of her choice."

All the food had been excellent. I wanted to vote for Tansy so that Cody could benefit from another year of free tuition. But my favorite meal had been the fried chicken dinner. I marked the ballot for Aja Freeman, folded it, and placed it in Nola's basket as she went by.

One table over, Cody Thompson sat holding his mother's emerald green hammered dulcimer case.

25

"What's the tune?" I asked Bliss, watching her strum the mountain dulcimer before the old-time ensemble class began.

"'Let Me Fall.' Like it?"

"Uh-huh." I listened, tapping my foot. "I take it you're going home tomorrow?"

She stopped playing. "The sheriff asked me not to." She thought about it. "But Edric said he has no right to keep us here, we should go home."

I nodded. "You have a funeral to arrange."

She looked uncomfortable. "Not for at least a week, the sheriff says. They're going to keep Shelby here for a few more days." Plucking the drone string on the lap dulcimer, she stared out the barn door. "We're going to have a small funeral, but a big tribute to Shelby. Bigger than the one here." She glanced over to where Guy was sitting. "After that, I . . . don't know."

Bliss returned to her tune and I concentrated on the others. Up on stage Vance looked more than happy. Deeply satisfied, I'd say, despite his tent being destroyed. Lafayette looked edgy, twisting and turning in his chair as if fire ants had invaded his tent last night. Maybe they had. Fonnie looked unhappy, as usual.

"Frank, glad to see you here." Vance paced the stage and fiddled as he spoke.

I nodded. "You play well," I said.

"This music is so infectious the notes play themselves."

"I don't understand why you didn't take the old-time ensemble class with the fiddle," I said. "Stubbs would have accepted you as a fiddler. Instead, you asked if you could play mandolin in class."

He turned red. "I couldn't live up to Shelby as a fiddler, so I wanted to play the mandolin. He had no right to turn me away! And it's none of your business, anyway!" Turning his back on me, he walked over to the other end of the stage and bent to speak to Guy.

I left them there and took the stairs to the upper level to check out the hayloft gate. From there I walked down the hill to the pigpen, where Richard lay in his corner wallow. Nothing much would happen until tonight, when I expected to catch the thief red-handed. That would solve the lesser of Mary's two problems.

In the vendor area Glover rocked back and forth on the heels of his cowboy boots. He touched the brim of his cowboy hat in greeting, I touched the brim of my baseball cap.

Kim, standing behind her table, yawned. "Good sales?" I asked her.

"Very," she replied, stifling another yawn.

"You taking off for home tonight?" I asked.

"No, I'll set up the table one last time after breakfast tomorrow, then leave around ten o'clock. Wisconsin's not that far away." She hesitated. "You might want to know that somebody stole one of my new guitar cases," she said, not looking at me. "I think it was during the storm."

"Did you tell the sheriff?"

"No, but I'm telling you."

Uh-huh. I wondered how many others figured I was a private eye. Maybe half the festival.

Kim told me the case was black with silver trim, soft-sided. "I'll catch you at the dance," I said, moving on.

Back at the corn crib, Raven played her autoharp and sang

"Will You Miss Me When I'm Gone." She knew she'd never be asked to teach at Midwest Music Madness again.

From there I walked to the kitchen, where Tansy and Aja washed the dishes in harmony. When they saw me, Aja began singing Robert Johnson's "Come on in My Kitchen." Tansy joined in by clanging two spoons together. Aja turned a wooden bowl upside down, beating on it with a wooden spoon. I applauded. They tried to feed me more cake and coffee, but I resisted.

Mary had turned the running of her class over to Cindy Ruffo, who stood with her mountain dulcimer strapped over her shoulder as if it were a guitar. Others joined in with their instruments or voices, singing "Sail Away Ladies." I watched Suzanne as she sang and played the tambourine. Coming to Midwest Music Madness had made her happy.

Truth: I'd miss it when we left.

I unlocked my Camry, got in, punched the air conditioning on high, backed out, and drove to Auralee. On Main Street I locked the car and walked toward Nola's house.

The gate to Nola's yard was in good repair, its latch well-oiled. In the back yard lay the red cedar. When she said the tree had just missed her house, Nola hadn't been kidding — its topmost branches lay three inches short of her back porch. With the cedar sprawled across the lawn, it was hard to tell what Nola's yard was like on a good day. There may have been a bird bath or two, even a vegetable garden. If so, they were buried under the fallen tree.

Some cops maintain that once your home is burglarized, you're safe for a long time. They operate on the theory that to the burglars, an unburglarized house is like a Christmas present; they just can't wait to see what's inside. After the present is opened, they forget about it and itch to move on to another unopened present.

I was banking on the opposite *modus operandi* for the instrument thief, who had returned to the same festival three years in a row and probably hidden the instruments in the same place: the black walnut tree.

The guitars wouldn't be strapped to a tree branch this time. The thief wanted them hidden but readily accessible. Her method was always the same: grab what's available, hide it someplace that couldn't be connected to her, pick it up later.

My eyes slid over the fallen cedar. The tight feeling in my gut got tighter. I walked to the base of the tree and searched, pulling aside branches, stepping between them, looking around.

At the halfway point, I found them. Two guitar cases, one brand new, black with silver trim, the other cracked cardboard. Mary's guitar was inside the new case, Booker's in the old one. Putting the branches back the way they had been, I crawled out, brushed myself off, and moved to my last Auralee stop.

I entered the sheriff's office and told Yale Davis everything I'd found: the fiddle in the bus depot locker, the two guitars under Nola's tree.

Davis was not happy about Stubbs' fiddle and bow. He blew heavy about how I should have come to him, steamed that the fiddle could have been taken out of the locker by now.

I told him I had no proof, that the proof had to come in catching the thief in the act of retrieving the goods from under Nola's tree.

"And the fiddle from the bus depot," he growled. "If that fiddle isn't there, you owe Mary thirty thousand."

"I need your help tonight," I said. "Somebody's got to watch Nola's backyard."

He wanted to know who the thief was. I told him.

He thought about it a few seconds. "Fits," he grunted. "Have you told Mary yet?"

"I'm not going to tell Mary — her behavior would give something away."

"You're right there," he said, his lips tight. "It's easy to see when Mary's hiding something."

"You going to let everybody go home after the festival?" I asked.

"I suppose you could have done better?" he shouted. "God damn it! What do you mean asking me a question like that — you know I've got no evidence."

Down-state cops can be touchy. Any cops can be touchy. "Got a suspect?" I inquired.

Sheriff Yale Davis studied me. "Do you?"

"I don't know who murdered Stubbs," I answered, shaking my head. I suspected, but I didn't *know*.

As he rolled back his chair and elevated his feet on the desk, I noticed his shoes were polished. I wondered how he kept the mud and farm dust off them.

"When it gets down to it, I have to go with English," he volunteered. "Motive, means, opportunity." He looked at me to see how I took his theory.

I figured that's how he was thinking. Cops don't go around looking at all the suspects. Instead, they choose the most likely ones and start building a case against them. "Motive?" I questioned.

"Bliss, naturally. He's her lover, he was jealous of the husband."

When you're wrong, you're wrong.

"He's not her lover — he's her father."

The sheriff's feet thudded off the desk. *"What?"*

I repeated what I'd said. Davis asked for proof. No proof, I told him, just a good guess. He wanted to know based on what, I told him the obvious. "There's no sexual interest in how he looks at her," I explained.

"Did English tell you this? Did Bliss?"

"Nobody told me."

"Mary thought—" he started.

"—that Honey Miller was Edric's daughter," I finished.

He stared at me without speaking.

"Bliss is his daughter," I assured him.

Returning his feet to their perch, the sheriff leaned way back. "Say it's true. That still gives English motive. He doesn't like the way Stubbs is treating his daughter, he gets rid of the problem for her."

"Doesn't hold water," I argued. "Divorce is easy. Bliss could divorce Stubbs any time she wanted to."

"Say she didn't want to, so English gets rid of him," Davis argued back. "Then Bliss inherits." He watched me. "If he's her father, why didn't she say so? Why didn't he say so, for that matter?"

"I don't know," I confessed. "Maybe she doesn't want to capitalize on his name, maybe he doesn't want to stick her with having an ex-con for a father."

Davis switched the subject back to the thefts and arranged for Toby Thompson to stay in Nola's house from 5 P.M. on. I'd meet the deputy there after the drumming class performed and, assuming all went well, we'd catch the thief when she came to pick up the guitars.

"And she'll come to look for the fiddle in the locker," Davis said. He was still stewing about that, I could tell.

I told him I didn't think so: I thought the fiddle was stolen by the murderer, not the thief. "He wanted to spread the guilt around," I explained, "point suspicion at four or five people, which is why he stole Edric's shoes, my clothes and hammer, took the fiddle, and planted the key in Booker's room."

Davis jumped on the pronoun. "He?"

"I think so, yeah."

"So you think when we catch her retrieving the guitars, she won't have the key? It'll still be in Booker's room where you left it?" he asked. Before I could reply he continued. "I'm not ruling out that Booker's the killer. He and Stubbs have had a few run-ins."

Now that he was back to the murder, Davis tossed a few

other names out — Lafayette's, for one, Raven's for another — but we weren't thinking along the same lines. The whole time, I could see him holding back on something. I thought I knew what it was.

"There's one thing," I said as I got up to leave. "Mary didn't do it."

Davis stood. Straightened his shirt and belt. "She's hiding something."

"She was," I said. "She stole Honey Miller's song and didn't want to tell you."

"She should trust me," he retorted.

"She didn't want you to know because she was ashamed."

He digested that for quite a while, then offered his opinion. "She's hiding something else, I know it."

Trouble was, I knew it too.

26

I arrived for lunch just in time to join the applause as Mary announced Aja Freeman winner of the cooking contest. Mary told Aja that everybody looked forward to seeing her as a student next year, then announced that Nola would be taking payment — total or deposit — on all black walnut orders.

When only Suzanne and I were left at our table, I told her about the guitars. She was about to ask me something when Raven walked up to us.

"I have a festival in August," she told us. "Much more fun than this one. I hope to see you there."

Mary, her arm still bandaged and in a sling, had snuck up on us to listen.

The three of us watched Raven go.

"She's getting together with Edric," Mary told us. "She talked him into forming a duo, English Hook. Raven and he were an item years ago, before Shelby stepped in." She grimaced. "I feel sorry for Edric."

I asked Mary to sit with Suzanne and me so we could speak in private. Then I told her I'd found the two guitars and that the thief would be apprehended tonight. Her eyes blazed with excitement. Revenge, too. She pushed again for the name, but I told her it was important she didn't know.

"How could that possibly be important?" she demanded. "I'm paying you big money to solve this case and stop the thief."

Suzanne coughed, earning Mary's glare.

"Don't you cough at me, Suzie. Two hundred dollars is nothing to cough at," she said. "In addition, there's the free tuition for yourself and Frank. A week at Madness is priceless."

"It's four hundred dollars, not two hundred," I said.

A shifty look entered Mary's eyes. "Two hundred. It was one hundred, and I doubled it."

"You doubled it from one hundred to two hundred Tuesday morning, when you sent me to find Lafayette. Then you doubled it from two hundred to four hundred this morning, on condition that I find and restore your guitar and Booker's guitar."

"Well, you haven't done that yet. Of course, if you told me the name of the thief and the location of the guitars, I would agree to the four hundred regardless."

"Listen, Mary, we don't have time to argue over this. There're two important things you have to do, starting now."

Not used to being on the receiving end of orders, she blinked. I had to give her credit, though: she straightened her one good shoulder and tossed back her braid.

I nodded at her readiness. "First, I want you to go around to several people and tell them — quietly and in private — that your guitar and Booker's guitar were stolen."

"What?!" she shrieked. "No! That would—"

"Just listen," I interrupted. "Tell them the thefts haven't been announced because you feel that would harm the festival. Tell them to guard their own instruments carefully. Ask them if they saw anything suspicious."

I paused to make certain she was with me.

"Tell them to keep it quiet. If they ask questions, answer them briefly however you want, but *don't* tell them the case is solved or indicate in any way we know who stole the instruments. Act upset." I considered what I'd just said. "On the other hand, watch that you don't over-act: I don't want the thief to spot it."

Mary inspected a bread crumb on the table, mashed it with

a finger, flicked each particle in my direction with a fingernail. "What is the purpose of this?" she asked.

"It's obvious, Mary. The thief has stolen two guitars and no announcement has been made. Don't you think the thief is pretty damned nervous by now?"

"Oh."

"He wants to put the thief at ease," Suzanne summarized.

Mary nodded. "Who all am I supposed to speak to?"

"Not Raven," I explained. "If you told her, word would get out by tonight's concert."

Mary agreed with that assessment.

"Tell Fonnie, Cindy, and Kim." I enumerated the suspects on my fingers. "And Vance and Lafayette. You have told Nola, haven't you?"

With another nod, Mary started to push away from the table.

"One more thing," I added. "Who determines the order the classes perform in tonight?"

"Why, Nola. I usually leave that sort of thing to her."

"This is important, Mary — you've got to make certain Kofi's drumming class performs first, followed by your roots of old-time music, followed by Raven's autoharp class. After that, the classes can perform in any order."

She repeated the order to me: Kofi's drumming class, roots of old-time music, Raven's autoharp class.

"I'm trusting you to carry this out," I told her. "Every single part of it."

As Mary marched off to her duty, Suzanne appraised me. "Drumming class first, roots class second. If I didn't know you better, I'd think you were trying to upstage me."

"Could be." I smiled.

"Raven won't like her class coming third."

"I'll have to console her."

Suzanne touched my five-day beard. "Sexy."

"Yeah? Let's go back to the tent," I suggested.

She smiled. "I can't miss the last class with Booker."

Win some, lose some.

"I'll walk you there." I pulled her to her feet.

The Old-time Songs in Black and White met in the back room of the farmhouse, where I'd found Mary drunk Tuesday night. I glanced in the office as we passed: Nola was busy. "How are you coming along carving Mary's pig?" I asked Suzanne.

"I finished it this morning. I oiled it just before lunch. Should I give it to her tonight, or tomorrow morning?"

"Tomorrow would be good."

Outside the classroom Booker leaned against the wall, strumming Kim's guitar. He looked up when he saw me, a question in his eyes. "Later," I told him under my breath. I rounded the farmhouse, rounded the showers, and approached the high ground near the pigpen for the last session of the African drumming class.

Today Kofi wore a kente cloth wrapped around his shoulders and down to his ankles. Everybody was dressed a bit better than they had been all week. Maybe I'd have time to shave before our performance. There was little chatter today: we practiced in earnest for two hours. I was going to miss my drum, more than I'd have thought possible just four days ago.

After class I continued walking the grounds. In the farmhouse, Nola studied a check.

"Bad check?" I asked.

"I hope not — it's from the lumber company. There's enough money here to run Madness for two years. So many people have already signed up for next year's festival that attendance will be up significantly." She looked around, making sure we were alone. "Mary told me Booker's guitar has been stolen."

I nodded.

"Do you know who— Oh, hi, Vance."

"The tree's not all gone, is it?" he joked. "I want a slab."

"The mill has the tree now," Nola informed him. "The wood will be delivered here next week."

Vance nodded and waited.

"A slab would cost you a fortune," she continued. "But we're willing to take your money."

I left them negotiating the price of the wood. Hitching up my carpenter's belt as if I meant business, I gave the grounds one final patrol. By the time I reached the sycamore, the appetizer class had already begun. Lafayette sat with an old washboard against his chest. Beside him sat Tansy with a pair of spoons in her hand. Behind them, Booker strummed his borrowed guitar while Edric plucked his washtub bass.

Either people really wanted to know how to play the washboard and spoons, or it was a Madness tradition to attend the last appetizer class: about fifty people gathered around. Suzanne handed me a pair of beat-up silver spoons.

"Where'd you get these?"

"Tansy had a bunch of them spread out. You have to return them," she added as I eyed the spoons.

"No spoons, no dinner?"

"Something like that," she said with a grin.

First we learned how to play the washboard for "Goin' Down to Cairo." I wondered if my mother would notice if I snuck the old washboard out of her basement for a few weeks.

After about twenty minutes Tansy took over, demonstrating how to hold spoons and how to play them.

Forty pairs of spoons didn't sound bad. Sort of like Metallica on steroids.

The appetizer class ended with everybody happy and about half the group going to the vendors to buy spoons.

Dinner came early, a cooperative effort of build-your-own sandwiches, hearty pasta salads, and sides of vegetables. During coffee and dessert Kofi came around to inform me that the drumming class was performing first tonight and I should be ready. I assured him I was.

Around me I sensed a certain haste, no lingering over the food, people pushing themselves away from the table and hurrying off. "Jitters," I explained to Suzanne.

"Uh-huh. You, of course, aren't a bit nervous."

"Who, me? About drumming in public? With a whole bunch of other people to hide my mistakes?"

She smiled and caressed my hand. "Just take a deep breath and do your best. It'll be fine."

In the barn Kofi lined us up near the stage stairs, our drums at our feet.

Arm in a sling, Mary walked on stage. Right behind her walked a contingent of students and teachers. She looked surprised. As the musicians set up, Guy announced they were playing a few tunes "in honor of Mary Ployd, organizer of Midwest Music Madness." She stepped aside as they launched into a series of pig tunes which Cody, standing next to me, giggled over. He named the various tunes for me: "Pig Town Fling," "Four Little Pigs," "Sow's Got the Measles," and three or four others. The audience laughed and applauded, Mary thanked the musicians for the tunes, and for not playing bacon songs.

The drumming class came next. Kofi led us on, we sat in a circle, he looked us over and beat out the call. The rest of us responded with the rhythm patterns we'd been practicing. After the first few strokes, I was loose, lost in the pattern, listening to my fellow drummers. We played well and when Kofi struck the signal we all stopped on cue, even Lafayette.

Mary's roots of old-time music class filed on stage as we took our drums to the back of the barn and lined them up neatly. The others went to find seats. I stayed back against the wall, near the door. Residents from Auralee and surrounding farm towns were still arriving. Nola sat at the door, taking their money. I stood there listening to Mary's class play and sing "Sail Away Ladies."

Suzanne stood up front, her alto voice harmonizing with the others. I applauded loudly and when Mary began to announce Raven's autoharp class, and Nola's eyes were on the money she was collecting, I slipped out to the parking lot.

Nola's house was dark, the back door unlocked. I walked in, closed the door softly behind me, and climbed the stairs to the second story. "It's Dragovic," I said into the dark.

"Come in," commanded a voice from a back room.

I walked in. Deputy Toby Thompson stood there, gun drawn. I stopped, put my hands in plain sight, and frowned.

"Just wanted to make sure," he said, holstering it.

We went to the window, which offered a clear view of the sidewalk that led into the backyard. From where we stood, we could see the middle of the fallen tree. "Where's Davis?" I asked.

"Base of the tree, far side. You can't see him from here, or from the ground — he had me check twice." Thompson glanced over at me. "We have somebody watching the depot, in case she stops there."

We spent some time waiting in the dark, conversing occasionally, mostly just wondering when it would happen. Eyes grow tired on a nighttime stakeout, staring out at dark shapes and darker shapes within those dark shapes. Lids grow heavy from boredom. You need a lot of coffee, a lot of mental games to keep yourself alert. I tried timing, letting my eyes scan the entire yard from front to back, then side to side, every sixty seconds. Then another sixty looking out at the moon and stars.

I saw movement outside. My left elbow prodded Thompson, who snapped to.

"That her?" he whispered as a figure moved stealthily below.

"Let's go," I said, moving toward the stairs.

We reached the kitchen together.

"Uh-uh," he grunted, pulling me back from the door. "The deal was you wait until we make the collar. As soon as I step out and tell her she's under arrest, you throw the light switch."

We looked out the window. She backed away from the tree, dragging two guitar cases with her. Thompson pushed open the screen, and shouted, "Stop! You're under arrest!"

Fonnie dropped the guitars and started toward the gate, thought twice about it as the lights went on and Thompson, with me behind him, reached it first. Turning in her tracks, she ran the opposite way, toward the back of the yard.

Right into the sheriff, who grabbed her. "Fonnie Sheffler, I place you under arrest for the theft of two guitars. You have the right to remain silent," he began, reciting her rights.

"I don't know what you're talking about." Her voice cracked. "I'm just leaving the festival and I came to say goodbye to Nola's tree. That's all."

"You came to retrieve the two guitars you had hidden here earlier," said Davis. "I have two witnesses."

She turned to look at the deputy and me. Him she didn't seem to recognize, but me she did. "What? — What are you doing here?" she stuttered.

"He's a witness," replied Davis. "A private investigator from Chicago, hired by Mary to track down who's been stealing from her festival."

"You!" she shouted. "You traitor! You rotten spy! I knew it! You're always snooping around, being everywhere."

When the sheriff cuffed her, Fonnie began to cry. By the time we were settled in the police station she confessed that she had stolen Cindy's mountain dulcimer the first year and sold it to the first taker she found a couple of weeks later. "I never figured it would end up back here at Madness," she wailed. "If it weren't for Bliss, I'd be okay," she rationalized.

Fonnie admitted she'd stolen Tansy's hammered dulcimer

case the first year, too, strapping it to a tree branch for the specific purpose of concealing a stolen instrument in it. "I stayed an extra day the first year. Then I climbed up the tree that night and unstrapped the case and took it to my camper."

As Davis questioned her about the second year, she admitted stealing a guitar and Raven's autoharp. "I meant to steal just the guitar," she whined. "But Raven left her autoharp out and it was easy to take. It's not my fault she did that!"

"You stole Mary's guitar when I drove you in from town," I said. "I ran to see what everybody was doing around the barn, and you were behind me, but not all the way."

"She deserved to have it stolen, leaving it out there like that!"

"Why didn't you steal her case?" I asked.

Fonnie shrugged. "I don't know, I seldom steal the original cases. It's bad luck. I took one of Kim's guitar cases during the big storm. People aren't suspicious if they don't see their own case."

"What about Booker's guitar?" Davis asked.

"I saw him go in the showers, so I ran into the house, up the stairs, and into his room. I took my old guitar case with me and put Booker's guitar into it." She wiped her nose. "Then I walked out to my car and put it in the trunk. Instead of going to breakfast, I drove to town and hid the two guitars under Nola's tree. I figured nobody would look under a fallen tree." She glared at me. "It was dumb luck you saw me in Nola's yard yesterday!"

I shrugged. It was luck that I saw her in Nola's yard, but she'd been my number one suspect for a few days: perched on her rooftop in the world's hottest weather, not to meditate but to scope out the scene; talking about the sacred spirit of trees not because she believed it, but to derail any questions she didn't like.

The sheriff asked Fonnie to empty her pockets. No locker key. He questioned her about that, but it was obvious to me she didn't know what he was talking about.

The fiddle was taken by the person who killed Stubbs.

27

"Everything okay?" Nola whispered, eyeing the two guitar cases I carried.

"According to plan," I replied, looking around for Suzanne. I spotted her dancing with Lafayette. The Stubborn Pea Pickers — Edric, Vance, and Booker — were going strong, Vance leading on the fiddle. "Where's Mary?"

"She left with Bliss. What should I tell Booker?"

"Tell him everything's fine. His guitar will be back in his room by the time the dance is done." A light went on in the farmhouse. I asked Nola to tell Suzanne I was back but meeting with Mary.

In the darkened farmhouse I took the stairs and checked out the south bedroom: Raven had packed and gone. I put Booker's guitar in his closet. Then I pried the key from under the dresser mirror, went back to my car, drove to Auralee, and removed Stubbs' fiddle from its locker.

In fifteen minutes I was back, looking at the crack of light under Mary's office door.

Holding a fiddle case and a guitar case, I knocked.

A scuffling sound, then Mary opened the door. "Oh. Frank. Come in. We were just having a drink." Two glasses and a bottle of Makers Mark sat on the desk. Suddenly it dawned on Mary that I was not only there, but back from where I'd been. "Oh!" she cried, grabbing my arm. "How did it go?"

"Perfect." I looked at Bliss, who watched us with interest. I held the fiddle case out to her and a light dawned in her eyes.

"Is that Shelby's fiddle?" she asked.

"It is." I handed the case to Bliss. "I think it should go to you," I said, "even though you weren't his first and only wife."

Mary coughed and moved back behind her desk, grabbing the bottle. She offered me a drink but I declined. "Do you want a report now, or later?" I asked her.

"Now, please. Tell us all about it. Bliss, Frank is a private detective I hired to discover who's been stealing our instruments."

Bliss looked at me in mild surprise. "A private in*ves*tigator? But . . . but Edric says you're such a good carpenter."

"Never mind that," Mary instructed. "Frank, sit down and tell us what happened tonight."

In the short time it took me to explain how I figured Fonnie was the thief, and how Davis and Thompson staked out and recovered two guitars, Mary downed her drink.

One look at her was enough to take the fun out of "Soldier's Joy." She cleared her throat.

Sensing something was coming, Bliss stiffened in her chair.

"Bliss," Mary started. Stopped. Poured another two fingers' worth into Bliss's glass, twice that much into her own.

"Bliss," she tried again, "about Shelby . . . . I'm— I'm — I'm going to give you the money," she blurted.

Bliss stared at her in confusion. She looked at me, back at Mary. "What money?"

Shaking her head, Mary played with her braid. "It's yours, really. I mean, it's mine really, but you earned it. No, I don't mean that the way it sounds, I mean by rights it should be yours." She sipped more liquid courage. "And I try to do the right thing. Even when it's hard."

"What are you talking about?" asked Bliss.

"Shelby."

"What about him? What's he got to do with this?"

"He left his money to his wife," explained Mary.

Bliss looked into her drink. "Wasn't that me?"

Mary shook her head. "Not legally — legally, I was his wife."

"What?" gasped Bliss. "You were married to *Shelby?* For *real?* "

Her face crimson, Mary stared at her desktop. "Yes," she admitted. "I was married to him nearly forty years ago. For a week. Then I left him."

"I don't understand what you're saying." Bliss shook her head back and forth and deposited her glass on the desk. "What are you saying?"

Mary gave me an imploring look.

"She's trying to say Stubbs' will leaves the money to her because she was his first and only wife, but she wants the money to go to you."

"That's right," Mary agreed. "That's what I'm trying to say. I don't want the money, I'm giving it to you. I don't care what you do with it, it's yours."

I wondered how difficult it was for Mary to say she didn't want the money.

Bliss stared at Mary as if the generation gap were a couple of centuries, not decades. "You mean you didn't get a divorce?"

Mary sighed. "I don't know why I didn't get a divorce." She hid her head in both hands. After a moment, she looked up. "Forty years." Mary shook her head. "Almost forty years ago I was in a band with Shelby and Waydell, the Boot Jacks. I— I was in love with Waydell." She lifted her glass and drank. "I was in love with Waydell, and Shelby saw that, and set out to steal me away from Waydell."

Draining the glass, she poured herself another, not so much as last time. "More's the fool I, that he did. We were married in New Mexico, just picked the first town we came to, and then he told Waydell. Gloated about it." Mary studied the bourbon. "I can still see the look on Waydell's face. How disappointed he was in me."

"Yeah," said Bliss softly, "I know what you mean." They sat there, looking away from each other. Eventually Bliss asked, "But how do you know that *Shelby* never got divorced?"

"I assumed he *did!*" shouted Mary. "I heard he married Opal, then I heard he divorced her and married Raven, so I assumed he'd gotten a divorce. Then I heard he divorced Raven and he married you. Then . . . " she paused. "Then I saw him at the Georgia Festival last year. I've gone out of my way to avoid seeing Shelby and I didn't know he'd be there, he just came around the corner at a vendor's stand and there we were, face to face." Mary rolled the glass against her forehead, as if the fumes could enter that way and wipe out thoughts of Stubbs.

"He said something like, 'Well, look who's here,' and I said, 'Hello, Shelby' and turned to go, when he grabbed my arm and said, 'Something I've been meaning to ask you if I ever bumped into you again, Mary,' and I said, 'What?' and he said, 'Did you ever divorce me?' and I said 'No, but I assume you divorced me,' and then he started laughing." Mary hit the desk with a fist. "Then he said, 'I never divorced you, Mary, you're still Mrs. Stubbs.'"

"Omigod." Bliss gulped. "What did you say?"

"I said, 'Shelby, I was never Mrs. Stubbs,' and turned around and marched on out of there."

Bliss nodded and sipped her bourbon. Mary nodded in return and sipped hers. I was a piece of furniture propped against the windowsill.

After a while Mary spoke. "Tomorrow Nola will talk to Yale, tell him my story. I suppose I'll have to be there, too." She scuffed her feet over the carpet, probably wishing she could crawl under it. "I've asked Nola to draw up a letter of intent, saying that I want the money to go to you." She held her head in her hands. "I've got a terrible headache, Bliss. I just want to go to bed."

"Okay," said Bliss, standing. "You don't mind if I sleep in your room one last time?"

Mary waved her upstairs.

Bliss paused. "Thank you," she said, then slipped out the door soundlessly.

Mary looked up at me. "Good work, Frank." Her speech was slurred. "Did I tell you that already? Good work."

"Thanks, Mary. You did."

"Where are the guitars, did you say?"

Which goes to show how far gone she was. I held out her guitar, snug in Kim Oberfeld's black and silver case. "Booker's is in his room," I added.

"Good." Her eyes closed. She might have been sleeping. Might have been faking. After a while, she peeked out of one eye, caught me watching, and sighed. "Good night, Frank. I'm very tired." She cradled her right arm, still in a sling.

"I'm not leaving."

Mary groaned a little, rubbed her arm. But that wouldn't work, and she realized it. "What do you want?" she asked.

"Who pushed you out of the barn door?"

"No!" she shouted. "Your job here is done, it was excellent work. I'll pay you tomorrow, I'll even give you a bonus, Frank, now let me alone."

"Murder," I said.

She went stiff. "What?"

"Somebody murdered Stubbs."

"Well, Yale is taking care of that. It's not your job."

I leaned forward. "Taking care of it? A fourth of the festival is leaving as we talk, the other three-fourths leave in the morning. That's the end of the sheriff's case."

"We'll have to live with it." She shrugged philosophically.

"No." I shook my head. "He tried to kill you once, he may try again."

"No, he— why would he?"

"Why *did* he, Mary? Only you know the answer."

She clammed up, and I could see she wouldn't budge. So I sat back and began telling her the story as I saw it.

"The way I figure it, Stubbs did something to somebody, let's call him X. Denied him his dreams, the way you put it. Stood in the way of whatever this person wanted most and snatched it away, or polluted it, or destroyed it."

Trying to act nonchalant, Mary leaned back in her chair and assumed a bored expression. But her eyes were wary.

"Whoever X is, he waited for a chance to kill Stubbs. The chance came here, at this festival. He took it. And then he tried to kill you."

"Ridiculous. Why would somebody wait forty years to kill Shelby?"

I looked at her.

"What?" she demanded.

"I never said it was forty years. I said Stubbs did something to somebody."

Mary swore, looked around for the bottle. I moved it out of her reach.

"That's okay," I assured her. "I figured it was forty years anyway. And whatever it was, you were there. So," I added, watching her carefully, "was Waydell."

"Don't you drag Waydell into this, he di-di-didn't do it. He saved him, he didn't hurt him. I won't have you taking—" Mary choked on her words.

I waited, knowing if I showed any sympathy she'd draw back into denial.

"I won't have you talking about Waydell like that," she finished. She pressed her lips together and straightened in her chair. Wincing, she pulled her arm out of its sling, crossed her hands over the desk and sliced them sideways. "Here's the way it was. The truth is better than your ridiculous guesses."

She took a deep breath. "It happened exactly seven days

after I married Shelby. We, the Boot Jacks that is, the three of us, had played Trinidad, Colorado, the night before and had a gig in Colorado Springs that night. Waydell said he was leaving the band. He made up some reason, I forget what it was, but I know it was because I'd married Shelby. Waydell was disappointed in me. Hurt." Mary hung her head.

"Shelby told him to go to hell, we could get another guitar player anywhere, he'd heard of one up near Salida who would jump at the chance to play with the Boot Jacks." Mary's eyes narrowed. "Shelby was so full of shit, as if anybody outside of a few barflies had ever heard of us. But he did it, he called this guy up near Salida." She rubbed her bad shoulder. "Bram. His name was Bram. I don't even remember his last name. It was raining when Shelby and I left Trinidad in the pickup. The closer we got to Salida, the harder the rain came down, pouring down the mountains like it would wash us away. I don't know how we found the place we were looking for, the guy lived in a little cabin way, way up in the mountains."

As she got into her story, Mary relaxed, her body visibly loosening. "We found the cabin. It had a carport or some kind of a lean-to that Shelby pulled into so fast I screamed. The rain was coming down so hard you could hardly see, and then he slammed on the brakes so fast my head went forward and hit the windshield." She moved some hair aside and fingered a spot just below her hairline. "I still have the scar. Tiny little thing, but I know it's there." She looked puzzled, her eyes unfocused from all the alcohol. "Where was I?

"Oh, the lean-to. If Shelby hadn't stopped, we'd be dead. Just past the lean-to, the mountain dropped off into nowhere, and down below was the Arkansas River." Mary shuddered. "There was this guy, Bram, standing in the doorway, a fiddle in his hand. Not a guitar. He played both, I guess. Whatever, he had a fiddle in hand, and held the door open for us as to come in. My head was bleeding and Shelby didn't care, but Bram bandaged me up. Then

— then he began to play the fiddle." She paused, as if remembering the music. "Beautiful. It was . . . masterful."

A scowl settled across her face. "Bram was a show-off, too. I'm not making excuses for Shelby, there are none, but it was almost like Bram set out to provoke him, to say, 'Bet you can't play the fiddle like *that*, Shelby Stubbs.'" She inhaled deeply and the scowl disappeared.

"Shelby didn't say anything, just told Bram to pack his guitar and gear, we had to leave if we were going to make it to Colorado Springs in time for the gig. Bram wanted to know if we wanted something to eat and I said yes, but Shelby shouted no, we had to get going." She rubbed her arm and looked past me, into her memories. "Bram took some things out to the truck. Shelby helped him. I saw Shelby grab the fiddle case to carry. I went to use the bathroom.

"When I came out, I heard Shelby start the truck. I ran to the door, because he was in the kind of mood he'd leave me behind if I wasn't there. As I was coming out the door . . . as I was coming out the door, I saw the truck backing up and I heard — despite the rain I distinctly heard — the tires go over an instrument."

Mary made eye contact now, knowing it was me she was talking to.

"I knew it was an instrument. I could hear the splintering of the wood, but just before that, a horrible sound, horrible, like — like something beautiful dying. It was the sound of strings." She shook herself. "The fiddle. I knew it in my gut, and I knew then that I was going to leave Shelby when we got to Colorado Springs, get a divorce, go find Waydell.

"I didn't know it then but Waydell had been following us. If— if I'd have just stayed . . . things would be different."

Mary stood, walked to the window, looked out at the night. "Life never turns out that way, does it? As soon as Shelby ran over the violin, he stopped the truck. He and Bram both jumped out. I can still see them, running 'round to the back. Bram running, Shelby swaggering. 'Look at that,' Shelby said, 'ain't that too bad. I thought I'd put that fiddle up front.'"

"Bram just stood there a minute. I thought he was going to cry. Then he kind of turned into a raging animal. I'd never seen anything like it. He jumped Shelby, went for his throat, tried to choke him. He was shouting the whole time, saying that Shelby did it deliberately. Which he did, I know."

Mary turned away from the night, toward me. "I wish he had killed him, I wish he had. Somehow Shelby fought back and tried to get into the truck, I think, maybe not, but they were moving toward the front as they were fighting, and then —" She turned back to the window, pulled the drawcord of the louvers open and closed, open and closed.

"Then?" I asked when it looked as if she wouldn't continue.

"Then Shelby pushed Bram over the edge," she said flatly.

"I can still see him falling. Screaming. I stood there, paralyzed. Shelby grabbed me, shoved me into the truck, and backed out of the driveway at top speed. We almost hit a car that was coming along the road behind us. Almost crashed head-on into another. I— I just sat there." There were tears in her eyes. "I'm so ashamed of going with him. I should have stayed." She looked at me. "Dark stormy nights — they bring it all back."

"Bram lived," I surmised.

Mary nodded. "When we drove off like that, I thought he was dead. Killed in the fall, or drowned in the river. But he wasn't."

I waited.

"That night, I didn't go on with Shelby. I don't know if he played or not. We had a huge fight. I checked into a hotel, sat there counting how little money I had, wondering how I could get back to Texas." She sat down hard. "I left the next morning, hitchhiking back." She bit her lip. "A couple of weeks later, Waydell found me.

Said he thought I should know that Bram . . . I don't remember the last name . . . was alive. The car we almost hit, you see, was Waydell. He'd come . . . he said he'd come to ask me to leave Shelby and go with him. Even in the rain, Waydell saw the smashed fiddle case on the ground. He got out of his car, and he . . . he heard Bram calling for help. Waydell saved Bram's life."

Mary broke down. "But when I ran away from what Shelby had done, and left a man to die, Waydell said he couldn't . . . he couldn't see our making a life together." Mary turned off a small desk light. She looked at the ceiling lights and grimaced. "After a while, I moved as far away from Texas as I could, and after a few years I ended up on the Apostle Islands. Which is where I taught Suzie music in kindergarten, and which is why you're here. I never did get that divorce. Frank, could you turn off the overheads? The glare is too much."

I got up, turned off the switch, returned to my chair.

The two of us sat there in the dark with our own thoughts. "So Bram waited until Waydell was dead," I said. "If he murdered Stubbs while Waydell was alive, Waydell might give the cops a lead. Midwest Music Madness presented him with the perfect opportunity — Stubbs and you in the same place." I leaned forward and switched the desk lamp back on. "Which one is Bram?" I asked, watching her face.

She shook her head. "I don't know. I just don't know."

"Is the answer in the testimony you gave to Nola?"

"No." She shook her head. "What's in there is what I'm telling you. I tell what happened, but I don't know who Bram is."

"Mary. Murder is a serious matter. And your life's in danger."

"It was so long ago . . . I just saw him for, what, ten minutes, fifteen, I've tried to remember what he looked like, but I can't, and it was almost forty years, he's changed, he could have grown a beard, a mustache, gotten bald, gotten glasses, I don't know I don't know I don't *know!*"

I believed she didn't. "Was he tall?" I asked.

"Oh, I don't know, he was about Shelby's height. They were about the same height when they were fighting. Shelby weighed more. Bram was thin."

"Say six feet, then, give or take an inch." I'd been thinking about it ever since the storm. I ran through it again in my mind. "The way I see it," I offered at last, "Bram is one of three people."

Mary looked at me in disbelief.

"Each of them is your age, each plays the fiddle, and each has a physical injury of some kind."

Mary looked confused.

"Chances are, Bram was injured falling off the mountain," I explained. "Jeff Glover can play the fiddle. He walks with a slight limp. He lives out west."

Mary considered it. "Who else?"

"Vance Jurasek."

"Vance has been coming here for years," she objected. "Why didn't he try to kill me before?"

"Waydell was alive," I reminded her. "Vance has a glass eye, an accident he doesn't talk about. He plays every instrument there is, fiddle, mandolin, guitar, autoharp. And," I paused, mulling it over, "he might see it as poetic justice, joining the Shelby Stubbs Band, taking over as fiddler."

She looked at me in dread. "The third?"

"Yale Davis. He met you at a festival out west," I began, "possibly made a point of getting to know you."

"No," she objected. "Not Yale. You're wrong."

"He has a scar on his face," I continued. "And he plays the mandolin."

"What's that got— oh. The fingering."

I nodded. "Same as for the fiddle."

Mary frowned. "You've picked up a little too much knowledge, Frank. I don't like this at all."

"The question is, what are we going to do about it?"

Mary looked at me. "Well, what *are* we going to do about it?"

I liked the *we*. Then again, maybe I didn't. "Do you have a gun?" I asked.

She didn't.

"I want you to be careful," I said. "Lock your door tonight, don't let anybody at all in for any reason whatsoever. I'll stake out the farmhouse, just in case there's another attempt on your life. When everybody leaves tomorrow — I don't know. That leaves you here alone. I don't like it, Mary."

28

"What are you doing?" Suzanne asked as I rummaged around the tent for the face blackening I'd left in one of the hanging mesh organizer bags.

I found it, rubbed it on, and told her about Fonnie, then explained about Mary being pushed, and my belief that the killer might try again. "I've got to go."

"But you don't have a gun!" she protested. "What if—what can you do? Shouldn't you call the sheriff?"

"No, I can't. But I'll ask Guy to help."

I unzipped the tent flap silently. Crawled out the door, listening for any sounds in the night. A few lanterns glowed from the direction of Cindy's tent. I looked back: Suzanne sat in the tent opening, staring out.

My intention was to stake out the farmhouse from the woods, where I could see both the front and back doors. But then I remembered Vance — was he spending the night on the sofabed again? If Vance was Bram, my being outside wouldn't protect Mary in any way. Keeping low, I crawled toward Vance's tent.

Nobody home.

I moved quickly toward Guy's tent and called out to him in the dark.

His head popped out of the tent flap, looking all around. But not down on the ground, where I lay. I got his attention. His mouth opened, probably at the blackening on my face. I crawled into his tent and told him I thought there might be a second attempt on Mary's life. I asked if he'd be willing to spend the night at the top of the stairs, guarding her door.

He agreed instantly.

My instructions to Guy were simple: if he heard anybody at all climbing the stairs to the third floor, he should shout as loud as he could, waking up everybody on the second floor. "Pound the door, scream, hit things," I told him. "Yell for help. Chances are that will make whoever it is back off — he doesn't want witnesses."

Of course, I intended to nab whoever it was when they came out running.

Guy pulled on his jeans and boots, grabbed a T-shirt and flannel shirt, and took off for the farmhouse. From his gear I figured he was eager to return to Maine. I waited until he entered the house, then slid out of his tent and belly-crawled behind it and toward the woods, stopping every few feet to listen. The farmhouse was over my right shoulder, the woods straight ahead, the barn directly behind me, the smashed pole barn and remains of the black walnut over my left shoulder. Every few feet I stopped and glanced all around me, then continued.

I had told Mary that three men fit the bill of murderer. In reality, my money was on one of them in particular: the one who had easy access to my hammer. The other two were simply outside possibilities.

I stopped crawling.

Lifted my head.

Flopped over and sat up, staring in the direction of the creek.

Shit!

A figure walked toward the black walnut.

Short, stocky. Striding purposefully. Weaving a bit.

Mary Ployd.

What was she doing? Hadn't I told her to stay put, go to

her room and lock the door? Why had I thought for even a minute that she would listen?

Why had Guy let her go? Why wasn't he at least following her? Then I remembered Bliss. He must have decided to stay and protect Bliss.

Quickly I reversed directions and moved across the ground. What I needed was a pair of elbow and knee guards from my skateboarding days. The pig came trotting out of its shed as I crept past the pen. Mary had reached the tree and was walking alongside it. I could hear her speaking, but not what she was saying. Was there somebody else down by the tree? I saw nobody except Mary. Don't tell me she was a Druid like Fonnie.

The pig and I made tracks together, Richard on the inside of the pen, me on the outside. Richard grunted a few times but did nothing else to give away my position. Probably thought I was crazy. I reached the corn crib and settled against its base, secure in the knowledge nobody could see me here.

A high piercing sound floated my way. Lafayette's bowed psaltry. I listened carefully, trying to decide whether the sound was coming from his tent. I figured it was.

Minutes went by. A quarter of an hour. Half an hour. What was Mary doing, giving the tree music lessons? Lafayette finished his serenade. In the quiet I heard the sound of a zipper as he put away his psaltry. Then I heard him humming "Mary's Cornfield."

Bugs crawled up my pants. Just behind the slats something gnawed away. Rat? If I stayed there long enough, it might gnaw on me.

Tires on gravel.

I looked toward the parking lot. No headlights.

A car door opened softly. Didn't quite close.

In the light of the moon, the silhouette of a cruiser. No dome light. Deliberately turned off, no doubt.

The figure of Yale Davis, square-jawed and straight-shouldered, moved toward the barn, one hand on his holster. He disappeared from my line of vision. Was he standing there, waiting? Or going around the perimeter of the barn? My ears strained to hear. Nothing.

I turned to see Mary heading back my way, walking unsteadily toward the farmhouse. I stretched quietly, releasing some of the tension from my shoulders, waking up my back, hips, legs, and arms.

Now what?

Mary stopped, looked to her right, up at the moon.

No.

Not the moon, the barn.

What was she looking at? I craned my neck, trying to see into the upper story, but couldn't from the base of the corn crib.

Flipping her braid over her shoulder, Mary turned in her tracks and marched toward the ramp.

No! I wanted to shout.

Step after step, stride after stride, oblivious to the danger, she marched up the gravel-covered hill, her clogs crunching loudly. I surged to my knees and knuckles like a sprinter, ready to take off.

She reached the top and I raced across the grass. At the base of the ramp I shifted right, stepping on the old stone blocks that embanked the dirt. Less gravel there, less chance for sound.

At the top, I paused, listening.

"Who's there?" asked Mary.

But she was facing inward, not in my direction. I stepped on the gravel. Careful, careful. Moved toward the door.

"Who's there?" she repeated angrily. "I saw your light."

As she spoke I slipped through the open doors and flattened myself against the stacked bales of straw, arms flat, head back, listening.

"Mary!"

A whisper. I didn't quite recognize the voice. Where was it coming from?

"Mary!"

She looked to her left. The granary? The loft above?

The stairs below. A head appeared. Shoulders, chest. The sheriff stood there, gun drawn.

"What are you doing here?" she asked in a normal voice.

"Get out of here," he whispered, "before you get hurt."

"Hurt? What are you talking about?"

"There's somebody here," whispered Davis. "Get out!"

She stood there frozen.

I had no weapon. I looked around in the dark for an implement, a tool, something. I inched closer along the straw.

"Yale, I don't understand." Her voice cracked.

The sheriff moved toward her.

Fell face down, the gun flying from his hand, skittering across the floor toward the granary. Twenty, twenty-five feet away. To reach it I'd have to cross the open door, the moonlight behind me.

Too far.

Mary gasped.

Glover stood there, a club in his hand. Glover — the one who stole my hammer when I raced out of the drumming class.

"You— you— you're . . . ." Mary stopped herself in time.

"Yes. I'm the guy you left to die," he finished. "I'm Bram Bailey."

"You pushed me," she said. "You tried to kill me."

He moved toward her, she stepped back. "You left me for dead, Mary Ployd. Stubbs pushed me off the mountain and you drove away with him."

"But I— he— Oh! You murdered Shelby! You— you can't get away with this. The sheriff knows. He's not dead. His deputy knows. Frank Dragovic knows. Suzanne knows, Lafayette knows." She was desperate, making up lies wholesale. "Get away while you can, go now."

Glover shook his head, grabbed Mary by the bandaged

arm. She cried out in pain and pulled back, but he held on. Dropping the club he pulled out a knife. Long, wide blade, thick shaft. I could rush him, but he could slit Mary's throat in half the time it'd take me to reach him.

"Waydell lied for you," Glover said, holding her close. "He saved my life, you know. When I got better, I went to see him, asked him about Stubbs and you. I think he knew I wanted revenge. Not for myself, a fight's a fight, I didn't hold a grudge for that. It was the fiddle — you know he ran over it deliberately. Waydell told me your name was Mary Ames, said you were his sister and that if any harm ever came to you, I was dead. I believed him."

"Waydell has a sister. Mary."

Glover chuckled. "I know. That's what had me confused for so long. His sister Mary. I assumed she was the one. I never looked her up. If I had, I'd have known she wasn't you. Never mind, though. I waited. It was Stubbs I waited for, and he's dead now."

"You killed him," said Mary needlessly.

"Smashed his head in. Fitting, don't you think, breaking his skull? Bone for bone — my left leg was shattered when he pushed me over the mountain. I heard him the day I drove in, standing on the porch ranting about purity of old-time music. He'd have done better to think of purity of behavior. He was jealous of my playing, wasn't he? He ran over my fiddle deliberately."

"Yes," whispered Mary. "He did. But I didn't. I left Shelby, you know that."

"Bram Bailey," he continued, listening only to himself. "BB. Best Bones. I changed my name so I could kill Stubbs some day, but I kept my initials on my bones. Every time I made a pair, I thought of standing behind him, slipping one over his head, and pulling against his windpipe."

Mary struggled. Glover gripped her more firmly.

With his free hand he held up the knife as if studying it. "But choking him with bones would have brought suspicion on me. Instead, I used what was handy."

Again Mary tried pulling away, again Glover held on.

I edged closer. My hand touched something hard.

"I sang when he was dead, you know," Glover continued. "I went out and sat behind the pole barn and sang rock songs. He knew his time had come when he first saw me — when he wanted to buy my fiddle. That's why he fell over, because he knew I was here for justice."

"You don't have to do this," Mary argued. "Go away, just go away. You can change your name again, I won't tell. I haven't told anybody."

Glover nodded in a distracted way, examining the point of his knife.

"It's your own fault," he said. "I didn't know it was you, that you were the Mary who was with Stubbs. But the night of the thunderstorm, when I was playing my song, you asked the carpenter to have me stop playing and singing. And then I crept close and heard you talking to him about being a singer with Waydell and Stubbs. About playing in the Boot Jacks. That's when I knew it was you, that Waydell had lied."

"He knows," Mary said. "Frank knows it's you! He's not a carpenter, he's a private investigator. I hired him. He'll find you. You can't get away."

Glover ignored her, holding the knife up to her face. "You weren't as bad as he was. I'm going to give you a choice, Mary."

Silence.

"What?" she asked at last.

"I can slit your throat," Glover explained, "or I can push you out of the barn again. There's no straw down there now. But you still might live. I fell and lived, and you might, too. What do you think?"

My right hand closed around the hard hickory shaft of the

pitchfork. Cindy had left it there, thrust into a bale of straw. I worked it loose.

Glover heard, jerked in my direction. When Mary pulled away from him, he let her go. She fell to the floor. Pitchfork in hand, I drew back my shoulder.

"Drop the knife!" I shouted.

Glover's feet moved, his knife arm went back.

I hurled the pitchfork.

Booker called Saturday's breakfast gathering to attention, hoisting his guitar in one hand, Mary's in the other. Booker told everybody they'd been stolen Thursday and Friday, but had been recovered thanks to me. When he explained that I'd been working undercover to find the instrument thief, all eyes turned in my direction.

Like me, Mary had spent the night in the sheriff's office, answering Davis's questions many times over. Dark circles lined her eyes, but she wore a fresh purple skirt and tunic with a bright red sash and her hair was freshly braided. One arm remained in a sling. I had managed to shower and change clothes. As Mary stepped up to the microphone I thought she moved with a lighter step than usual. She announced that Fonnie Sheffler had been the thief, that she was barred from Midwest Music Madness, and that people should spread the word about instrument thieves.

I concentrated on my French toast and scrambled eggs, aware of many eyes on me. "I had no idea," said Vance, studying me suspiciously

Guy took the hurdy-gurdy bag off his back and set it down. "I feel better now, Frank. That is why you knew how to twist my arm, *non?*"

Cody came up to me. "Is it true, Frank? Did you kill Jeff with a pitchfork last night?"

The French toast was dry going down. "I don't know, Cody. He might live." Which I doubted. "He was going to kill Mary. Probably the sheriff too."

Cody patted me on the arm. "I'm glad you know how to throw a pitchfork, Frank."

Under the table, Suzanne took my hand.

Tansy rushed up and ushered Cody away.

The table was quiet.

"Sheriff Yale Davis wants to say a word," continued Mary, "and then I have an announcement, and then we have a special treat from Lafayette. Please, everybody — please don't leave for home until you hear from the sheriff, me, and Lafayette."

I guess the reason Davis showed up, head swathed in bandages, was because Mary had returned after being pushed off the barn's second story. I guess he felt he had to show he was as tough as she was.

Which he was.

He said a few words about what happened last night, left out the gruesome details, thanked me for my help, and said he hoped he could attend next year's Madness as a student, not a law officer. A polite smattering of applause.

Mary stepped forward with her announcement. "Everybody who attended old-time week this year will receive a *twenty percent discount* on next year's festival. That's my way of thanking you for the terrible things you had to put up with this year. And I promise they won't happen again!"

A moment of silence, then applause and happy whisperings among the crowd.

Booker stepped forward again, his guitar strapped in playing position. "Now we'll hear from Lafayette," he chuckled.

Lafayette pulled a chair up to the mike, which he bent toward his psaltry. "Early this morning, a *tyoon* called me. I followed it. This is for Frank," he mumbled. "I call it 'Frank's Find.'" He lit into a four-four number with an interesting melody, but the melody disappeared as soon as it began. We sat there listening, others understanding the music, me counting the beats.

"That's unusual, to end the tune like that," said Suzanne.

"Yeah," Vance agreed. "The way he started out with that little melodic bit in the A part, then it disappeared, but popped up again at the end of the B part."

"Ah," said Guy, "it doesn't seem like an end, it seems like another beginning." He thought a while. "That is it! Lost and found! I get it!" he said, applauding loudly.

I applauded, too, pleased to have a tune written in my honor.

Breakfast over, we said our goodbyes. Suzanne gave Mary the wooden pig she had carved. I thanked Lafayette for the tune and gave him my card, asking him to send me a tape of the song. He beamed with pleasure. "Do you really like it, Frank?" I assured him I did.

The sheriff approached and Lafayette left. Davis wanted to make sure I'd return for the coroner's inquest. I said I would. Then he reached into a bag he'd been carrying and pulled out a hammer. I could see that it was a Klein straight-claw smooth face. "Here," he said. "I thought you could use this one until I return yours."

I thanked him and took the new hammer.

"I understand about your hammer," he said. "I'll do everything I can to get it back to you."

I hoped he would.

Suzanne and I went to load the car.

We had just finished when Mary arrived, envelope in hand. "This is for you," she said, handing it to me. "Your pay. Four hundred, minus the one hundred retainer." She winced as she handed it to me. I couldn't tell what hurt, her arm or her pocketbook. "Also," she said, "also, Frank, there's a bonus in the envelope."

"Thank you, Mary." I thought it might be fifty dollars or

even another hundred, which for Mary was humongous. Then I realized she wanted me to open the envelope.

Inside were three crisp one hundred dollar bills. And a piece of thick paper. I pulled out the paper.

It was a handwritten certificate, made out to Frank Dragovic and Suzanne Quering, offering each of us one free week of tuition, room, and board at Midwest Music Madness "as long as Madness exists."

I showed the certificate to Suzanne. "Oh, Mary," she said, giving her a hug. "This is wonderful."

Mary was giving me the most priceless thing she could offer: the gift of music. "I don't know what to say," I said.

Mary patted me on the arm, then hugged me.

Suzanne insisted on driving. "You haven't slept all night," she pointed out.

She was right. I handed her the keys and settled in the passenger seat.

As she pulled out of the parking area and onto the county road, Suzanne asked, "What about the sheriff and Mary?"

I turned around and looked. Mary and Davis stood side by side. Close, but not touching. They were both waving. "Don't know," I replied, "but I think they'll work it out."

Suzanne rested a hand on my thigh, giving me hope that we could work it out, too.

The barn glinted in the sunlight. I took one last look at it, then glanced into the rear seat at the two washtub basses, the box of bones and spoons, and my new Ewe drum.

Barbara Gregorich's works include the novel *She's on First* as well as the nonfiction work, *Women at Play: The Story of Women in Baseball,* which won the SABR-Macmillan Award for Best Baseball Research of the Year. Her novel *Dirty Proof* introduced Chicago private eye Frank Dragovic. *Sound Proof* is the sequel.

Gregorich studied at Kent State University, the University of Wisconsin, and Harvard. Before becoming a writer she worked as an English instructor, a typesetter and a letter carrier. She lives in Chicago with her husband, Phil Passen, who plays the hammered dulcimer. Her web site is www.barbaragregorich.com

Made in the USA
Lexington, KY
02 June 2011